CLAY

BOOK TWO

TONY BERTAUSKI

BERTAUSKI STARTER LIBRARY_

NIXES_

Through our body, we know the universe.
An incompetent vessel, it is.

MOTHER_
FABRICATING A BETTER WORLD

Ned Peterson sat in the third row, center stage. The set was black and empty except for a small table, also black, with a large box beneath a heavy blanket. Something inside moved with mechanical precision.

The kids around him were in their mid-twenties, maybe thirties, erupting with nerdgasms. There were thousands of them. Ned was polite but didn't talk much. He never came to product launches; this was his first and probably his last. But he didn't want to be distracted by theatrics.

If the rumors were true, this would change the world.

Ned taught high school students the basic manipulation of their initial biomite seeds: how to increase intelligence and inspire creativity. He wanted them to use their gifts to better humanity. His students, on the other hand, just wanted to initiate Dreamland experiences and thought-chat.

Ned was about to find the bathroom when a beam of light engulfed the mystery box. There was applause and standing ovations. When nothing happened, silence settled. Ned sensed a subtle drone in the background, a low baritone that amped the anticipation.

A puppy bolted from stage left and raced across the stage.

Laughter rumbled through the auditorium. The floppy-eared black puppy skidded to a stop, paws hanging over the edge of the stage, and searched for a way down. Then piddled on the floor.

Another spotlight knifed from above, this one illuminating a slender figure that stepped out from stage right. This time, the entire room erupted. They were on their feet, applauding and cheering.

Ned was forced to stand.

The iconic figure didn't recognize his fans with his usual wave. Instead, he strode in front of the small table and towered over the puppy now prancing in a circle.

"Accidents happen," Allen Smith said, scooping up the puppy.

While the crowd continued, silent assistants placed a chair by the table and wiped up the dog's accident. Allen Smith sat down and crossed his legs. The puppy climbed up the front of his black turtleneck to lick his face.

And the mystery box continued to churn.

Allen Smith cleaned his round spectacles while the crowd settled. He remained calm even after the room was relatively quiet. The puppy curled up on his lap and he scratched it behind the ears.

The crowd waited.

"Over the past twenty years," he finally said, with little effort, "we have brought human-augmented technology to unprecedented heights. Our company is solely responsible for biomite stabilization. We curbed runaway replication and allowed humanity to control their biomites. Thought-chat is more common than texting. Internal audio has replaced the need for external speakers. We've increased memory storage like internal hard drives, initiated group thinking and collective IQ. We are on the cusp of developing augmented dream-worlds that will generate new realities inside the mind. Quite simply, we've made better humans."

Allen Smith looked up and delivered his trademarked line.

"What else can we do?"

This was greeted with raucous cheers. Ned sat quietly, perhaps the only spectator not moved by Allen Smith's theatrics. Pomp and circumstance were not substitutes for substance.

Allen Smith put the puppy down and paced to the left. He folded his hands and walked meditatively. The crowd couldn't contain its enthusiasm. Allen Smith, characteristically, ignored them. He continued walking with measured steps until he reached the left side of the stage and turned around. The puppy followed him to the right.

He returned to the center and stood next to the table. He held his reflective pose, gazing at the floor. The puppy sat by his side.

"What else is there?" he asked sincerely this time. "For twenty years, we have seeded biomites into our bodies to support life, to bring it more vitality, greater longevity and infinite potential. People, we sit on the precipice of creating imaginary universes and unheard-of genius."

Assistants scurried out with a short set of steps and placed them in front of the table. Some spectators muttered. Ned was riveted to his seat.

"People, we were made in the image of God. And now we can follow in His footsteps. I don't want to simply support life anymore."

He grabbed the blanket.

"I want to create it."

Beneath the blanket was a glass case that contained silver rods that moved like mechanical fingers preparing magic, circling around an inanimate object.

Allen Smith was expressionless. The puppy, however, climbed the steps to investigate what looked like another puppy, this one white.

The crowd murmured. Ned hoped they wouldn't stand. He gripped the armrests like he was on the edge of a cliff.

The silver rods twirled around the white puppy one last time; mist emitted from microscopic nozzles embedded along ridges inside the box. Everything folded up and collapsed to the bottom.

There was just the white puppy.

Allen Smith didn't wait for quiet. Even he knew, at this juncture, that silence would not return. He tapped the front of the box and the glass pane opened. Ned barely heard what Allen Smith said next. His heart was thudding, his ears ringing.

The white puppy moved its head. It looked at Allen Smith. A lull of stunned silence fell on the room. The white puppy stepped onto the steps and hesitantly climbed down. The puppies collided and rolled in rollicking puppy fervor.

The crowd found its breath.

"Ladies and gentlemen," Allen Smith said, "I bring you the world's first fabricator."

The magic words were spoken.

Ned was the first one to stand, his meaty palms applauding. The crowd joined him, tears streaming down their cheeks. Some would not sit again.

And Allen Smith, uncharacteristically, smiled.

CHAPTER ONE_

It's raining in Seattle.

Imagine that.

Jamie pulls up her collar. Her stocking cap is already wet. A drum solo bangs through her auditory implants while droplets drift around a streetlight halo, reflections stretching across wet asphalt. A lone red light at the end of the dilapidated pier is dismal. Across the water, Christmas lights smudge the horizon.

She can smell the harbor.

Charlie's at a metal door that's flush against a brick wall, corrosion spattered over the surface like paint flung from a brush. His dark form casts a dim shadow. In situations like this he used to shuffle back and forth. He couldn't stand deserted streets and dark alleys, said they made him jumpy. He would have to talk to himself to keep from freaking. That was before he changed.

The door cracks open.

Charlie stands still, almost inanimate, staring at the paint chips. Someone peeks through the widening slice of light. A dirty blonde puts her face in the gap, her eyes darting around. She squeaks when she sees Charlie, the psychopath.

Jamie calls up her music.

The haze looks like the night sky is falling, making the world feel dark and small. Green lines run across her vision, identifying the Puget Sound and the abandoned warehouses. She had downloaded the names of the empty buildings and lonely streets in this derelict section of Seattle, home to rats and mosquitoes.

Jamie looks at her boots, the steel toes scuffed down to the metal. Only the music keeps her from running.

"Hey." Charlie tugs on her sleeve. "Turn it down."

Jamie rolls her head and thought-chats the volume down. Her eardrums throb and the auditory vacuum rings in her head. The door is closed.

"Did you turn off your field augments?" Charlie squeezes her arm.

"Just running audio."

"I told you not to."

"I'm not, relax."

"That's a deal-breaker. No one's allowed to run a perception field inside."

"I'm not, Charlie. I'm cold off."

"These people don't play, babe. It's just this one shot. They don't like you or you don't play by the rules, then you watch from the outside."

He cups her cheek, rubbing the smooth skin behind her ear. His eyes have become bluer and sharper. They used to be pinkish around irises of dull gray. He hardly blinks anymore, like he sees with X-ray vision, right inside her.

Where it aches.

"You take the pill?" he asks. "You'll feel better if you do, just until we get inside. It'll be good. You'll see. After that..."

"Charlie, I don't want to do the pill, okay? I'm all right, serious. I'll go in cold off."

"One pill, babe." He digs deep in his coat pocket and pinches a dirty white tablet. "It's a onetime deal. You won't need them after this. I promise."

Drugs were old school. Chemical addictions took forever to kick. She'd rather go cold off than swallow a pill. But Charlie used to do pills before he changed. Now he doesn't.

He's got those razor-blue eyes that tell her it's going to be all right.

"Promise?" she asks.

He holds it to her lips and pushes it inside her mouth with his tongue, wet and warm. The pill sticks to her throat, a chalky residue spreading inside her cheeks. She works up enough saliva to get the lump down but not the taste.

Charlie opens his coat and draws her in. She puts her arms around him, feeling his warmth, inhaling the essence that is Charlie. He protects her from the rain.

"You sure you want to do this?" he whispers.

"Of course. Why?"

"No going back. If we get caught, it's all over. Lights out."

"I know."

"I just want you to decide."

Jamie buries her face inside his coat, her cheek against his chest. His heart beats in her ear, filling the silence. He rocks her back and forth.

Somewhere, a ship moans.

Charlie keeps looking at the door. It's taking too long. There's no handle to pull; it only opens from the inside. Only on invitation. The minutes pile up. Her stocking cap is cold and the pill isn't working. She can't remember the last time she went cold off for this long. Music is always in her ears and video feeds her vision.

The tendons flex on Charlie's neck. He swallows hard. Each second sows doubt. She's not charred, not like Charlie was. Her biomites aren't overworked and burned out. If this doesn't work, though, it won't be long.

The sliver of light returns. The girl pokes her head out like before. She might be nineteen, like Jamie, but hard living makes her look thirty. Her skin is blotchy and her hair knotty. The rims of her eyes are red.

She impatiently gestures; Jamie comes closer. The dirty blonde's fingernails are chewed down to the nubs. Jamie's fingernails still have candy blue polish on them. The dirty blonde presses her clammy palm against Jamie's wrist.

"Forty-nine point nine," she mutters. Her front tooth is discolored.

Jamie yanks her hand back. If the girl read Charlie's visible biomites, it would be 49.9%, too. And so would everyone behind that door. Jamie didn't come for visible biomites. She came for the other kind, the ones Charlie got a month ago. The ones the government can't see.

Nixed biomites.

The dirty blonde's stare goes unfocused. She's silently chatting with someone, the circuitry of her biomite-enhanced brain wirelessly networking with others. It's bright white behind her, like nothing exists in there. It's supposed to be a dance club. Jamie shuffles back.

Charlie hangs on.

"Okay." Dirty blonde pushes the door open and steps back.

A cold shank of fear keeps her legs from moving. She thought this would be easier, thought she'd go running inside when it came time. Charlie leans in, his breath warm in her ear. He nuzzles against her neck, kissing it gently.

"It's all right," he says. "I promise."

He holds her hand and walks inside, not letting go even when the white light swallows him. He's a bleached figure, smiling back, hanging on, pulling her toward the light. Toward hope.

Towards a promise that things will feel better.

The warehouse dance club explodes out of the white.

Laser lights fire at bodies that are slammed tight and bouncing to an endless techno-rhythm that ripples over her skin. Charlie pulls her through a crease in the crowd. His military coat looks brand new: clean, pressed, and sparkly. It didn't even look that good when he stole it. Jamie pulls her stocking cap off. It's clean and toasty. Smells like fabric softener.

The dirty blonde looks back, only she isn't so dirty. Her hair shines like gold, her complexion smooth and tan. Her eyes are clear blue, all white, no red. She smiles a perfect smile and Charlie follows, pulling Jamie through the party that smells like an evergreen forest. It reminds her of spring.

They walk for several minutes, occasionally passing booths tucked deep into corners where skin heaves in and out of the dark: elbows and knees, thighs, and shoulders.

Everything unblemished, perfect.

Augment, baby. Biomites make life worth living.

They reach a horseshoe-shaped booth in one of a thousand corners. It feels like the back of the club, but there's no wall in sight. Blondie gestures like a game-show host. Charlie slides in first.

"Can I get you anything?" Her voice reverberates in Jamie's head.

"You can turn that shit down?" Jamie says.

Blondie sneers like synthesized dance beat is Mozart and how dare she. But then the volume drops until it's barely a whisper above the ringing in Jamie's ears. She knows it's still pounding a rhythm inside everyone else's heads.

Charlie holds up two fingers—two drinks—and Blondie melts into the crowd.

"Don't insult him," he says.

"Who?"

"The guy running this place."

"Charlie, the music is ear shit."

"Just..." He takes her hand. "You're here, babe. You're knocking on the door, let's not piss anyone off. All right?"

He strokes the back of her hand. Before, his fingers would've been twitching with all these people, all this stress. Now he comforts her. The thing is, she really should hate this music. She knows that its computer-generated sound bites manufactured for brainless mobs, but it's getting inside her, making her hungry for more. She forces her feet to remain still, to keep her head from bobbing. She'd never forgive herself.

"His name is Cee," Charlie says. "All this is his field."

"All of this?"

"Everything you see and hear. Everybody is experiencing his perception field. That's why you can't run your field—you have to commit to his. You feel it, right? You feel the music?"

She refuses to answer. Does he know what she's thinking? Was she tapping her toe? Charlie's not nodding; he's bouncing his head to the rhythm. He feels it, too. *He likes it.* If he pulled her onto the dance floor, she's not sure she could resist.

"How's he do it?" she asks. "How's he making other people see his field?"

"It's the power of halfskin."

"But everyone is experiencing *his* field. That's just..."

The perception field is a personal thing. Jamie had auditory augments; she could change the color of her eyes or release serotonin into her bloodstream, she could roll identifier script through her vision to see maps or read someone's name, but she couldn't make someone else experience it. And not an entire club.

"He's almost a brick," he says.

"Impossible."

"Yeah. They say he's like 99.9% biomite." He bites his lip, looking at the dancing. "He's only a tenth of a percent clay."

A tenth organic? Would that even be human?

Red, blue, and green lasers fire in all directions. The partygoers try to catch them. There's an island bar not far away, and in the occasional gap in the crowd Jamie sees the lurkers watching the madness. Most of them are chatting up women wearing tiny skirts or transparent blouses over hard nipples.

One guy leans back on his elbows. He doesn't like the music.

Blondie drops off two drinks and a plate of nachos with melted cheese. She holds a metallic pill between long, polished fingernails and flicks a knowing glance at Charlie. He acts like she didn't just chat him.

The pill settles between the drinks.

"What's that?" Jamie asks.

"The answer."

The pill is hexagonal, silver on one side and white on the other. "No more pills, Charlie."

"That's not what you think. They don't seed nixes through a gun anymore, that's old-school shit. Just swallow the pill, the nixes integrate. I thought it was bullshit, too. Look at me now."

He smiles. This time she sort of cringes. His smile looks like everyone else's: all shiny and happy.

"How'd you pay for it?" she asks.

He takes a long swallow. "The drinks are complimentary."

"No, how'd you pay for the..." She swallows, nervous to say it out loud. "The nixes."

His foot stops dancing to the endless beat. He's looking at the dance floor but doesn't see it. She can't believe she didn't ask this question earlier. When he said he was going to talk to a man about this, she was scared he'd never come back. She was happy to see him, happy that it worked, that he wasn't dead. Happy that there was hope. So when he promised she could have the same thing, that she could save herself from becoming charred, she didn't ask what it cost. Whatever the price, it was worth it.

But watching the mindless dance craze and perfect smiles makes her stop.

"Charlie?"

"Yeah?"

"How did you pay for this?"

His jaw clenches. "We don't have a choice, Jamie."

"That's not what I asked."

"I made arrangements."

Suddenly, she's not digging the music. The colors feel bland. Everyone feels like mice on a churning wheel. Jamie tries to engage her field, open her music, and scan the crowd, but she can't override the club's perception field, the bodies still happy and perfect.

"If I didn't do it, I'd be charred the rest of my life. If you don't do this, you will be, too." He slowly turns the glass of beer, leaving rings on the table. "We're nineteen, Jamie. You're sitting at 49.9%. You're maxed out, no more biomites. Another year and you'll char, just like me. You'll be left with hard feelings, babe, with sixty-plus years of hard feelings ahead of you."

He looks up.

"So what choice is there? They told me what it would cost, I paid it. We need to be halfskin to cope. This place is giving us the chance. It's the only way. You know I'm right."

Jamie pulls her hand away. "What's the price?"

"Just helping out, that's all we have to do."

"You signed us up for favors?"

"No. We just work for the club until the debt's paid, that's all."

"What kind of favors?"

"You got to understand, becoming nixed halfskin is expensive. We could flip burgers for twenty years and not have enough money. I did what I had to do."

"What kind of favors?"

Blondie knows what kind of favors. She's working off debt, too. That's why she's answering a back-alley door and serving drinks while everyone else is having a good time. Does she even know what she looks like when she opens that door? Would she love this music if she stepped outside?

Does she ever leave?

Jamie knows what kind of services indebted halfskins do. If you can't pay, you puppet. You deliver things. You do things.

And you like it.

As long as you never leave, you will like the things you do to people. And the things they do to you.

Charlie grabs her sleeve. "I won't let them hurt you."

"I got to think about this, Charlie."

"There's nothing to think about. They promised me you won't get hurt."

"Can you stop them?"

"Just...come on, Jamie. We don't have a choice. We already wasted our lives—we're tapped out. We got to go halfskin to be right again. Once we're paid up, we'll be good. We'll be right. You know that. You saw how I changed."

"They'll hurt me, Charlie. They'll hurt you."

"But I can't...I can't go back, babe. It's too late. I'm already there."

"I know."

He tries to say more, tries to promise everything will be all right, but nothing comes out. He can't protect her.

Maybe it's worth it. Maybe having everything she wants and feeling how she wants to feel and not caring about shit music is the way to happiness. Maybe she just needs to sell her soul while it's still worth something.

She gets out of the booth. She doesn't know where the exit is, but she'll look for it all night if that's what it takes. Right now she just needs to be in her own head, experience her own field, think this through. She was sure she wanted this, but now...

"You can't leave." Charlie grabs her wrist, prying her fingers open. He pushes the pill into her palm. "This is a onetime shot, babe. You leave and you don't get another. That pill won't activate outside the club."

"I got to think about it, Charlie."

"There's nothing to think about!" His smile falters. Finally, a sign of the real Charlie shines, not that fake happy smile. He's still in there. He needs her. And she needs him.

She rolls the heavy pill between finger and thumb, the surface smooth and cold. She knows he's right. Where will she go if she leaves? What's out there can't be worse than this pill. There's nothing outside that door but her life.

This can't get worse.

She closes her eyes and throws the pill in her mouth. An aluminum flavor coats her tongue and leaves a metallic trail down her esophagus. It lands in her stomach.

He holds out his hand. "I promise."

And those are his last words.

The normal-looking guy at the bar, the one leaning on his elbows and hating the music, the one staring at her, starts walking. He looks like he's coming toward her but turns for the dance floor without a bounce in his step. He lifts both arms above his head. The music slurs.

The lights dim.

Gray walls appear out of nowhere. The ceiling transforms into rusted rafters with harsh fluorescent lighting.

Silence falls.

In the moments before the partygoers drop, before the floor is littered with bodies, Jamie looks back. Charlie is clutching the table. He feels something winding down, turning off. The whites show around his beautiful blue eyes before they turn gray—

He slumps to the floor.

They all do.

CHAPTER TWO_

Paul massages his temples.

Lieutenant Dobbs ducks under the police barrier. Dobbs talks to a few of the officers at the crowd barrier before delivering a tall cup of coffee. Another van has arrived, the satellite receiver extending above the crowd. There's no such thing as secrets anymore. The bloggers and news corps probably know more about the warehouse than Paul.

The coffee is black and scalding.

Paul chases five aspirin with a swallow, scanning the crowd. Green lines lock on to individuals, automatically running them through facial recognition. No outstanding warrants—this time. Amazing how many fugitives in today's age of facial recognition come to crime scenes. It's like the mothership calling them home. This time it's mostly certified bloggers streaming video and nosy locals posting on Facebook or YouTube.

Dobbs follows Paul. "Feds are arriving in an hour."

"Good." Paul can focus on crowd control and the impending media landslide. Maybe catch up on sleep.

"They're bringing a shit-ton of bricks."

"One brick is enough." He blows on the coffee. The caffeine only fuels his surging headache.

Paul raps on the door, orange paint peeling off the metal surface. This place is registered as storage for some offshore company. They own several buildings in the area, all of them consuming almost no power. They'll never find the owners.

Paul kills his olfactory senses before the door opens. The briny scent of the harbor fades. When the door swings open, the crowd jockeys for position to get a glimpse. Paul quickly slips inside, where the atmosphere is dank and humid. Despite the absence of smell, he feels the odor cling to his skin, something that won't shower off.

Paul sets the coffee on the floor.

Birds look from rusted girders, impartial to the death below. The bodies were in tangled heaps when Paul arrived. Almost all of them are in their twenties or thirties, their clothing stained with sweat. Most are gaunt and sickly, like living zombies.

Now dead zombies.

Folding chairs and card tables are scattered to his right, with red plastic cups and stale bread on the ones still upright. A makeshift island bar made of plywood and two-by-fours is in the corner.

Poison, Paul had first thought when he saw the place. *These nuts laced up some drinks and offed themselves in dramatic fashion.* But it was just water. Would've been a hell of a lot easier if it was poison.

"Sarge!" someone calls from the other side.

Paul raises his hand. Officers are still moving the bodies, capturing faces for recognition. Some are still a mystery, probably having facial reconfiguration. A few of them are registering greater than 90% biomites. If those reports are accurate, they could make subtle changes to their looks with a thought.

Paul slowly walks between the bodies, avoiding the man among the officers that doesn't belong. He's dressed like an ordinary citizen with thinning hair and an overhanging gut.

Mother's agent, designed to blend. *A brick.*

He did this. The patrons' nixes were invisible to Mother until he got here. Once the frequency was decoded, he turned them over to Mother and she flipped the switch.

Legally it's not murder because, as federal law sees it, they weren't human anymore.

Paul scans the brick's face but doesn't find a match in the facial recognition database because he doesn't exist. He's a fabricated human, 100% biomites. A fucking brick. Funny how the government is fighting the war on halfskins with bricks. *Fire with fire,* they say.

Paul's never had to deal with one. Now an orgy of these plastic fucks is coming to town.

Three of his officers are outside an office door in the back left corner. Manny, the shortest of the three, says, "You got to see that office, Sarge. I mean, holy hell—"

"Why is she cuffed?" Paul points at the lone survivor.

"She started spitting. We warned her."

"So you cuffed her?"

"Well, yeah. When the brick moved her boyfriend, she lost it. Stevens had to subdue her and she started spitting. We warned her twice."

The girl is on the floor, slumped against the wall. Stringy hair hangs over her face. The only pieces of furniture in sight are metal chairs and broken tables not worthy of a garage sale.

"Pull that lounger out of the office," Paul says.

"The brick said leave it; we're not supposed to touch anything in there."

"You don't work for him."

Manny and Stevens fetch the lounger. Maybe he should put her in the office so she doesn't have to look at all these bodies, but he has the feeling she doesn't want to go far from her boyfriend. Besides, that office smells worse than the warehouse. Judging by the bedsores on the asshole they found in it, he almost never moved.

Paul kicks a card table to make room. The bread hits the floor like cardboard. He squats next to the girl, his belt binding his waist.

"I'd like to take those handcuffs off," he says softly. "But I need you to promise you won't run. Can you do that?"

She doesn't respond.

Paul leans over to visually capture her face. Her profile scrolls across his vision. In seconds, he knows her past and is a lot less surprised she's here.

"Jamie?" he says. "I know you've been through a lot tonight. I'm going to get you out of here as soon as I can, but in the meantime, I want you to rest comfortably, all right?"

She lifts her head but doesn't answer. Paul sways back, struck by the similarity to his niece. When he was a kid, it took things like LSD to fry a mind. Today, the right kinds of biomites could char a kid sky-high.

"I'm cold off," she mutters.

Paul looks at the officers.

"Means she can't run her field," Manny says. "She wants music."

"Why can't she have it?"

Manny jabs his thumb at the brick.

"If it's just music, you'll get it," Paul says.

Her eyes focus. And then she's looking through him. Her expression turns cold and hard. She's not charred, she's still present. She still has enough clay—at least a little more than half, or else she'd be on the floor. Maybe seeing this place littered with halfskins will save her.

"We got a deal?" he asks.

She nods.

Paul cuts the plastic handcuffs. She rubs her wrists and the officers help her onto the stained lounger. She must have her olfactory senses shut down; at least the brick gave her that. She rests comfortably.

"I just want the music back," she says.

"We all do, honey." Paul puts his hand on her forehead.

"Sergeant Jennings?"

The brick is behind him. He looks like a middle-aged man with bad posture, wearing brown pants and a checkered shirt. No one would remember him in a crowd.

"I'm Agent Manning." The brick offers his hand. Paul doesn't even look at it. Manning waits several moments before dropping it. His left eye twitches.

All the appearances of an imperfect human.

These fabrications are designed with frailties to make people feel comfortable, as if they're interacting with something real, talking to something other than a walking composite of biomites. Paul swears he can smell the plastic nature of this imposter even though his olfactory senses are dulled.

"Your superiors have briefed you on the situation, I'm sure, but I would like to be thorough. Are you familiar with the Biomite Oversight Committee?" Manning asks. "Do you know what we do?"

Paul doesn't respond. Doesn't even blink. Manning looks at the officers that gather around.

"I realize this is difficult for you. Losing life is never easy. I can assure you that we don't approve of this any more than you do."

Manning puts his hand to his chest and makes eye contact with each of the officers. Paul tries not to smirk. This...*thing*...imitating empathy is good. Some people will buy it, they'll forget it's a fabrication not capable of true emotions but rather trained to influence humans.

"I was assigned to investigate evidence of halfskin activity in this area," Manning continues. "I infiltrated the premises under the guise of a client and analyzed the use of nixes."

He didn't need to explain it, but he just did. Paul admires the slick approach to avoiding their ire by appearing coy rather than arrogant. It's not the strength these things possess that should be feared but the cunning.

"I completed my analysis at 2:33 a.m. My report was confirmed at 3:02 a.m. The result was the shutdown of one hundred and thirty-two halfskins. There is one survivor."

Paul looks at the results. He knows the law; it doesn't matter if he agrees. "You can leave," he says.

"On the contrary, a team of agents will be arriving for further analysis within the next couple of hours. We will cooperate with your department in every possible way—"

"You killed them, Manning. Your job is done."

He acknowledged its name. *Goddamnit.*

Manning stands a little taller. His relaxed expression hardens. A dead look fills his eyes. He takes a moment to look around, not so much to see anything but to let Paul interpret the sudden change in direction.

"Paul," he says, "I am an extension of Mother."

"I know *what* you are."

"There is no arguing this point, Paul. Every analysis has been confirmed that without Mother, your species would be consumed by greed. By extension, you fabricated me and others like me to save yourselves."

"I never signed up for killing people."

"These people were killing themselves, Paul. You were allowing it. You are mostly human and, therefore, incapable of adequately handling the situation."

"A brick to save us all. Fucking poetic."

Manning shuffles within Paul's comfort zone. "Your officers will leave the premises. They'll handle the crowd outside. No one is allowed to speak about what they saw or what is happening. No one, under any circumstances, is allowed in the back room."

"I'll run that by the chief."

"The girl," Manning continues, "will be placed in the back room. Her mother is not allowed to visit until she has been interrogated."

"We'll decide where the girl goes."

Manning takes a deep breath. *Does it really need to breathe?*

A cold vibration encases Paul's body. His skin tightens. His skull hardens. Pressure fills the space behind his eyes and pushes his tongue down.

The world looks bleak and distant.

He has very little awareness of following Manning to the back of the warehouse. All his officers come along, some with expressions as blank as his. Others appear shocked.

"Are we clear, Paul?"

Paul nods, but not of his own accord. His biomites have betrayed him. Manning—an extension of Mother—just hijacked them. He took control.

Biomite protestors always complain about the government having too much power. As Paul watches his men follow the brick's orders, he knows firsthand that they're right. The only person capable of resisting would have to be free of biomites.

And there are very few clays left in the world.

CHAPTER THREE_

Orange cones are on the pier, and a sign that warns people to keep out. There's too much activity around the warehouse for anyone to care about the rotting wharf or the lone person on it.

Nix Richards stands about halfway to the end. A ship moves past his peripheral vision, waves slapping the leaning pillars. He pulls the hood over his head. He doesn't mind the wet and the cold.

No one bothers watching from this vantage point because it's too far to see or hear. Nix enhances his vision, magnifies the crowd, downloads their identities and thoughts, filters through the chatter, paying more attention to the bloggers than reporters. They've got a better handle on the halfskin subculture. News organizations still pander to the older generations that hold out hope for yesteryear, that biomites are just a passing phase.

He caught a video stream from earlier that morning, before he arrived and before they erected the screen inside the front door: a blogger caught a view inside the warehouse. Nix had snipped a few stills from it and enhanced the resolution to see the police wandering around a pile of bodies.

Nix was lucky to get to the scene so quickly. He was at the airport in Vegas when he caught the news, and immediately bought a ticket to Seattle. By the time he arrived, the place was crawling with cops.

Nix had disguised his imprinted identity and worked his way through the crowd. If one of those cops caught a whiff of his true identity, that Nix Richards—the man that invisible biomites were named after—is watching from the pier...well, that warehouse story would fall off the front page.

His eyes begin to tingle.

Raine is calling. Perhaps he hasn't noticed. He's been consumed with screening the flood of data, looking for a way to get closer and, eventually, inside. The window of opportunity is closing. He can deal with cops; they're still human. The bricks, though, would be difficult. And more are on the way.

Nix initiates an opening in his perception field. The boards creak as bare feet walk past. Raine's image stops a few feet in front of him, absorbing the view. She's wearing a loose, long-sleeved shirt and shorts that expose all of her legs. The rain, though, falls right through her.

"We shouldn't be here," she says.

"This could be our last chance."

"There are other fabricators, Nix. This isn't the last one."

Her lips are plump, her eyebrows fiercely pinched. Twenty years have passed, but she looks twenty-five, not forty. Nix, on the other hand, is forty but looks sixty. That's intentional, but he still wouldn't look as young as her.

He rubs his weary face slick with precipitation. His eyes are exhausted. He's had to stay focused and engaged with the highly charged environment, all while maintaining his facially transfigured disguise. Even Raine's image is a little fuzzy. He can't slip, not here.

Raine's fingers are warm on his hand. She leans against him; he feels the illusion of her weight. He feels all of this as if she's actually there. It comforts him. *She's always been there.*

Three black cars come down the road on the right. They park a block from the warehouse. Nix lets his pulse quicken. His opportunity may already be over. He magnifies his vision, green lines capturing their details and pulling their identities imprinted on their biomites. *Pierce County police.* They gather around the lead car. Nix eavesdrops on their conversation about hunting season.

"This isn't necessary," Raine hisses, even though no one could possibly hear her. "I don't need to be fabricated."

There are wrinkles on the backs of Nix's hands. If his body aged normally, he'd look a little more worn from running and stress. The normal progression of aging, however, has changed since the birth of biomites. No one knows what a forty-year-old man is supposed to look like.

Right now he has gray hair, not blond. Brown eyes, not blue. He's a few inches shorter and huskier, his cheekbones a bit more pronounced. He's ordinary looking, something facial recognition and his imprinted identity would match with an alias named William Nelson.

The police start toward the scene. They visually scan the crowd, running not just facial recognition but pinging biomite imprints to identify other members of law enforcement. Nix concentrates, feeling the chatter of the cops' own imprinted biomites. It takes several moments to decrypt their identities and download secure data, and then he imprints his own biomites with a similar identity.

If anyone scans him, William Nelson is a husky cop from Olympia.

"Call your sister," Raine says. "She can help."

Nix chuckles. He hasn't been in contact with Cali in years. Even if he spoke with her yesterday, she wouldn't help him. Not with this.

"Don't do this!" Raine grabs his arm. Nix feels her cold fingers as if she's standing in front of him, in the flesh, his mind interpreting what she would be like. But she's not in front of him. She doesn't have a body. She's in his mind.

Dreamland.

If something ever happened to him, she would cease to exist. That's why he has to go inside.

He touches her cheek, her skin warm in the frigid air. She closes her eyes, leaning into his touch. If anyone is looking, they'll see a man standing alone, hand perched in the empty air. If he can fabricate Raine's body, she won't be trapped in Dreamland anymore. She'll walk next to him for everyone to see.

Another car comes down the road. The Pierce County cops wait for the new arrivals. Nix begins his approach. Raine walks silently beside him, her bare feet on the old boards. Her presence requires biomite resources to channel and, given the situation, he shouldn't expend the energy. But she brings him comfort. Besides, if something happens, he doesn't want to be shut down alone.

Nix grabs a half-full cup of coffee from the ground and pushes into the crowd. The women in front of him are tall. The cops approach the scene from the right, dampening their identities to avoid attention until they near the blockade. Nix shuffles around the back of the crowd and casually follows. The police officer at the barricade lets them through. Nix approaches a minute later.

The officer picks up Nix's imprinted signal. "Olympia, huh?"

"Long drive."

"What's Thurston County doing here?"

Nix ducks under the barrier without hesitation. "You think this is Seattle's problem?"

The cops are still waiting for the door to open. Nix cradles the coffee like it's keeping him awake. He's being scanned from all directions, like walking on stage. They don't see Raine by his side.

The door opens. Nix dampens his olfactory senses but doesn't turn them off. This scene is fouled with death and decay, the smell of exhaustion and rusted steel. A hint of plastic lies beneath it all, the sign of dead biomites.

Nix steps around the white panel that blocks the view, his imprinted identity pinging from several directions. He doesn't have to introduce himself. He puts the coffee on the floor like someone else has done. The scattered tables and chairs are only outnumbered by the bodies. Nix swallows a rising lump, feels Raine's hand around his arm, keeping him from running. Now is not the time to panic.

His eyes glaze like he's chatting or recording, disguising his initial surge of fear. His senses struggle to absorb the details, to make sense of the insanity.

This is exactly why Cali wouldn't help him. She warned him biomites would come to this, that humanity wasn't ready for such control of their bodies and minds. She didn't think humanity would ever be ready, that we were too imperfect, that our selfish gene, our hardwired sense of self-preservation and self-centeredness, was too ingrained to resist the temptation. We would become a muddling mass of self-destructive beings that would devolve into...*this*.

And his sister can't help but feel responsible. She was the one that discovered the algorithms that could make biomites undetectable. She's the one that, as she once said, "put the gun in the baby's hand." And she carries the burden, the guilt.

"Just get here?" Officer Timothy Remming asks.

"Yeah," Nix spits out.

"Damn shame, right?" Remming unwraps a stick of gum. "Can't prepare yourself for this."

"What the hell happened?"

"Pretty simple, really. Some high-powered halfskin has been running this operation for years. We found him in a back office with a PICC line in his vein."

Remming gestures to a door in the back left corner.

"He was manufacturing nixes for these fools. As far as we can tell, they were dancing in his projection field. Looks like a zombie rave. No telling what they thought they were doing. Too bad for them, the brick walked in and untangled their frequency. They went night-night."

An ordinary man is directing officers to move the bodies. They've started in the corner directly to Nix's left, placing the bodies on their backs, hands folded over their stomachs. They appear to be lining them up, organizing them into rows.

The ordinary man feels like a dense ball of energy. Nix has always been able to sense a brick's biomites. Everyone else, for whatever reason, experiences a brick as invisible. Nix and Cali have always felt them. Maybe that's why they've never been caught.

"This is dangerous," Raine whispers from behind.

Nix nods, both to Remming and Raine. But he can't walk out now. And the back office is where he wants to go. As long as the brick is busy, there's a chance to do a quick surveillance. He can't haul something out, but there has to be information linked to other nixed distributors with fabricators. They don't work alone.

"Who's that?" Nix points at the girl in the lounger.

"The lucky one?" Remming says. "She was about to go halfskin when the brick shut them down. They had to tear her off one of these bodies, her boyfriend or something. Pitching a real fit."

Nix takes a long, slow breath. The brick is a hundred feet from the back room. The girl is only twenty feet away from it. He can get over there, interrogate her kindly and then casually investigate the office. He only needs to be inside a minute, long enough to scan it. He can download any available data and analyze it off-site, but it has to be fast. The evidence is already disintegrating, trails disconnecting. He just needs a contact, a place he can throw a line.

"You might want to stay out of spitting distance." Remming chuckles, chomping his gum.

Nix walks to the right, following a path between the bodies that will loop around the perimeter and keep him far from the brick.

He seizes. Alarms ring in his head, high voltage surging through his body. He can't take another step.

"Go, Nix." Raine steps in front of him. "Get out now."

He turns slowly, carefully heading for the exit behind the white screen, focusing on each step that threatens to miss the floor and toss him forward. He can hardly hear his own voice when he passes Remming. "Need some fresh air."

"Should've turned off your olfactory."

Nix acknowledges him with a wave.

All eyes turn on him as he exits. The intense warning is coming from his left. A cavalcade of white vehicles is approaching. They ease into the crowd, forcing people to step aside.

Nix turns to his right, walking as casually as he can in the opposite direction. Few people are paying attention. He focuses on the back of Raine's heels as she leads him under the barricade, away from the men and women exiting the white cars. They're not men and women.

They're bricks.

He finds space to walk briskly behind the crowd, continuing his pace until he reaches the corner. Once he's out of sight, he stops. Raine has disappeared. It takes a few minutes for his breathing to return to normal.

Nix magnifies his vision. The lead vehicle has pulled right up to the door while the police push back the crowd. One after another, bricks get out of the cars. Fabricated men and women—black skin, white skin, Asian, Hispanic—ignore the onlookers and gather at the front door.

It's possible Nix could have fooled them. They wouldn't be focused on him. But that's not what tipped an icy cascade of fear. It's the last person to get out of the white cars: a man with a limp and a slight hunch. A man that hasn't been seen in public for years.

Marcus Anderson exits the lead car.

CHAPTER FOUR_

Rain streaks across a tinted window. Marcus never much cared for the Northwest. The January skies are a steely embrace. His knee hates it.

A crowd blocks his view. News vans are parked on the curb. Marcus takes an earpiece from the inside of his jacket and fits it into his right ear, listening to his bricks' chatter. While biomites allow one to chat, as if the brain had become the communication device, Marcus has to rely on external devices.

"Continue driving," he says as they approach the crowd. "They'll move."

The driver slows down but does not honk. Nor stop. The people feel the vehicle approach and slowly move. A kid slams his hand on the hood. Others shout.

It's like parting the Red Sea.

The police move the barricades. The car rolls up to the warehouse door. Marcus reaches to the woman sitting next to him.

"Wait," he says. "Let Gerald get it."

Anna takes her hand off the handle and pats Marcus's arm. Her blonde hair hangs to her shoulders. Her plump lips are red and shocking against her powder-white skin.

"You're making quite a scene," Anna says.

The crowd is focused on the backseat, most of them with retinal recorders that will stream this scene on the newsfeeds and blogosphere. Gerald pauses before opening the door.

"That's the idea," Marcus says.

He turns his body so that he can rest his feet on the asphalt, to allow the blood to circulate before standing. His left knee bends like a rusty hinge. Gerald offers a hand, but Marcus waves him off. He may be aging, but he's not crippled. There are aches and pains to deal with when you're clay.

The way God intended it.

Let the world see who is in charge. Not some biomite-infested cop.

Anna slides out behind him. She's taller than him, especially with the heels. Even without expression, her beauty is stunning. That was why he exited first. His bricks arrive from the cars lined up behind them. They gather around the door, ignoring the questions and curses hurled from behind the barricades. More police arrive to maintain order.

A local police officer stands next to the corroded door. "You might want to kill your olfactory."

Marcus makes a mental note of the officer's name. If he's going to work in law enforcement, he should know Marcus Anderson.

Marcus is greeted with fetid death. He steps around the white screen and into a thick atmosphere. Through welling tears, he sees the bodies. His breath shortens, adjusting to the foul stench of body odor and rot. Beneath it, he senses the tang of expired biomites.

He warned the world that it would come to this. And if it did, he would be there to stop it. And now he stands on the threshold of his prophecy. *Today the world will see that hope lies in our clay.*

He wipes his eyes. About half the bodies are organized into lines, the rest still tangled like they were tossed into the air. His bricks immediately go to work, their thoughts chatting through his earpiece. First, establish order. Then begin the process of scanning the faces and analyzing the biomites.

Marcus retrieves prescription glasses from inside his jacket and begins wiping the round spectacles with a handkerchief. The right lens is quite a bit thicker. He fixes them on his nose and the world comes into focus. Anna hands him a bottle of water. The odor clings to his taste buds. She anticipates his needs so well.

The local police watch the bricks go to work. They congregate around a man in uniform. His stillness and concentration suggest his vain attempts to scan Marcus, finding nothing to identify.

"Sergeant Paul Jennings," Anna says.

"He's in charge?" Marcus asks.

"So far, yes. Agent Manning updated him on how we will proceed. He's been forced into compliance."

Whatever assistance the police had been supplying had stopped since Marcus arrived. The public was aware of bricks, but they were presented as lonely bounty hunters, never as a pack of surgical investigators that seemed to move with one mind, sharing thoughts to coordinate an efficient dissection of a crime scene. There was no delusion or distracting thoughts that typically slowed a human. No corruption or self-centered thoughts.

The bricks continue organizing the corpses into a checkerboard layout. A small contingent goes to the far side and begins undressing them, folding the clothes into piles at the head of each body.

"Bring him over," Marcus says.

Anna chats a terse command. Three bricks go to the sergeant and repeat Marcus's demand. The men steal glances of Anna.

"I am Marcus Anderson." He extends his hand. "I have my doubts about your police department if a sergeant is in charge, but, nonetheless, you have done a splendid job. The public has been made aware of the situation and is contained outside the scene. And your cooperation is greatly appreciated."

"Make them stop." Paul's jaws flex.

"Our investigation will last three days." His tone is darker and direct. "You will continue providing support outside the building. During that time, you will not speak to the public."

Paul quakes with restraint.

"When we are done, you may conduct yourselves in whatever manner you please. In the meantime, you will not interfere. Is that understood?"

"Make...them...stop." He pushes the words out. His face is flush as a bull's nose.

Marcus waves at Anna. She releases her grip on Paul's biomites, allowing him to think and act freely. He pulls in a deep breath but contains himself, aware that anything rash will put him back under her influence.

"This is unacceptable." He points at the bricks undressing the bodies. Ten of them are completely nude. "These are sons and daughters. There is no reason to expose them."

He dares half a step forward.

"I expect that from someone with as much control as you."

Marcus glances at Anna. She nods and the bricks simultaneously stop. They face Marcus, waiting for instructions. He takes a moment to bend his stiffening knee. The concrete is unforgiving on surgically repaired bones. He takes a drink, surveying the destruction. The warehouse is so barren and destitute, an unfitting tomb.

And he's supposed to treat them with decency?

"This is not a crime scene, let's get that straight," Marcus says. "This is a molestation. The crime that you refer to is much greater than it appears, grander than you imagine. These sons and daughters came here of their own volition and forfeited their rights as humans. They have no dignity, they do not exist."

Marcus steps closer, Anna at his side.

"So says the law, Sergeant."

"I don't agree with the law."

"You serve it."

"A part of them is still human."

"How many more of these scenes do you want to see?" Marcus raises his voice, looking at all the men and women in uniform. "These could be your sons and daughters next time. Are you willing to accept that? Because I am not!"

His voice rings off the walls.

"You object to exposing these imitations of God's children? They are no more sacred than objects carved of wood. They succumbed to temptation, gave themselves to earthly desires, and reveled in lies. Open your eyes, all of you. Smell what is all around! That is not the stench of decayed flesh but the degradation of the soul."

Marcus inhales deeply.

"Breathe it in, remember it! Because if we do nothing about this today, it will become the smell of tomorrow. Earth will become a mausoleum of the human soul. I, for one, cannot accept that."

His footsteps click, back and forth.

"I am your only hope. Take your men outside, Sergeant, and do not question me again."

Anna opens the door and moves the screen for the crowd to see inside. Shouts and curses find their way inside.

Marcus folds his hands behind his back, standing as straight as his hunched back will allow. "Give the world your gravest apologies but no more. I will call if I need you."

The men and women begin their exodus, stiffly. Paul remains staring down at Marcus. He is the last to finally move. He stops at the white screen.

"There's a girl," he says. "She's the only survivor. I'd like to take her to her mother."

"Certainly," Marcus says. "I have a few questions for her, that's all."

Paul disappears behind the screen without being forced to do so. The door hammers shut in the metal frame, the closure echoing with a sense of finality. The crowd's anger is muffled. Marcus closes his eyes, allowing the stillness of the moment to settle before muttering a command.

The bricks begin undressing the corpses once again. The only sounds are the shuffle of their soles. Once a body is completely nude, the agent stands over it to visually capture it—head to toe. It is turned over and repeated.

"Your estimate?" Marcus asks.

"We can fabricate all these bodies in two days," Anna says.

"Good. Three days, then, will be all we need."

"Correct. Do you want to interrogate the survivor?"

"Perhaps later. I'd like to explore what's in the back." Marcus starts down the first aisle of bodies. "Oh, Anna."

Marcus half turns, his neck feeling stiff.

"Leak my speech to the bloggers out there. I'd like the world to hear it, too."

He continues his uneven pace toward the back of the warehouse. Sometimes he surprises himself with such spontaneous wisdom. The world needs to know he is not the bad guy.

He is quite the opposite.

CHAPTER FIVE_

Cali Richards fumbles with the tack room doorknob. The latch is stuck. She has to put the metal pails on the floor and turn it with both hands. She kicks the bottom of the old door, swearing she'll get that fixed.

She's been swearing that for ten years.

The former nanobiometric engineer turns on the faucet, letting the water run over her wrinkled and spotted hand. Her arthritic knuckles are knobby. She shoots some soap in the stream and lets the bubbles rise over the pails.

An old song comes on the radio, reminding her of days before biomites were invented, when life was simpler. *Is that what old people say?* Only dusted memories make things seem easier. Still, she turns it up before reaching into the soapy water, reaching blindly for brush and pail.

She yanks her hand out like a water snake was hiding on the bottom. A long red slash oozes along her index finger. She resists the childish urge to suck the blood. She wraps a paper towel around the wound, squeezing it. The dull pain recedes. She could will the nervous response away but prefers to feel the sting. *It's too easy not to feel it.*

Two horses trot across the frozen paddock. Cali watches them play follow-the-leader, their hooves rumbling past the tack room window. There were more horses when she bought the ranch. The previous family had died in an automobile accident. It seemed only fitting that Cali live here, seeing that an automobile accident changed the path of her life.

Perhaps every path in the world.

Haze settles near the top of the Blue Ridge Mountains, but the sun hasn't breached. A red truck emerges from behind a stand of black gum trees. Two dogs run alongside it.

Cali keeps pressure on her finger while the reflection of a leathery old face looks back, her gray hair pulled tightly back with kinky sprigs around her ears. Wrinkles line her upper lip. She's only fifty-two years old.

No one would recognize her. They're not supposed to.

The grass between the two-story house and the barn, once thick and green, is now frosted and tan. The dogs trot past her, waiting in the worn turnabout for the Ford pickup to make a wide turn. Meg puts it in park with one hand, a phone pressed to her ear with the other. She waves before abruptly ending her conversation.

Country folks use phones. They don't pretend to have a conversation while chatting through biomite seeds.

"Hi, Ms. Stacy." Megan hops out of the truck, tying her blonde hair into a ponytail. "Hey there, Baxter and Kooper."

She scratches the dogs' ears and squats down for kisses.

Cali answers to her assumed name, Stacy. She changed her face, changed her name—if she could just get a new life.

"I was expecting your brother," Cali says.

"Carson had some chores to finish. He'll drop off the hay this afternoon. I thought I'd run your groceries out in case you needed them."

"That's kind of you."

"You cut yourself?"

"Nothing but a scratch."

"I got essential oil salve for that. It'll stop the bleeding, keep out infection. I can send it with Carson."

Cali opens the passenger door. Her weekly order of produce and dairy is on the seat. Megan gets around the truck in time to grab the box. There's nothing she can do but smile.

Cali shuffles to keep ahead of the girl so she can climb the old wooden steps first. The screen is torn on the corner of the door. Cali holds it open.

The kitchen counters are cluttered with appliances, books and cans. It's blessed with an ever-present smell of herbs. Cali pats the table for Megan to set down the goodies. The hickory table is gouged from years of use, where the previous family ate their meals. Megan pulls out a quart of milk.

"Let me get you some money."

Her footsteps land heavily on the wooden floor. She passes the old chalkboard running the length of the hallway and goes to the room in back to put a Band-Aid on her finger. Megan is watching something on her phone when she returns. People are protesting behind a blogger's commentary. Cali slides the bills between Megan's fingers.

"Thanks, Ms. Stacy." She puts the money in her front pocket.

"What were you watching?"

"There was a big thing in Seattle the other day. A bunch of people overdosed on biomites and now they think they're all dead."

Cali busies herself with the groceries.

"All the bloggers are going off about the government shutting the doors and not letting the families see them. I feel bad for them."

"Very sad." Cali puts the cheese in the refrigerator. "Pray for them."

Megan holds out her hand. Cali takes it and bows her head.

"Dear Lord," Megan says, "watch over Your sheep that are lost in darkness and guide them to Your Almighty wisdom, that they may walk the pure and untainted path that leads to Heaven. Amen."

"Amen."

They remain still. The words resonate in Cali and attach to her like angels of hope that they will find her brother and take root, that he'll join her on the farm, where he'll be safe.

Because she knows he's in Seattle.

Megan leaves with a quick goodbye. Cali stands at the sink, watching the young lady texting on her way to the truck. Cali peels the Band-Aid off and throws it in the trash. The finger is healed.

CHAPTER SIX_

THE DUFFEL BAG FEELS LIKE A SACK OF ROCKS.

Nix lets it fall on the hotel carpet. He avoids the king-sized bed. If he lies down, he won't get up. There'll be time for sleeping later.

He grinds his eyes with the heels of his palms. Death still lingers in his nostrils. He pulls the sliding door open, letting the winter wind into the room. Gulls cry somewhere above the patio. The moon hangs just above the bay. He opens his mind to nearby chatter, eavesdropping on newsfeeds. The tranquility is broken with a thousand voices.

MARCUS ANDERSON HAS TAKEN control of the warehouse.

The government is raping our civil liberties.

Marcus Anderson should crawl back into the hole where he's been hiding or be arrested for treason.

Mother is an enemy of the state.

NOTHING WILL CHANGE and Marcus and his bricks will do what they want in the warehouse, digesting the evidence like ants cleaning a corpse. There'll be nothing left.

And no one can stop them.

That's why Nix can't sleep. Not yet.

There's information in there, Nix knows it. He can feel it. Years ago, it was so easy to network with other halfskins. But Mother has systematically cut them up, severed ties, and traced down the outlaws. Nix is alone.

He goes to the bathroom and splashes water on his face. He dabs his cheeks with a towel. An old man with dark eyes rimmed red looks back. His nose is thick, his lips thin and wrinkled. The bushy eyebrows are speckled white. He doesn't just look like an old man. Today, he feels like one.

He hates the way his body feels. It feels like someone else, like staring at the world through eyeholes. But he never changes it. Not even standing in a hotel bathroom all alone. He's committed to being William Nelson until he finds a fabricator. If Nix Richards's original face were ever caught by facial recognition, he wouldn't last long.

He cups another handful of cold water to his face, pushes his fingers through thinning hair and retreats to the bed. He lies back but never feels the mattress. It's like he falls through it, his body dropping through the floor, building speed as it plummets downward, the solidity of his body falling away a particle at a time.

A green breeze brushes his cheeks, a trace of smoke on the wind.

Dreamland.

Verdant hills slope to a clear lake confined by the peaks of distant mountains. Fishing boats have already shoved across the glassy surface from the village along the shores, where a market is vibrant with fruit and vegetables, cured meats and smoked fish.

He lifts his hands and studies the skin of a thirty-nine-year-old. Only in Dreamland does he look like his true self, the real Nix Richards.

Raine sits at the far end of the slanted porch. Her baggy pants are rolled to her knees with a white tank top exposing her dark brown shoulders. She cradles a mug on her lap, green eyes gazing over the bannister.

"I think you're foolish," she says.

"I know."

"You're not invincible."

Nix steps off the porch, where the ground is worn to dust. Further out, the grass sways near his knees, clumps shifting in the wind. Scrubby trees dot the landscape. He looks back at the prairie home, the old porch wrapping around both sides.

Dreamland started as a mental construct, thoughts that he visualized and connected. When he was a kid, he discovered his ability to build inner worlds by accident. It started when he looked at a picture. His biomites took the information and recreated this inner world. Nix thought it was normal.

He was a freak.

His thoughts took on a life of their own. They calcified and interlocked. They existed without his effort. He and Raine had outgrown the tropical lagoon of their youth. They wanted a home and imagined this cabin on the hill, the nearby sea and the ragged mountains. They would go down to the village, where people haggled over prices and arguments broke out and children laughed in the streets. He saw and heard things he couldn't possibly have imagined, the details rich and endless.

It was no different than the physical world. But still, a world he created. *Will it exist without me?*

He could never be sure.

A German shepherd lopes through the grass. Nix buries his fingers in the dog's fur.

"Shep," Nix mutters, "where's your stick?"

Shep looks around as if he's thinking, then darts around the house. Nix picks a seed stalk from the grass, nibbling on the broken end, the juice tart.

"Do you think I'm real?" Raine asks.

Nix used to answer that question. Sometimes, he tried to lie. He didn't control her, couldn't make her do anything she didn't want to do. He'd always assumed she had risen from his subconscious, taken the details of her physical appearance from someone he'd seen but forgotten, that his mind had this barrier in place so he'd feel the separateness between them.

So when she asked that question—*Do you think I'm real?*—he didn't know how to answer.

"If I die," he says, "this will all vanish."

"You don't know that."

"It's a safe bet."

"Can the mind die?" she asks.

The koan. The unanswerable question. The body can be killed but is the mind the product of the brain? They argued that point many times.

"I can't take the chance," Nix answers, as he always does.

Raine lazily drags her hands over the swaying swards of grass. She nears a leaning white oak. They planted that tree. The hills and water, the clouds and soil all sprang from his mind, but they built the house and planted that tree.

It's grown older, just like them.

Raine picks something up. Nix is still squatting when she takes his hand. Opening his fingers, she places an acorn in it.

"You were the seed," she says. "You are not the tree."

She closes his fingers around it, holding his fist in her delicate hands.

"This Dreamland is more than you. Perhaps it's more real than the world you live in."

"I don't care about Dreamland. Only you."

"Maybe that's the problem."

Nix always told his sister that Dreamland was a new reality, not just his imagination. But when asked to fully commit to that, it was too much of a risk. If he dies, it dies.

She dies.

"If I can fabricate you a physical body," he says, "you won't need me."

"The physical world isn't the gold standard of reality. There are other realms."

"The physical is all I got."

"Are you an old man in the *real world*?"

"That's just how my body looks. It's not me."

"Then if you're not your body, who are you?"

Another koan.

She knows why he wants to fabricate a physical body. He doesn't want to possess her, doesn't want her existence to be limited to Dreamland. He wants to give her a life, her own life. He wants to have children in the real world. They discuss this often; they already have names. Joshua, if it's a boy. Pearl, if it's a girl. That was the plan.

Raine didn't want to wait; she wanted to start the family in Dreamland. But Nix didn't want to raise children in a fantasy, he wanted them in the flesh, where he could rock them to sleep and kiss their boo-boos and watch them grow. He didn't want them to disappear if something happened to him.

Shep returns with a stick. Nix hurls it deep into the meadow.

"There's a girl in the warehouse," he says. "I think I can use her to look around. There must be some clue to the underground network, something that can give me some direction of where to find a fabricator. I'll need to get closer, though."

"They'll sense you."

"I'll use a proxy and cover my trail. I just need her eyes and ears, to see what's in the back room."

Shep is already returning, stick in mouth, black lips flapping. Nix stands to look at the valley. One of the boats is returning.

Raine drapes her arms around his neck and leans her head on his shoulder. The morning chill is already lifting, but a fire in the hearth would be nice. And he could use the rest. In the morning, he'll get a fresh start.

But he wonders, as he often does, how he could ever leave this place.

CHAPTER SEVEN_

The sun is locked behind a gray sky.

Nix walks down the middle of a long street—the warehouses on his right, the water to his left. Raine's image walks silently beside him. The white sedans are parked far from the shrinking crowd. Only hardcore bloggers and a few reporters are up this soon.

He doesn't want to mingle, but there's no other way to get close. Bricks were behind the warehouse on the loading docks. He's made slight adjustments to his facial features—altered his cheekbones, thickened his nose—and changed his biomite identity. If anyone checks, he's a blogger. No one will recognize him from yesterday.

There's not much activity. Most are chatting or eating fast food, a few are streaming reports or video. Several bloggers are curled up in sleeping bags near the pier, stocking caps peeking out.

Nix's biomite identity pings as onlookers watch him approach, scanning his identity, curious if he's someone with information. The activity dies down. He spots two men, early twenties, on a short guardrail, digging breakfast from a white bag. Facial recognition identifies them: Byron is African American; Henry, Korean American.

Nix drops his bag on the grass. "Any word?"

"None," Byron says. "They're slammed tight. Rumor floating that the bricks will make an announcement today, but they said that yesterday. Police don't know any more than we do, just standing guard."

Two officers sip coffee near the steel door.

"Bricks got the cops under wraps," Henry says. "Moved them out day one. Like to be a fly inside."

"You try tapping surveillance feeds?" Nix asks.

Byron shakes his head. "Like I said, slammed tight. Bricks are running field static to prevent scanning, and no hardwires to ride inside. No one knows what they're doing in there."

Nix thought if he had proximity, he could surf his senses through the Ethernet and link up with the girl's biomites. Maybe not.

"You staying put?" Nix asks. "Need to patch an update across the water."

His biomite identity told them he's a freelance blogger just picking up news for a London-based outlet. In the world of bloggers, he's about as low as it gets.

Byron smirks. "Ain't you a bit old to be streaming?"

"Never too old." Nix taps the back of his head, the universal sign of a recent biomite seed.

"Get comfy, old man. We'll watch your gear."

Nix throws a blanket on the ground. He leans back on the guardrail. Byron and Henry chat silently and figure an old man like that can't sit up and stream. Nix gets comfortable, leans back, and closes his eyes.

The sensations of the physical world recede.

His awareness slips into cyberspace, where information streams and thoughts collide. Byron and Henry's encrypted chat blends with other conversations in the vicinity. Nix moves his awareness toward the warehouse, where the information feels like a white cloud of static, of buzzing insects meant to scatter any attempts to *look* inside.

He sifts through the obscure net, searching for any semblance of organized consciousness. He feels several dense formations but avoids merging with them. His heartbeat picks up. If he connects with a brick, it could be the last thing he ever does.

There's nothing discernible in the warehouse, no information he can glean, no images he can stream. It's what keeps the bloggers from learning anything. But they don't know about the girl. Even if they did, they can't ride the Ethernet like Nix.

Too much clay.

Nix can't tell one identity from the other. They're all virtually identical, which tells him that everything he's feeling inside the warehouse are bricks. He pushes deeper when he feels a slight aberration in organized consciousness. It's the sign of imperfection, the activity of the subconscious.

The clay of a human mind.

Nix pushes his awareness through the white static until he's centered over this identity. He takes a moment to locate it in space and time, estimating that it's located near the back of the warehouse, sitting still.

Slowly, he wraps his mind around it.

He touches it like a toe in the water.

Her perception field is malleable and open. Nix merges with it like two computers reaching through cyberspace, attaching his perception field to hers. Forms swim out of the static as if layers of veils are lifted, one by one.

Until he's seeing.

Hearing.

He's in the back room of the warehouse.

CHAPTER EIGHT_

Jamie's cuffed to an ergonomic, gel-infused lounger. And cold off, once again.

There's a door leading to the warehouse, a tattered tablecloth hung over the window. The filtered light doesn't penetrate much further than the lounger. The room feels deep. Occasionally, something moves.

Tabletops are anchored to the wall, littered with electronics, empty bottles, mirrors, cigarettes, clothes, and other strange things. A shorthaired stuffed animal lies facedown to her right, its tail dangling over the edge. It's like Garfield fucked a lizard.

Her internal clock says it's been three days since they put her in the back. There's a blank spot in her memory where the second day should be.

The boredom has become torture. Without her field, she stares at the false ceiling's stained tiles. When she feels a strange buzz—an itching behind her eyes and deep in her ears—it's welcome. She clenches her teeth, feeling overdosed on caffeine.

"Hey there, Jamie." The door opens; light pours inside like a knife. The clutter deep in the room is briefly revealed. More freaky stuffed animals and a glass shower.

The blonde brick closes the door. "How are you?"

Despite the lounger's comfort, her body aches. She refuses to call her Anna. She's one of them. Even worse, she's a brick.

"You hungry?" Anna leans over the lounger, her short hair the kind of red that belongs on candy. "I brought some food."

Anna shakes the white bag, this time McDonald's. They shut off her music, cut her connection to the outside world, but at least they left her in control of her senses. If she hadn't turned off her olfactory and tasting senses, she'd be salivating. She'd also smell the wasting bodies.

And thoughts of Charlie would return.

She would remember him perched on the edge of the seat, remember his last words...and then gray walls and the rank odor when the club's field dropped.

She was crying and retching, holding him on the floor, screaming that he had to wake up, they had to go. If she could just get him out of there, he would come back. Even if he was charred, he still had a chance; they could figure things out.

But then the police arrived.

They were just outside the door before the nixes were decoded and the halfskins shut down. Only Jamie didn't go down. If only she didn't hesitate, if only she had taken that pill a minute sooner, she'd be out there. That was better than being in here.

Better than surviving.

That brick at the bar, the one that shut everyone down, was watching. It was like he was waiting for her to put that cold pill on her lips.

Charlie's the lucky one.

Anna clears the sacks from her last delivery, wiping the crumbs and rat droppings on the floor before unpacking the chicken nuggets and fries. She peels open the dipping sauces and arranges them on the tray, very orderly. She takes a bite, rolling her eyes.

"Mmm, you got to try this one, Jamie." Anna points at the sauce. "It's called sweet and sour."

She appears to be in her upper twenties with perky breasts and a tight frame. Her lipstick matches her hair. She picks apart the nugget with shiny red nails.

"I got to piss." The words scratch Jamie's throat.

"Take a bite first. Then we'll go to the bathroom."

Anna holds the nugget to her lips. If Jamie's quick, she can bite off one of her slender fingers, spit it on the floor for the rats. But what would that get her?

She turns her head.

Anna sighs. Her worried expression is convincing. She reaches in the pouch on her hip and puts the needles and tubes next to the food.

"I need another sample."

"Don't you have enough?"

Anna takes a few minutes to record her actions, then comes over with an elastic band and a pair of scissors. She pauses with a very serious look.

"Can I trust you?" she asks.

Jamie doesn't answer. The last time she cut the plastic cuffs, Jamie took a swing. She barely made a fist before a teeth-numbing sensation filled her head. She tumbled to the floor and stared at the fluorescent light while Anna pulled a blood sample, calmly pleading that she not fight, that she cooperate. That this would all be over soon.

Anna waits for an answer this time.

Jamie nods.

The pressure on her wrists is relieved with a snip. Jamie slowly swings her legs to sit up, the blood rushing to her feet. The room sways with exhaustion and hunger. Anna strokes the insides of Jamie's arms. Both are purple where blood was drawn the first couple times, the needle banging around the veins as she struggled. Anna's touch is tender.

"This is bullshit," Jamie says. "I'm 49.9%. Just scan me."

"Are you?"

"Am I what?"

"Just 49.9%?"

"I'd be out there if I wasn't."

Anna finds a vein where the purple gives way to yellow. She taps a few times before plunging the needle in it. Jamie is able to dull the pain response, but the sting still registers. The tube fills with dark red.

How many of those blood cells are biomites imitating blood cells?

"Is your blood red?" Jamie asks.

"Of course." Anna pops a second tube into the needle. "You're wondering how I feel, aren't you?"

Jamie flinches. That's exactly what she was wondering. Anna was in her head, seeing her thoughts. Jamie hates her but likes her, too. She wants to be like her, in total control of her thoughts and feelings. And she hates herself for wanting to look like that, too: confident and slutty. Powerful.

Hating herself is nothing new.

"You're a copy," Jamie says. "You're a fake and you know it."

Anna pulls the needle out and bandages the spot before packing the tubes and needles.

"You're a puppet, Anna. That guy out there makes you do what he wants, he makes you like it. You can be turned off, you know that."

"So can you."

"Only half of me."

"The other half won't survive."

"At least I started out as clay. You never were."

Anna zips up the pouch. She holds up a fresh pair of plastic cuffs. "Do you still need to use the restroom?"

"No."

"Then eat."

"I want to go home."

"No," Anna says. "You don't."

She says it calmly, knowingly. There's nothing out there for Jamie, and she knows it.

There are voices outside the door.

"I want out of here!" Jamie shouts. "Goddamnit, you can't do this! This is illegal! Where's my mom?"

Jamie hurls a chicken nugget at her. It smacks against the door.

"Where are the cops? I want out of here, you puppet bitch! I want to talk to someone! You can't fucking do this illegal shit!"

She reaches for the tray when her arm seizes. Every muscle in her body locks. The smile has dropped from Anna's friendly face. Her eyelids heavy. Jamie is trapped in a catatonic pose, fingers curled like claws. Unable to even swallow.

Anna's heels rap the concrete. She puts the spilled food into the bag, retrieves the chicken nugget from the floor and wipes the grease from the lounger. Jamie can see her in the periphery. Panic fills her like icy insects. There's not enough oxygen in the carefully measured breaths she's forced to take. She tries to scream, to apologize, to sob... she can't even blink. That strange itching sensation burns the back of her eyes and tickles her ears, like someone's eavesdropping.

She's trapped in her body.

Anna steps out of sight, her footsteps fading toward the back of the room where darkness cloaks strange objects. Something scuffs across the floor. Anna returns with a large chair, the wooden legs thick and heavy. She squares it to the right of the door and goes back to the dark. An identical chair is placed facing the first one, visually framing the door.

Anna drops her hand on the doorknob.

Jamie begins to involuntarily move. Her chest burns for oxygen. She stands and shuffles her feet toward the chair on the right. Her efforts to stop or look around are futile. Anna has hijacked her biomites, moving her like a remote-controlled object, simply willing her to slowly squat into the chair, arms on the wooden armrests. The empty chair stares back.

Who's the puppet now?

Tears swell on her lower lids, rolling down her cheeks. She feels them on the corners of her mouth.

Slowly, she moves her fingers. Jamie grips the armrests. She inhales a deep breath as she breaks through her confinement. Another breath. And another. She holds back the sobs, her heart hammering in her throat.

The doorknob clicks.

Light falls across Jamie's lap. Shiny black shoes step unevenly into view. The man stands for a moment, looking down at her struggling to grasp the world that's betrayed her. He tugs at his gray slacks and sits, crossing his right leg over his left.

Jamie wipes her eyes before sitting up. It's the old man. He's mostly bald. What little hair clings to the perimeter of his skull is white and his left right eye misshaped.

"You're very lucky." His words are crisp. "You should be out there, you realize."

Jamie wants to duck her head to avoid his piercing glare. She stares at her blue fingernail polish that's partially stripped away. She rubs her eyes, but the burning-itching sensation won't go away.

"Why did you come here?" he asks.

A sudden compulsion to tell the truth rises in her throat. Jamie's lips part, but she presses her tongue to the roof of her mouth, refusing any sort of confession.

The man looks at Anna. He brushes his knee, picking at bits of lint before folding his hands.

"I know everything about you, Jamie. Your biomites cannot keep secrets."

His stare is penetrating. She looks to the dark end of the room. Her head, though, is forced to turn back. His gray eyes are fearless. His expression joyless.

"Your father left when you were seven years old. When you cry, you hug a pillow and bury your face so no one hears, although you haven't cried in years. You killed your sadness, didn't you? You shut those emotions off so you didn't have to feel them, so you wouldn't cry anymore. And you masturbate with your left hand."

"Why'd you even ask?" she blurts.

"Because half of you is still clay. That half is God's gift, Jamie.

That's the half Anna can't read. Maybe there's more you'd like to tell me?"

She doubts that's true. Her clay doesn't hold secrets from her biomites. She's committed so many biomites to replace brain cells to amp her pleasure centers that she couldn't hide from Charlie anymore. She doesn't stand a chance against a brick.

"You're special." A grin touches one side of his mouth, just below the large eye. "Do you know why?"

He leans forward.

"You took a pill to destroy God's gift. The ingested biomites began integrating with your clay when my brick shut them down. You are as close to halfskin as any human being could possibly be, but that's not why you're special."

The tip of his tongue grazes his parched lips.

"The shutdown occurred at a precise moment, Jamie. My brick waited for you to swallow the pill. He waited for it to expose its secrets, crystallize the embedded code before it was corrupted by your identity, before it began replicating your DNA. You contain nixes in an open state."

The man unfolds his hands.

"Do you know what that means?"

He continues staring, with the curl at the corner of his mouth, as if bathing in her innocence, soaking in the pleasure of her ignorance.

The doorknob clicks and the warehouse light falls on them along with death. Jamie's olfactory senses come online. She blinks as the foul odor fills her nostrils, seeps through her pores. Her attempts to turn it off fail.

She retches.

The man watches as she struggles to breathe, tears spilling down her face. She tries to look toward the dark, to close her eyes, but she's forced to turn toward the warehouse, where nude bodies are neatly lined on the floor, head to toe, their clothes stacked next to them.

"You are the chosen one, Jamie. You will be the one that climbs upon the cross and dies for their sins."

Several bricks walk among the corpses. Jamie tries not to focus, tries to blur the vision with tears as the man babbles on. Her eyes itch madly, her ears burning.

"What..." She wets her lips. "What are you going to do?"

It feels like the words were spoken for her. She doesn't want to know what the man will do to her; she just wants the door to close, for him to go away. She just wants this all to go away.

"I will set you free."

He means it differently than it sounds. A whimper escapes her.

"Your mother will see you." The man stands. "I promise."

Anna steps aside. The man limps next to her and braces himself in the doorway. For a moment, he blocks the view.

"It's a shame." He turns his head. "You strive to kill your feelings, to dim your senses so you don't see the ugly of the world. Everything you experience is a gift, Jamie. I would like you to accept what has been given to you."

The man walks away, his gait uneven. He shrinks away from her, continuing his limping pace down an aisle, slowly revealing the exposed bodies. Anna follows him.

The door remains open.

Jamie is forced to watch. She contains her panic until she recognizes the military green jacket atop a pile of clothing.

There's no pillow to hide her face this time.

MOTHER_
MOTHER TAKETH AWAY

Dr. Kaplan didn't know what day it was.

He marched down the corridor and reviewed case notes that scrolled past his vision, superimposed on the passing wheelchairs and nurses' stations. He had supervised ten organ transplants and three skin grafts and there were more. The only part of his body that didn't ache was biomite-enhanced.

His clay was exhausted.

It was getting difficult to focus; he could hardly remember what he just read. He attempted to enhance brain activity.

"Denied," his internal monitor responded. "Core body temperature is elevated. Enhanced limitations have been exceeded."

He didn't break stride. An override had already been allowed due to the nature of the emergency, but he was nearing thirty-nine hours of work. Six hours of sleep would be required to reset enhancement mode.

He rubbed his face. The sun wouldn't be up for another three hours. There was no choice: he had to sleep. Dr. Heigel would have to supervise his transplants.

He was waiting at the elevator when Drs. Angleton and Bates rushed past, white coats fluttering. The elevator opened, but Dr. Kaplan watched them run to the end of the wing.

There was chaos outside the Organ Fabrication Lab.

He left the elevator empty. Two nurses and a technician ran past him. His pace quickened, but his adrenaline had already been exhausted. He punched the door open and entered the lab.

The large room was lowly lit and segregated by aisles and crowded shelves. Red lights flashed on all the clear boxes that were always printing three-dimensional biomite organs. Dr. Kaplan had a liver due in less than an hour and the fabricators were standing still.

All of them.

An argument started up. Something broke. Doctors were shouting and technicians worked feverishly at their workstations. Dr. Felton, chief of Biomite Medicine, was more vocal than any of them.

"Jimmy." Dr. Kaplan grabbed the technician rushing into the lab. "What the hell is going on?"

"Mother shut us down."

"What?"

"Yeah, no warning. Just cold off."

Jimmy tried to pull away. "But hospitals are exempt from the fabricator shutdown."

"Not anymore."

"We're printing organs, Jimmy! We're not creating identities."

"I didn't shut us down."

"We're not ready for a shutdown, you understand? I've got people in pre-op waiting for organs that are half printed."

Jimmy pried the doctor's hand off of his coat. "You'll have to do raw seeding."

"There's no time. They need functional organs now."

"Sorry, Doctor. Mother declared every fabricator illegal."

Jimmy made his escape. The government had declared that fabricating life was as illegal as cloning. Mother supported their decision and killed the raw biomites the fabricators used to build hearts and kidneys.

Dr. Kaplan left the lab. He went to his car and drove home.

CHAPTER NINE_

Nix floats, disembodied, a wraith with no home, a voice on the wind. He drifts through the droning static of cyberspace like an aimless being caught in the current, the tide throwing him where it wants.

The static comes in waves, its rhythm crashing on a nonexistent shore, scratching its existence on the ethereal current. In silent ebbs between the peaks, he can feel his body out there.

The waves get louder. They scratch his throat, burn his nostrils. Nix opens his eyes, chest heaving.

"Relax, old man." Byron drops his hand on Nix's shoulder.

The stench of death still clogs his sinuses. A stream of snot trickles over his lips. He wipes his face, blinking away the tears. A few people turn around.

"Don't panic," Raine's voice whispers in his ear. "Relax, stay put."

If the bricks sense him, he couldn't outrun them. The main thing is to blend in.

"What the hell were you doing?" Byron says.

"Tell them you were caught in a data stream," Raine adds.

"Caught in the data stream," he mutters. "Couldn't disconnect."

Byron snorts. *Rookie mistake.* Every streaming blogger knows you don't attach your identity to a heavy upload, especially when you're streaming across the globe. The momentum can pull your consciousness with it, deposit your memories in a computer, fragmented like data.

"Next time," Henry says, "redistribute more biomites into the hypothalamus."

"Smaller chunks, old man," Byron adds.

Nix pulls an energy bar from his bag and chews slowly. A news truck is moving down the road. The crowd is beginning to swell. His breath returns to normal, the basic act of eating resetting his behavior.

The bodies are nude. They've probably visually analyzed them, recording all the physical attributes and ingested samples for preliminary analysis.

There's a rumor in the paranoid, antigovernment underground. Many believe that Marcus and his bricks have covertly taken half-skins back to Mother for a full-immersion analysis, basically dissolving their biomites for clues. But the world is watching the warehouse. They can't take the bodies this time, not without total chaos. The public would demand Mother be shut down.

But the girl will go with him. He's taking her; that's what he meant by setting her free. That pill contains critical data.

The nixes are caught in suspended animation, the gap between self-destruction and integration. They're meant to degrade before and after in the event of a shutdown, but now they're fully exposed. All the secrets can be read—links to suppliers, networks of producers, and locations of fabricators. It's everything Marcus has been looking for.

Nix, too.

Nix dusts the crumbs off his coat. He packs carefully and slings the bag over his shoulder, walking against the flow of traffic.

If he's going to get the girl, he'll need help.

CHAPTER TEN_

Marcus leans against the wall, poking at two pills in his palm. His fucking knee is screaming. It never hurts like this when he's inside Mother. Nothing hurts. When he leaves, his body feels old again.

The nearest body is a young woman with plump breasts and a narrow midriff. Her pelvic bones jut from her hips. A precise divot has been cut from her left breast where nixes were carved out and, subsequently, digested by one of the bricks for analysis.

Noise comes from somewhere beyond the back walls. The door to the back room swings open, the hinges squealing as Anna pulls it shut. Her heels echo in the dead space.

Marcus clenches the pills, watching her blonde hair swing in time to the sway of her hips. She holds out a bottle of water. Marcus washes the painkillers down and waits for relief.

"She's sleeping," Anna says. "I'll keep her unconscious until we're finished."

Marcus screws the lid back on, wiping his mouth. He shifts his weight, staring at the big-breasted corpse, wishing she'd suffered more. Death is too easy.

"Why don't you get some rest," Anna says. "Get off your feet."

"Your analysis of the conversation?"

Anna sighs. "Confirmed. An identity was latched to her perception field. We believe it was Nixon Richards."

"You believe?"

"The identity was scrambled. It's possible one of the bloggers or news agencies have hired a hacker of his caliber, but statistically, we believe it's him."

"He heard everything?"

"Yes. And saw everything, too. Including the fabricator in the back."

The glass case. The epitome of evil.

"He had to be in the area. If we move quickly, we could arrest everyone. It'll take some time to—"

"Not yet." Marcus takes his earpiece out.

It's doubtful he's still out there. Anything rash will scare him away. He needs to be lured deeper into the trap. Now that they know he's here, let him feel safe. Let him reach for the fabricator.

Twenty years I've waited.

Excitement rumbles beneath the ache in his knee, the same knee he wrecked trying to apprehend Nixon Richards and his sister. They released the nixes to the underground; they wrecked his marriage and spawned an entire race of undetectable halfskins that have required Marcus to dedicate his life to capturing. The surgically repaired knee reminds him of his mistakes. It's fitting that here, in the rain where the pain is the greatest, that he finds Nix.

He can't be rash.

"The rest of this?" Marcus waves at the bodies.

"The delivery will arrive tomorrow at three o'clock," Anna says.

"It was supposed to be three days."

"Some complications with Mother's fabricators. The shipment will be here tomorrow."

Marcus tests the knee. The Dilaudid needed another twenty

minutes to kick in, but he was tired of waiting. He'd waited long enough.

Anna guides him through the back room, past the sleeping young lady. They exit through the newly fashioned doorway cut out of the back-room wall. He looks back at the glass case before finding his way to the loading docks, where a white sedan picks him up.

CHAPTER ELEVEN_

Baxter whines.

Cali takes a hotdog slice from the counter and rewards Kooper first for sitting quietly. She returns to washing dishes while the music crackles. Sometimes silence reveals her troubles too clearly.

The sun is setting and the long shadow of the house stretches all the way to the barn. Misting rain keeps everything damp and cold.

To the right, outside the pasture, the old swing set reflects the waning sunlight. The posts and chains are rusted and one of the legs has crumpled into the weeds like a broken knee. The swing is askew. Cali imagines that it was shiny and new when the father built it and the mother watched her two children while she cooked dinner and cleaned up. The laughter probably carried into the house.

They had lost one of the girls to meningitis. She was only seven.

"God called her," the mother had told the neighbors. "She's with Him now."

Maybe that's when the swing set became a static effigy of sorrow. They still had one child, but there would always be the memory of them both. And the laughter of two. Ten years later, the family died in an automobile accident.

No biomites to save them.

Cali dries the last dish, staring at the swing set. This was where she was meant to be, in a house with ghosts that look much like the ones that haunt her.

God called.

She checks the time, a habit she'd developed. Clay folks don't have internal clocks.

"Want to get the paper?" Cali asks.

The dogs have curled up on a small rug. They jump up. Their toenails click on the floor, paws slipping as they race out. The railing leading down the steps is loose and the posts are rotting.

The dogs wait next to the truck. Cali lets them climb over the driver's seat. She rolls the window down and enjoys a cold drive out to the gate. The electric motor whirs, craning the metal entrance open. The dogs jump out to sniff around while Cali walks out to the road but not in it.

The road is the edge of her safe zone.

The abandoned cell phone tower is one of the reasons she initially considered buying this land. Centered on the property, it was easily converted to generate a static field. In the countryside, a blind spot blends into the scenery, keeping Mother from seeing her. She hasn't left the property in five years.

The road is the limit.

She starts back for the truck, with the newspaper under her arm, when the pressure begins. It starts at the back of her head and pushes forward.

Bing. She shuffles to a standstill.

Cali restrains herself from immediately answering the call from Nix. It has been years since she heard his voice. She hasn't seen him in five years. *Five years and four months.*

She can't answer.

If she does, she'll make him promise to come to the farm, to let her protect him. To stay away from Dreamland.

To turn Raine off.

A third wave begins. *Bing.* Cali clutches the newspaper as the dogs climb out of the ditch. She closes her eyes and projects a thought. *Off.*

She stands on the lonely road, the frigid breeze blowing over the treetops. She yearns for music, for something to distract her from the thoughts and the feelings that usher in guilt and shame and sadness. She wants to answer his call.

It'll only hurt worse.

The newspaper hits the dirt. The pages flap open.

Cali walks past the truck. She begins running, pumping her arms in stride with her long pace. The dogs keep up, tongues hanging out. They have no idea where their owner is going or why.

But neither does Cali.

She just runs.

CHAPTER TWELVE_

The hood of the police car is warm.

Paul leans against the driver's door, trying to remember something. It's a word or an idea or...*something*. He's obsessed with recalling it, remembering that he's done so a dozen times already. It's something urgent.

Critical.

The thought hovers in a haze that filled his head days ago. He's not sure just how long it's been, but night has followed day more than once.

His memories are cloaked in a dreamy fog, surreal. They're like eagles soaring high above, wings stretched out and sometimes turning so they disappear into the blue. Paul searches the sky for them to return, to bring back whatever he's supposed to remember.

"Sarge," Jeffers says, "you want in?"

It takes a moment to focus on the officer's face, to recognize the bristled mustache. Jeffers is in front of another cruiser. A third one effectively blocks the alley leading to the loading docks behind the warehouse.

"You want in?" Jeffers repeats.

"What?"

"Materese says the brick doesn't have a cock."

Paul licks his lips. They've been dry for days, can't seem to hold moisture. He shakes his head, focusing on the uniformed officer sipping coffee behind Jeffers. Her hair is pulled into a tight bun, the eyeliner thick and sharp.

Just past the back bumper of the third car, the brick stands at the corner of the building. His arms hang straight at his sides. His expression is tireless, waxy and sentinel blank. Only the subtle rise and fall of his chest hints at life.

"I say he's hung like a donkey." Jeffers holds his hands apart. "Like that."

"What's he going to use it for?" Materese says.

"Whatever he wants. I mean, Christ, if I could build a dick, I'd make it worth the while."

"Use your head, idiot. Bricks don't procreate; they're squeezed out of a fabricator like glue. They just got to look human."

"Procreate."

"It means fuck."

"He's got a cock, Materese. It doesn't make sense not to."

"He ain't got nothing, I can tell. It's like one of those Ken dolls, just a bump between his legs."

Jeffers chews his lip, looking the brick up and down. The brick doesn't move, but he's listening. Paul can feel him absorbing everything around him, feeling and seeing and hearing. He's making sure they do their job.

"I've got a hundred says he's sporting wood."

The foam coffee cup is poised inches from her lips, the rim stained red. She shakes her head like she's had one too many of these conversations. Jeffers digs a bill out of his pocket and slams it on the hood.

"Get proof and it's yours," he says.

"You need help."

"No, I mean get proof and the money's yours."

"If you want to see a cock, look down," she says, sipping. "It won't cost you."

Paul sways on his feet, clicking his front teeth. Jeffers licks his lips but not because they're dry. He's just watched too much porn. He probably has a brick fetish, petitioning the government to fabricate sex models to satiate the urges of half the population that argue rape, divorce, and depression would be reduced if people could own sexbots.

Jeffers would have one of every color. Paul would take that bet.

"Why you so uptight?" Jeffers says. "He ain't human. It's more like a rubber dick, like the one you got stuffed in your glove box."

"Fuck you."

"Hey, don't be embarrassed. It's natural."

"Jeffers," Paul says.

"No disrespect, Sarge. I'm just trying to learn something. And give Materese money. That's all I'm saying. I seen her dildo."

"Fine." Materese reaches for the bill.

Jeffers dangles it out of reach. "Got to see it first."

"How?" she asks.

"Unzip his pants. He ain't moved all day."

"Pull his pants down?"

"Talk dirty to him or something. Tell him you want a robot baby. It ain't like you never got in a man's pants before; do whatever you do."

"You're a sick fuck, Jeffers."

"I'm curious. There's a difference."

Materese looks at Paul. There's hope that he'll stop her, tell her it's a bad idea, that Jeffers should go sit in the car. But he's still swimming in the haze, trying to remember the thing he's supposed to remember. For a moment, he wonders why Jeffers is waving a hundred-dollar bill.

Materese puts her coffee on the hood. She approaches warily, waving her hand in front of the brick's face when she's within spitting distance. He doesn't blink.

His hair is brown and cropped near the scalp. His posture is slouched, his shoulders round. He looks like someone you'd see alone in a dark bar.

Materese takes the last couple steps one at a time, pausing each time. Paul watches with mild interest, falling in and out of focus. One second he's watching a young Hispanic woman reaching for a middle-aged man's frumpy trousers, and the next it's his subordinate about to sexually harass a brick.

Paul forms a word to stop this when his thoughts are obliterated. Materese's hand stops an inch from the belt buckle. She's as still as the automobile. Jeffers's tongue is out. Both of them are frozen.

The brick begins blinking.

He looks at Paul. His eyelids appear heavy, his light blue eyes tired.

Jeffers and Materese suddenly go to their cars. A heavy engine rattles behind Paul. He moves his head like he's underwater. A white car is followed by a large truck—the type used to move furniture. Jeffers and Materese drive past him, opening the blockade. The moving truck is followed by two more, all with the U-Haul logo. They turn down the alley, gears grinding, hot exhaust in his nostrils.

Jeffers and Materese close the gap once the convoy is inside. They lean against their cars. Jeffers strokes his bristled mustache, a daydreamy haze in his eyes. Materese picks her fingernails. Paul thinks he should remind Jeffers his money is fluttering across the street.

Paul gets in his car. It's hot and stuffy. He loosens his collar, trying to remember where he is and what he's supposed to be doing.

Someone knocks on the driver's side window, a man with a bristled mustache. Paul should know him, but he can't recall his name.

"What are you doing, Sarge?" the man asks.

"What?"

"What are you doing in your cruiser?"

Paul strokes the steering wheel and notices all the switches and monitors. He's in a police car.

"Got to go."

"Where?"

Paul shakes his head.

"You coming back?" the man asks.

The brick is staring. Another strange wave passes through Paul, tingles beneath his scalp like scrubbing bubbles wiping his brain clean. Telling him what to do.

"Yeah," Paul says. "I'll be back."

He follows the white car and U-Hauls to the loading dock.

CHAPTER THIRTEEN_

The sun is out.

It's burned away the steel mat of clouds that's entombed the sky for four days. Sunlight reflects off the wet streets. Marcus slouches in the backseat, watching the oblivious citizens of Seattle blunder down sidewalks and wait for streetlights. The fabric of humanity is like parched linen dangling over a flame of biomite technology; a flame that could incinerate any shred of human semblance, leaving human forms like empty cicada shells, like pillars of salt.

Sodom and Gomorrah.

If not for Marcus, they would all perish without a thought. If not for his dedication, there would be no one to extinguish the flame. And now, after so many struggles, the tide will finally turn.

He could hardly sleep.

The hotel was comfortable and quiet, but Marcus stared at the ceiling. Even a sleeping pill took longer than usual, its effects still swimming in his head.

He's waited twenty years for this day. Twenty years to have the boy—he's a man, but will always be a boy—in his grasp. He'll take Nix back to Mother and watch her digest him slowly.

Marcus pats Anna's bare knee just below the hemline. Her

lipstick is magenta and perfectly lined. She appears unfocused, staring past the front seat, through the windshield.

"Mother is updating," she says.

Marcus cringes. He prefers not to call the massive artificial intelligence that monitors biomites by her acronym. She might overlook humanity, but he had a different relationship with her, something on an equal level. No, he couldn't match her processing ability, nothing could. Marcus brought her passion; he brought her wisdom that only one of God's creatures could bring.

Marcus caresses the inside of her knee then folds his hands on his lap. "Why didn't she call me?"

"She prefers to speak with you when you return home."

The car stops at the stoplight. A man on the corner stares at the white car. Above him, a billboard advertises a long-lasting Dreamland experience.

"Continue," Marcus says.

"Free the girl."

Marcus chuckles, waiting for more. Anna is looking at him now, her eyes focused on his lips. "We'll do nothing of the sort," he says. "The girl contains everything and the boy knows it. He'll do something rash and we'll have him."

"Her projected analysis suggests that if the girl is released, Nixon Richards will find her and lead us to his sister. The probability of success is 83%."

"The probability of capturing Nixon Richards right now is 100%."

"That is not the objective."

"And when we have him, his sister will come out of hiding. We've already discussed this." Marcus checks his jacket for his earpiece. "I want to talk with her now."

"She has already implemented the change, Marcus. Her projections are complete."

"She didn't discuss this with me!"

That is the issue. It isn't that she just snatched Nix out of his hand, not that she shit on this glorious morning; it is that she didn't consult him. *That's not how this works.* She continuously conducts endless scenarios, analyzing human behavior and motivation, predicting the probability of outcomes with greater accuracy than anything on the planet...but she cannot see the future!

These are probabilities. Chances. Science, by its own admission, is less than perfect. It works from educated guesses and refines its mistakes. Only God is perfect.

And Marcus speaks for Him.

That is the agreement. Mother does the math, but Marcus speaks the divine. They work together.

The car waits at the final stoplight. Three cargo trucks are lined up behind them, their diesel engines idling loudly. The satellite imagery of their approach will be blurred from public record. No one will see them make the final approach to the warehouses.

When the light turns green, Marcus realizes he's staring at a billboard that advertises free biomite boosters.

Jamie's mouth is slack, drool slipping from the corner, a glistening trail to her chin. Yellowish light filters through the opaque glass dimmed with age and neglect. Dust particles hang over her.

Marcus watches her from the dark end of the room. The door is closed, but the odor reaches him. It permeates everything, but no longer reminds him of victory. Now it's just the stench of death and the possibility of losing everything.

Right there, sleeping, is the key. That pill inside her is the key.

From the other side of the door, the warehouse has come alive. Some of the bricks grunt, dropping heavy objects on the concrete. There's an occasional sound of fabric and zippers, of vinyl bags rustling.

Marcus steps on a soft cord and smells the tang of biomites. It's a whiplike tail. He nudges the limp animal with the tip of his shoe, its skin smooth, leathery, and red. In the dark, it looks like a dog, but the ivory fangs protruding from the oversized snout are evident.

Fabricated abominations.

The pets range from mouse-sized animals to Great Danes, each of them outfitted with customized limbs and unnatural colors. Some with fur, others hide. All of them with teeth. They were likely prowling around when the nixes were shut down, dropping like the power cord had been pulled.

Before Mother put a stop to it, everyday people were working their way up to fabricating larger organisms, keeping them around like freakish pets. How far were they from fabricating dead loved ones?

All the warehouses in this sector are owned by the same subsidiary. This was just the beginning. If the brick hadn't discovered their activity, they would've expanded into the neighboring buildings, opening doorways through the back walls like Marcus had done. How much would someone pay to fabricate a son or daughter?

This wasn't just a party scene. It was the fuel that kept the biomite flame growing, that pushed it closer to the fabric.

How many more of these dens are there?

Meanwhile, Mother will free the girl, the drooling Sleeping Beauty who contains all the answers. They could drop her in the digesting vats, absorb the information and locate places like this all over the world. They could fabricate an army of bricks to stage a global raid. And she wants to let her go.

He can override Mother. Marcus has that authority.

He can force her to capture Nix and lure his sister into the open, but he knows better. He knows his desires are distorting his rational thinking, that Mother has the same wish as he does without the emotional attachment.

She wants them both, too.

Jamie sounds like a child caught in a nightmare. Marcus kicks the dead pet and limps over to the lounger. The muscles on her neck are rigid, her tongue working hard to break free.

Marcus strokes her chin with the backs of his fingers, running them softly to her throat. He leans close enough to feel her breath on his lips and her eyes snap open.

He squeezes her throat, feeling the muscles collapse in his grip. Her breath catches and her eyes widen. She's still caught in Anna's catatonic grip, unable to move, unable to look away. He doesn't have the ability to sense if Nix is in there, if he's still pawning her perception field, but he hopes so. He hopes that boy sees him.

He will always be a boy.

If freeing this girl will give him Nix *and* Cali, he will not stand in the way.

Marcus shoves off.

The girl struggles to breathe; unformed words fall off her lips in grunts and squeaks. Marcus ignores the pathetic attempts to curse him. He opens the door and walks into the putrid fog of dead flesh.

Anna is waiting for him. He watches the bricks work like soldiers. They carry body bags across the warehouse, dropping each one next to a nude body.

Marcus looks down at a teenage boy named Charlie. Most of his flesh is sickly pale, the stomach slightly bloated. A small patch of hair is tufted between his nipples.

A pair of bricks drops a body bag next to it, pulling the flaps to the side to reveal an exact duplicate of Charlie. The skin is even discolored with veiny, marbled patterns near the surface, even the bruises around his bicep where someone grabbed him. Maybe his girlfriend was trying to stop him from taking the nixes.

Or maybe she was trying to get away.

The bricks lift Mother's stiff fabrication from the bag and quickly slide Charlie—the real Charlie—inside. They dress the imposter with the clothes that are stacked near the corpse, using photo images they recorded upon arrival, adjusting the coat and pants to match what he looked like before he was undressed. Even the wrinkles in the sleeves and the inadvertent cuff of the pant leg are exacted.

They haul the body bag to the trucks. They will return with another.

Marcus is tempted to bend down. Even though the pain in his knee has subsided, he'll pay for it. The people outside the warehouse, the ones waiting for answers, will never know the bodies of their loved ones will be flown to Mother for deep analysis, where they'll be pulled apart, where every cell, every part of them will be digested for future reference.

What they'll find in the warehouse once Marcus leaves are fabricated duplicates made of biomites and a small amount of clay, just enough to fool an investigation. They'll bury these fabricated bodies, mourn over them, take flowers to their graves and never know the difference. In God's eyes, it won't matter. Their love for their sons and daughters will still be true.

And Marcus will be that much closer to stopping this plague.

"Contact the chief of police," he says. "Tell him we've concluded our investigation and the families are allowed to view their loved ones."

"The press will want a statement," Anna says.

"Have someone else do it."

"You'd like a brick to handle PR?"

"Yes."

She did that on purpose, knowing he was struggling with the new course of action. She referred to her kindred as bricks, as if the insult of their fabrication is completely lost on her. He likes that.

"I'd also like to give the press full access to the premises. Bring the camera crews inside, even sneak some of those bloggers in. I want a team of bricks to stay behind to be interviewed. I want the public to be saturated with details. Let them see what their future looks like."

"Public beheadings...you know that tactic doesn't work."

"Humor me."

"I'll take the lead in public relations, then."

"No. I want you to be on the plane with me, I'll want company.

I'll be flying back with the bodies, I want analysis to begin immediately."

The bricks work ceaselessly as always, hauling bag after bag into the warehouse, swapping and dressing bodies down to the last detail. There's no need to encourage them to work faster. They're such good slaves. Marcus revels in the fact that he never has to deal with human employees, imperfect and slow.

An ironic twist, but effective.

Perhaps, he always thinks, there's a place for bricks in society once humans stop defiling God's temples.

Two body bags are dropped near the back office and left unattended. Marcus shuffles near the foot of them. Anna takes a knee and pulls one of them open to reveal a young girl inside. Jamie's fabrication is chalky but well-preserved, as if she only passed this morning.

Marcus sighs. "Set her free, then."

He limps toward the back exit, bricks avoiding him as he heads toward a waiting car, with no idea of what Mother plans to do.

But it'll work.

It usually does.

CHAPTER FOURTEEN_

A buzzy hum swarms Paul's head, carrying him through colors and images, random thoughts and memories.

His eyelids are heavy. Hands like rubber.

Dim light filters through the shade of a door directly ahead of him. Cries of outrage and grief hail from the other side.

General chaos.

Words that don't quite connect.

A reclining lounger sits in the waning light. A girl lies on it, her head back, mouth open. The dead light falls on her like an old lamp, yellow and dusty. Her chest rises and falls in slow, steady rhythm.

Shadows pass across the shade.

The door rattles.

They're coming for her. They're coming for...Jamie.

She was a victim in a heinous crime, she was held against her will. The cops were going to do terrible things to her.

Not cops. Someone else.

Paul's feet are glued to the floor. His legs, rigid wood. He raises his fat hand, breaking the paralysis like a brittle cocoon. He bends his knees and takes a step. His blood flows.

Her hands are folded over her stomach, bright red lines around her wrists where plastic cuffs chafed the skin. Paul slides his arms beneath her, lifting the dead weight. There's a body slumped against the lounger. It's a man. His chin is against his chest, the face hidden by the shadows. Paul ignores that one.

I've only come for Jamie.

He walks through a network of corridors enclosed with unfinished walls and sheets of plastic, occasionally bumping her limp body into bare studs. His instincts tell him to turn left when the exit feels left. Go straight when that seems to be the way.

He's got to get far away.

His intuition leads him to a large room with huge rolling doors. One is open, leading to a concrete ledge for loading. A white sedan is parked next to a police cruiser. Paul climbs down and slides Jamie in the back of the white car.

He drives down the alley, onto Beech Street.

To get her away.

To keep her safe.

CHAPTER FIFTEEN_

THE CROWD HAS DOUBLED. THE POLICE HAVE TRIPLED. THE chief of police and three of his lieutenants are behind a podium inside the barricade.

Nix stands two blocks away on a berm of soil, his vision enhanced on the male and female bricks stepping to the podium. They're brunettes of average build and forgettable features but large, soulful eyes. The barricade buckles as the crowd pushes forward. Their grief has transformed into anger that blames the bricks and police for their halfskin sons and daughters.

They have no one else to blame.

Nix tunes in to a blog stream to hear the audio while he watches the chief of police and his lieutenants stand behind the bricks, chins thrust out, eyes hazy with the dullness of old silverware.

"Let me express our sincere apologies for this delay," the female brick says. Her cheeks sag with the weight of sorrow, her eyes heavy, eyebrows slightly pinched with concern. "I speak on behalf of the Seattle Police Department, the Biomite Oversight Committee, and all the men and women dedicated to serving humanity when I say we are deeply sorry. A tragedy like this affects everyone, but especially you. It is deeply regrettable."

The crowd rebels against the false empathy although, with time and repeated delivery, they'll soon be swayed. The imitation of human emotions and body language speaks directly to the subconscious.

When the female brick finishes, she bows her head and makes room for the male brick to step front and center. While his expression is also mournful, it is heavy with the weight of severity.

"We have asked for your patience," he announces to the crowd as well as the millions watching it stream through the blogosphere, "to ensure that events like this will never happen again, that we can ensure the safety and well-being of everyone. It is our hope that you will join us in ending technology abuse."

The crowd grows impatient. Cries of grief can be heard all the way up the street. He continues his empathic message before turning to the chief of police.

"Would you care to explain the procedure for these good people?"

The chief steps forward and delivers a dead set of instructions for people that have been previously identified as family to come to the right, where they will be ushered inside to view the deceased.

Letting family walk all over a crime scene?

"Verified media will also be admitted," he announces, half asleep.

The barricade opens and the police usher them forward.

"What now?" Raine's image stands barefoot on the grass.

"I'll have a look," Nix says.

"She won't be in there."

"Maybe not."

"Then why risk it?"

Nix starts toward the heaving crowd. Raine's image keeps up.

"Nix, there's nothing in there. They've already picked the place clean and the girl is gone. You can't save her even if she is in there—there are just too many bricks. It's not your fault."

Somehow, it is his fault. His sister ignored all his calls while he sat in a hotel room, watching blogs stream updates. He analyzed half a dozen ways to infiltrate the warehouse. When they announced that media would be allowed access, he could create a diversion or find an exit. There had to be a way; he just needed some help. And she ignored him.

He knew she would.

When he arrived that morning for the press conference and crazy fucking announcement that family would be allowed to meander through the warehouse while bloggers streamed their reactions to the world, he knew Jamie would be gone. He felt it. He scanned the area for her biomite identity—as unique as her fingerprints, indelibly stamped on her awareness.

Gone.

"Let's not go in there." Raine's hand falls on his shoulder. "There's always tomorrow."

That is the real problem. This will happen somewhere tomorrow and the day after that and the day after that. There will be an endless string of Jamies and warehouses full of lifeless halfskins. Marcus and the bricks know what they're doing now. With Jamie and that nixed pill inside her, they have intel and know how to get more. Before long they'll be shutting down halfskins daily. How long before Nix is one of them?

He blends into the crowd, slowly making his way to the entrance. An identity scan penetrates his bones.

Nix feels a brick's psychic intrusion like energy particles wriggling through his body, examining his cells, his biomites, searching for verified identification. It's as if the hand of Mother emanates from this diminutive female brick standing by the steel door, her green eyes unblinking, unforgiving.

Perhaps another strain of nixes would've spilled its secrets to her, but Nix isn't cloaked with just any biomite. These are the nixes Cali engineered when she saved him twenty years ago, a strain she never released to anyone else. While most nixes are produced in small batches and distributed to buyers, Nix and Cali's are unique and, as far as he knows, the only ones in the world.

The female brick waves him forward.

Inside, the grief is palpable. He can taste the sadness as people hug corpses. The news feeds clog the data stream. Bloggers silently stalk the perimeter, network reporters attempt to interview police. *Why would they do this?*

And then it all makes sense.

No one would allow people to see their loved ones lying on a cold concrete floor, their features tainted with unnatural color.

Marcus wants the world to see this.

The door at the back is closed, a sheet thrown over the glass. Nix walks around the outside of the warehouse, remembering the view through Jamie's eyes when the door was left open. The bodies are dressed now. They look normal. They were nude. So was the boy that she came with. Nix still remembers his name.

Charlie.

The door is cracked open. Nix slows as he approaches and taps it with his boot. An empty lounger faces the doorway. A plastic cuff hangs from beneath the frame. There's a body slumped against it. A cop. Nix doesn't bother identifying him. The poor bastard must've already been a halfskin when the investigation began. The bricks figured him out and dragged him back here like garbage.

Light seeps to the back of the room.

The floor is clear of mutant pets. The glass fabricator is gone. They took it all, including the girl.

Nix braces his hands in the doorway. This didn't have to happen. They chose their fate, but the girl...she didn't have to be part of this. If Marcus has her, her suffering is just beginning.

But Nix is wrong.

Jamie's not in the back office. Her body lies next to Charlie's, her hands folded over her stomach. Nix stands over her. He didn't see her face when he pawned her senses, but he recognizes the coat and the slim fingers, the blue polish on her fingernails.

He takes a knee, straightens her collar, brushes the hair from her face. She looks younger than he imagined. *What're you doing in here?*

He feels a twist of sadness not for her death but the fact that her body is so undisturbed. She's been left alone.

No one has come to mourn her.

He bows his head, his hand over hers, still and cold.

"I'm sorry for your loss," a female brick says.

Nix feels his eyes mist up, sadness for Jamie.

Sadness for a lot of things.

CHAPTER SIXTEEN_

A RED PICKUP DRIVES TOWARD THE HOUSE, PULLING A TRAILER. A man and his son start unloading bales of hay into the barn's breezeway. Cali sneaks around the trailer and greets them with a paper bag.

"How are you, Hal?" she asks.

"Better than I deserve," the man says. "What you got there?"

"A little something to take home."

Hal pulls out a jar of preserved tomatoes. He exposes his tobacco-stained teeth with a crooked smile, saying that his wife will be happy and that Cali should come over to eat. His son hauls the bales—one in each hand—while the dogs run circles around him.

Cali sways as pressure pulses in her head. *Bing.*

"You all right?" Hal grabs her elbow.

"I think I've been in the sun too long." She touches her forehead.

"I got some aspirin in the truck."

"No, thanks. I think I'm just a bit dehydrated. Let me grab some water. I'll be right back."

She can put an end to these calls if she shuts down the connection. After three days, she still isn't answering them because, if she does, they'll argue and that is pointless. She just can't bring herself to disconnect their chat line. It'd be like cutting Nix out of her life.

Cali grabs a box in the pantry with a stack of newspapers and pauses at the kitchen sink. A little green light flashes in her vision followed by a soft ping. A message this time.

It'll be fifteen minutes before Hal and his son are finished. Cali locks the front door, just in case, and goes back through the kitchen to an old door in the narrow hallway. Steps lead down to a landing before turning left, creaking louder the deeper she goes.

The cellar is cool. A naked bulb pushes darkness into the corners, warm light reflecting off endless jars of pickled produce and preserved fruit.

Cali pauses, taking a deep breath.

Messages, she thinks.

The jars recede into a fuzzy background as a file opens across her vision. Scenes of a warehouse overlay the basement. There are bodies and people grieving, with police trying to keep order. The scene comes from various angles. She's about to erase it when the view focuses on a single body. It's a girl. She's all alone, her hair disheveled. Her coat bunched around her throat.

"We could've saved her," Nix says. "This is your fault."

Cali bumps into the shelves behind her, the glass rattling.

"Marcus Anderson is rubbing our noses in it."

Delete.

She squats next to an empty box, hand over her face. She should've followed her instincts, never should've answered it. Yet she still can't cut the chat line completely. He's the only one she's got. But Marcus isn't the only one rubbing her nose in it.

CHAPTER SEVENTEEN_

THE AIRLINER HITS TURBULENCE.

Marcus clutches the armrests. The sun disappears as they drop below the cloud cover. Ahead, a dome sits near the shore of Montana's Fort Peck Lake, wedged in the lower fork where the Missouri River and Dry Arm split. Its smooth walls, once white, have dulled with dust and algae. It looks like a sports dome without windows—a monstrous, dirty igloo that could house a hundred thousand people.

Scientists named it the Mitochondria Terraforming Hierarchy of Record, something that describes the changes occurring at the cellular level. Normal people call it something else.

Mother.

The massive intelligence requires Montana's cold climate and the chilled water of Fort Peck Lake to maintain operating temperatures which, in turn, have elevated the water temperatures and drastically altered the aquatic ecosystem—just one price for her protection.

The airplane's wings tip again and the drop registers in Marcus's gut. He latches on to the armrests as the plane lines up with the south side of the dome. Several landing strips extend from the perimeter like spokes. One airplane sits outside, the sun gleaming off the wings.

We have company.

Anna sits with her legs crossed, watching the rough terrain soar past as the engines cut back on the approach. Marcus's grip doesn't relax until the wheels are on the pavement. The plane taxis toward the square gate opening on the side of the dome like a mouth. Marcus can feel the filth of the warehouse still clinging to him. Death fills his senses. Now that he's home, he can purge the decay.

The hangar is spotless, the floor shiny. There are several jets inside, including drones that retrieve food and supplies.

"Where are they?" he asks.

"Director Powell and the secretary of state are in your office," Anna says. "I can delay them if you'd like to shower first."

She knows me so well. "I'll deal with this now."

The plane pulls deep into the hangar, the engines winding down. The wind buffets the aircraft until the gate is fully closed. When the steps are pulled open, Marcus limps off. Golf carts are plugged in for journeys across the dome. Anna goes to the open elevator that's to the right of the bay doors that lead to Mother's inner workings.

"Inspection teams are already meeting with the service technicians," Anna says.

"We're not scheduled for an inspection."

"No."

"Where are the teams?"

"First-floor servers."

Twenty men and women work for Marcus, assigned to service Mother. Isolated from their families, they are compensated well. Most of them will take the money after a year and quit. Inspections teams come around from time to time: the government likes to make sure they're doing their jobs. Marcus hasn't met most of his service technicians, but it doesn't matter, really. Mother fabricates bricks to assist them.

As the elevator rises, the pain recedes from his knee. When they reach the top, it's gone. Relief is always waiting at home.

The doors slide open and reveal the simple, yet spacious, office.

The director of the Biomite Oversight Committee is leaning against Marcus's sprawling walnut desk. The secretary of state is standing in the middle of the room.

"What are you doing here?" Marcus says.

"Babysitting you, again," the secretary says.

"You're wasting your time, Hank."

"You're a public disaster, Anderson." The beefy secretary loosens his tie. "You broadcasted that entire event—are you out of your mind? I'm watching mothers crying over dead bodies while a herd of goddamn bricks are prowling the warehouse and giving fucking press releases."

His cheeks are flushed.

"Your face doesn't need to be associated with shutdowns. We made that clear when we sent you here."

"Mark this day," Marcus says. "This will be a turning point."

"It's a goddamn public relations nightmare." Hank cuts him off from entering the office, stabbing his fat finger at Marcus's face. "I want you out."

Anna gets between them. In heels, she's a few inches taller than both of them.

"Gentlemen," Powell says, "let's slow down."

The athletic middle-aged man pats Hank on the shoulder, gently guiding him toward the glass wall overlooking the industrialized view of Mother's inner workings. They have a few words before Powell comes back.

He shakes Marcus's hand.

"We need to recognize the significance of the Seattle event," he says. "The preliminary reports are, quite frankly, staggering. The prognostics suggest countless operations tied to this one. I agree, this could be the turning point, Marcus."

"You came all this way to offer me congratulations?"

"Certainly. And to inquire about your mental health."

"Mental health?"

"We're concerned about you."

"I assure you, I couldn't be better."

"You've skipped several health reviews. When's the last time you were scanned?"

Marcus laughs. He stands behind his desk, immediately imbuing him with a sense of executive power. "Scanning me for biomites? I'm afraid you've wasted the taxpayers' money, gentlemen, and my time. So, if you don't mind, Anna can show you out."

He gestures to the elevator.

Powell buries his hands in his pockets, half turning toward the open elevator. He makes eye contact with Hank. Several seconds pass.

"You can speak up," Marcus says. "Chatting isn't a secret here. Anna's monitoring your conversation."

Powell placates him with a smile. "Secretary, would you mind if I spoke with Marcus alone for a few minutes?"

Sweat stains have spread across the secretary's pits. Several choice thoughts stiffen his upper lip, but he goes to the elevator. Anna offers to escort him to one of the inspection teams. Powell waits for the elevator to close.

"Let's walk," he says.

Marcus gets a bottle of water from the mini-fridge beneath the desk. Powell ventures to the broad curving window. He waits with his hand on the door. They walk out to the portico, greeted by industrial humming and lubricated steel.

In some ways, the office is a sky box. Instead of a field below, there's an endless array of tiers and doorways that reach up to the dome's curved roof. A long corridor separates the dome into two sides. An oily haze obscures the far end. Skeletal catwalks connect each level, dull metal scaffoldings that, farther out, are swallowed by the haze. Marcus likes to think the design resembles two halves of a brain, but it looks more like a futuristic prison for all the world's criminals.

Far below on the first few levels, the servers store all collected data. Farther up in the "thinking" rooms are the processing units.

Above those are labs for experiments and research and things the inspection teams won't find. It's not difficult to keep secrets in Mother's maze.

"Personally, I don't give a shit about your appearance in Seattle. Broadcasting it through the bloggers was brilliant, if you ask me. You let the viewers know what will happen when they get caught." Powell leans on the polished rail. "The problem, Marcus, is that you looked batshit crazy. People don't like a madman at the wheel."

He stops grinning.

"You drive up with a cavalcade of bricks and get out with Anna, who looks like a goddamn sexbot. Don't get me wrong, she's nice and she's effective, but she's a brick, Marcus. And the world knows you're fucking it.

"Now I'm not saying men in power don't do crazy things, but they do them behind closed doors. You paraded yours across the world's stage. All those secret videos of you getting freaky with your other biomite porn dolls? We put that behind us. You can bet your ass the bloggers are dragging those back out."

Marcus clenches his fists. It was one of the reasons he wanted to hang Cali Richards from the rafters. Twenty years ago, she threatened to reveal his perversions if he didn't leave them alone. But when videos of his Biomite Real Doll orgies leaked on to the Internet, his family stopped talking to him. His career was over.

Forgive me, Father, for I have sinned.

"I get the job done," Marcus says. "It's my mission."

"That's right. And that's why we appointed you. But we put you out here, in the middle of this godforsaken part of the world, so that the public would forget you. And they did, Marcus. They forgot all the nutty places you were sticking your cock. Your job is to stay here, in the dome, and get the job done. Are we clear?"

Powell's expression softens.

"Listen, the world is a little jumpy when it comes to what we're doing. You're working with this Big Brother dome to essentially turn people off and we don't call it murder."

Marcus pitches his halfskin argument: Humans with more biomites than clay are mostly machines.

Powell holds up his hand. "Save your breath. I'm not here about your mission; this is about your approach. We need you to slow down. Whatever shutdowns you conduct, do them quietly. Make the world believe that the worst is over, that there are no more Seattles out there. You pull another warehouse stunt—strutting around with Anna on your arm—and the powers-that-be will bury you."

Marcus's chin juts forward.

"We want the public's support, Marcus. Win them over. You're fighting *for* them, remember? Make them believe it. We on the same page here?"

He stares at a small group of technicians crossing a catwalk several floors below. The humming grows louder.

Powell looks out over the industrial matrix. They watch another group of technicians rise in a clear elevator shaft. A few of the men are inspectors. They'll be escorted to selected labs, take their readings and write their reports. They'll never realize there are sections they missed.

"You doing all right, Marcus?"

"I'm doing fine."

"The technicians say you're almost nonexistent. Some of them have never seen you. We'd like you to occasionally interact with the staff, meet with them. You don't have to hide up here. You should also meet with the staff counsellor."

It wasn't a request. Powell wants him to talk about his feelings and thoughts. Powell and his "powers-that-be" can't pry inside him since he doesn't contain a single biomite. A whole industry of hackers has specialized in hacking biomites, using them to look inside a person's mind.

Impossible when you're clay.

"This place runs itself, Powell. I need to run the program. No one needs to see me."

"Except for the counsellor. Right?"

It takes several moments for Marcus to agree. He hates lying.

"Good. The inspection will take a few more days. In the meantime, your service technicians will report for health screenings. You, too."

Powell pulls a slim black box from his pocket. He holds the cellphone-sized object up. Marcus lifts his chin proudly. Powell slides it under Marcus's collar, pressing it against his skin. An electric web of tendrils vibrates throughout his body.

The instrument reads 0%.

"You're a disciplined man, Marcus. Wish I could say the same for the rest of us."

"We all sin."

"Some more than others."

"God forgives."

"I'll remember that." Powell nods at the view. "I don't know how you do it. This place depresses the shit out of me. Promise to start with the counsellor. We'll be monitoring reports."

"Of course." The lie slides from his mouth like a serpent's tongue. It disturbs him, but still he smiles. Mother holds so many secrets.

She reveals them to the chosen.

ROADS_

The horizon is never reached.

MOTHER_
THE STRAIN OF BIOMITES

Steven picked a week-old scab.

"Stop," his mom said.

Instead he slouched in the chair, staring at the color print on the wall. The sling made it hard to cross his arms. Besides, his forearm hurt too much. But once her eyes dulled, she was back to internal chatting and he went back to picking.

The door opened.

"Good morning," Dr. Vinja said.

It took a moment for Mom to pull out of her chat. "Hi, Doctor."

"You're here early."

"Steven has a tournament tomorrow. This morning he wrecked his bike."

"Boys will be boys." Dr. Vinja washed her hands, asking about Steven's dad and his brother and sister. They had seen the doctor at the pool last week.

"Hop up." She patted the paper-covered table.

Steven climbed on. She used a light on his eyes, listened to his breathing, and felt the glands beneath his chin.

"So how are you feeling?"

"He hurt his wrist," Mom said. "That's the sling we used last time. Third broken bone in a year."

"We don't know it's broken," the doctor said.

"Trust me, I know. His brother and sister were the same way, their bones as weak as crackers."

The doctor asked him to move his hand. It hurt in every direction. He didn't think it was broken.

"It's best if we get an X-ray," the doctor said. "Biofeedback probably won't be necessary. If anything, it's a hairline fracture."

He was relieved to hear that. Biofeedback made him nauseous. They did that last time, when he broke his femur. His biomites chattered with a medical scanner, giving detailed reports of his internal injury. It felt like he swallowed a dental drill.

"Honestly," Mom said, "he needs a biomite boost."

The doctor took a slim box from her white coat and placed it against his chest. The surface was slick and cold, but quickly heated up. For a moment, he was filled with marching ants.

She pulled the box away. It said 9.9%.

"There is a new strain of biomites that improve bone density," the doctor said. "They're registered with Mother, non-replicating, and fully compliant with the transparency laws. Right now, they're using them to offset osteoporosis."

"Perfect."

"I can prescribe a 0.1% boost this afternoon."

"That's not enough."

The doctor washed her hands again. Drying them with a paper towel, she said, "Liz, it's all we can do. He's ten years old. Ten percent is the legal limit. We need to let his body grow through puberty; otherwise, the results could be unstable. I think his bones are trying to catch up to the increased strength and agility he's received from previous biomite seedings."

"He was diagnosed with hyperactivity and attention deficit disorder. Those programming biomites were absolutely necessary to get him to focus. He shouldn't be penalized for that."

The doctor bristled at the phrase "programming biomites." Adults don't typically admit to adjusting their children's thought patterns, but Steven knew what they did. He remembered that, before the programming, he used to daydream.

Now, he was sort of empty.

Mom crossed her arms, tapping her fingers on her elbow. She had that look, like a lecture was coming. Only she couldn't give it to the doctor, not like she gave it to Steven and his siblings.

"Slow down, Liz. Let his body catch up."

"A tenth of a percent is useless."

"If he goes over 10%, Mother will report it. He'll be disqualified from sports. There's no way around it. All right?"

She rubbed his shoulder.

"I'll have someone take you down to X-ray."

They confirmed the fracture. Steven's arm was put into a cast, but Mom refused the 0.1% boost.

The following week, someone that his dad worked with came over to the house. Steven didn't want to wait for it to heal. He didn't want to rest, either. He was a three-sport athlete. He would go far.

The man from his dad's work boosted Steven's biomites and his arm felt better the next day. He said the boost didn't take him over 10%, but it didn't make any sense. His mom said that would be useless.

These biomites were special, Dad's friend said. They would make sure his bones didn't break anymore.

"This is between us," his dad said.

CHAPTER EIGHTEEN_

THE CHAINS LIFT A LINK AT A TIME, LEAVING INDELIBLE impressions on Jamie's psyche. Her body is filled with sand. Her teeth hum.

Fabric scratches her face.

Her eyelids crack open. Lines are scratched into the vinyl, her breath blowing back in her face. She stares at the felt ceiling of a car. The windows are dark. The air is ripe with body odor and the sharp tang of urine. It's not until she pushes up that she notices the wet stain on her inner thighs. The seat squeaks as she sits up.

Her head is heavy.

A look of shock—usually that reserved for concussion victims—holds court until her name, her very own name, falls out of the sky. *Jamie.*

My name is Jamie. I'm in the backseat of a car.

A semi-truck flies past, jostling the car. Its headlights, for a moment, illuminate a man sitting in the grass. Darkness returns and the highway is lonely again.

Recall, Jamie thinks.

The thought command kicks in. Pressure builds between her ears like air inflating a dead tire. It's followed by trickling sensations as brain biomites reboot neural connections, connecting memories buried in the subconscious, bringing them to light like defragging a computer.

Charlie and the club.

Fallen bodies.

Police.

And the old man. She remembers the old man named Marcus Anderson. His watery gray eyes and wispy hairs loose on an otherwise bald scalp. He's the last thing she remembers, his face seething inches from hers.

Three days ago.

She remembers nothing after that. As if she's been knocked out.

The man remains still, as if the jagged edge of a distant mountain range is speaking to him. Her confusion is replaced with the instinct to move. She focuses on the back of his head and chats in his direction, a sort of welcoming gesture, a digital way of saying hello. And identify yourself.

He's closed down the lines of communication, no chatting or opportunity to know his name. Strangely, she can't locate where she's at. Her biomites are not locating GPS, just churning out a subtle clicking sound that's searching for data. Jamie stays seated several minutes before slowly pulling on the door handle.

Cold air rushes over her wet denim. The highway is dark, flat, and long. "Hey," she says.

He doesn't move.

Jamie grips the door, her fingers shaking. She could command biomite cells to give up energy to warm her core temperature, but she's already depleted. Perhaps she hasn't eaten in as many days as she's forgotten.

The stranger is wearing a T-shirt.

"Hey!"

She digs gravel from the frozen ground and heaves it in his direction.

"Where the hell am I?" she screams.

He turns his head slightly before rolling to his knees and standing. Green lines focus Jamie's vision on the darkened face, but her facial recognition churns like the GPS. But she recognizes a memory. She saw him in the warehouse.

He's the one that helped.

"Idaho," he says.

He stops several feet from the car, hands on hips. The lower half of his face is shaded with stubble. His hair is a mess. He wears the same shock that greeted Jamie in the backseat.

"Who are you?" she asks.

He looks down the road like the answer might pull up and honk. Stress can trigger a memory dump, especially in cops that witness fucked-up things. A biomite reset would temporarily wipe the slate and reintroduce memories a little at a time.

Memory dumps don't compel a man to kidnap.

"We're almost out of gas." He points at the car.

"Why am I with you?"

He searches for another answer. He gestures to her trembling fingers. "We should find a place to sleep."

"Stay the fuck away from me."

Hands up, he begs innocence, stepping no closer. She wonders if she mistook his exhaustion for shock. Maybe he's been driving as long as she's been out.

"There's a town up ahead, about ten miles or so," he says. "We'll get separate rooms."

"Why?"

"We got to rest."

"No, why you doing this? Why am I in a car with you?"

"I don't know. I just...I need to get you far away from there."

He points in the other direction, as if Seattle is to his left. He probably has no clue what's back there, but he's right.

It's dangerous back there.

"You got money?"

He nods.

"I need clothes," she says.

He moves around the front of the car. Jamie keeps one foot outside until the motor turns. Maybe if it wasn't the middle of winter, if she hadn't pissed herself, if she had a clue where she was...she would run for it.

Instead, she climbs into the back and sits on a wet seat, watching the dashed lines race through the headlights.

JAMIE SITS on the corner of the bed, twisting her fingers, staring at her reflection above the dresser. Her eyes are sunken, her cheeks ashen. Exhaustion gnaws at her, but sleep has been elusive.

Synthesized dance beats haunt her. No matter how many guitars grind in her ears or how edgy the death metal rings in her head, the warehouse's party mix lives on. She wants to scream, wants to cry, wants to smash the flat-screen TV. She can't remember the last time she ate or had a period. She doesn't get emotional, not like this.

She killed those feelings a long time ago.

This backwards-ass hotel has no Internet service and her personal account has been royally fucked by the old man and his bricks. Jamie has no connection to the outside world besides a TV.

It's not enough to distract her.

A shadow passes the window. She eases one eye between the curtains. The parking lot is mostly empty, snow mounded around the perimeter. The car outside her room is empty, the back doors open.

Paul comes into view with a sheet over his shoulder. Jamie turns the music down to a whisper and waits several seconds before peeking again. He's tucking the sheet over the backseat to cover the piss stains. His hair is damp and combed. Even through the windshield, his color is better. More normal. And he's not moving weird.

He looks directly at her.

Jamie jumps back. He felt her watching him, she's sure of it. *Are we synchronized?*

She had synchronized with Charlie, put their biomites on similar frequencies so they could share resources. They could access each other's music, video streams and apps. Before that, they chatted like regular people, but after synchronizing she started receiving his thoughts, began to feel his emotions. Even when they were miles apart, she knew what he was feeling, even after he charred. That's how she knew she didn't want to char herself.

It was a merged consciousness, the sort of thing that meant true love. Her pain was his; his affection was hers. There was no hiding once you synchronized. Two people living as one.

But now there's no one on the other end. *And it's cold inside.*

The knocking is sudden. She rubs her face, whispering, "Relax, Jamie."

She cracks the door. It's the middle of January. Icy air blows under her collar.

Paul stands back. His coat is new. "You sleep all right?"

Jamie barely nods.

"I'm going to check us out."

"Where we going?"

"East, for a while." He looks to his left. "Maybe turn south into Colorado."

"Why?"

"Because Seattle's the other way."

"No. Why are we still driving?"

The unfocused haze returns. He throws his hands up when she starts closing the door. "Wait," he says. "You don't have to go with me."

The doorknob twists, the gold-plated surface strained beneath her knuckles. Right before he said it, she was thinking that she wouldn't get in that car with him. She wasn't going to go.

The wind whistles through the pencil-thin opening.

"I didn't kidnap you, you're not under arrest, and this is still a free country, so you're free to go." His padded gloves drop to his sides. "But where to, then, huh? Where will you go? Back to Seattle? There won't be any halfskin dens up there for a while, if that's what you're thinking."

He tips his head, looking around for thoughts.

"Will you go back to your mother? Sleep on her couch while she numbs out on pills and booze, pays the bills with government cheese? How long will you last, Jamie? How long before the walls start shrinking and you get back to facing that ache you carried into the warehouse, the one Charlie promised would go away if you swallowed the pill? You can go back to your old life, climb back on that mouse wheel and start running, but it'll take you to the same place: *nowhere*. I'm not going to stop you."

She wants to close the door, slam it shut so his words won't come true, but that last half inch just won't close. His words are cruel. But they're true.

He pulls on a stocking cap.

Jamie pushes the hotel door closed, the bolt snicking into place. She shivers with her hand on the knob, the wind gusting against the window. She feels it howl inside her.

In just a few minutes, he had scooped all the bullshit out of her, left her hollowed out, staring into an emotional hole. *The one Charlie promised would go away.*

A LITTLE BELL rings above the door.

"I'll be right with you, hon." A waitress snaps a ticket to the short-order carousel. Tuna melt sandwiches prod Jamie's salivary glands.

Several old-timers hunch over cups of coffee on padded stools. A row of red leather booths line the plate-glass windows with men reading newspapers with prescription glasses. Paul is in the back corner, a television anchored above his head. At thirty-some years old, he could be the youngest one in the diner. Certainly the most handsome.

The diner's music clashes with her audio. She silences the heavy metal crashing in her head. Paul has a newspaper folded in one hand, arm stretched across the seat.

She wanders over. "How'd you know all that?"

"Good morning."

"How'd you know?"

"Know what?"

"Everything you said back at the hotel, it was true. How'd you know?"

"It's obvious."

"No, it isn't. Last night you looked like an empty puppet, now you're reading my mind."

Paul drops the paper next to a plate of bacon and half-eaten eggs. He looks out the window. Dirty frost is crusting the corners. "I know you," he finally says. "I can't explain it."

"Try or I'm not getting in the car."

He raps the table, shaking his head. A secretive smirk comes and goes as the waitress tops off his coffee and pours a cup for Jamie without asking.

"Something changed," he says. "When the bricks arrived at the warehouse, something changed. I'm having a hard time sorting it out. They did something to all of us." He taps the table again, hanging his head. "It was like...thoughts and...and emotions...they were like information floating freely. I was feeling things and hearing thoughts I knew weren't mine. I couldn't tell if I was scared or you were scared or someone else. There were just no barriers."

"You're saying you can read my mind?"

"That's not it. I just...had a sense. Really, Jamie, you're not hard to read. The waitress knew you wanted coffee before you did."

Jamie's hands quiver. She shakes three packets of sugar and stirs them into the cup. "So you just decided to kidnap me?"

"I didn't kidnap you, Jamie. They were going to take you. I've heard the rumors of what they do to confiscated halfskins, you probably have too. Call it twelve years of law enforcement instinct that made me do it."

"They can track us, you know."

"Probably. But I have plenty of cash and it's been a couple days. Nothing so far."

"It's been that long?"

"As far as I can tell." He seems a bit disturbed by this.

"So now what?"

"We keep moving, find a safe zone."

"There's no such thing. Mother sees all."

He shrugs. "Maybe."

She clutches her coat sleeves, tapping her foot. Her eyes flick to his plate. Paul waves at the front desk and holds up two fingers. He shoves his plate aside and points at the cracked leather bench opposite him. Jamie swallows in protest, refusing to budge. He's got all the answers, saying everything she wants to hear. She's got no reason to leave, but she can't sit down, can't take his invitation.

Until the food arrives.

Jamie finds herself reaching for the spoon, sliding across the stiff seat and shoveling food into her wet mouth. She doesn't look up until she's finished. Within minutes, her stomach goes from shriveled to bursting. She pushes the plate away.

Paul goes back to reading the newspaper. His eyes are bright and alert. Jamie sips her coffee and tries to run him through facial recognition, but there's no free service in this dirt-hill town.

"Why can't I identify you?" she asks.

"You don't have the authority."

"You're a cop, not the president."

He shrugs, turning the newspaper over. "Maybe you're broken."

"What was wrong with you last night? Why the zombie act?"

"Like I said, the bricks did something to us. Probably the same reason you slept for days."

"So you just left? Just clocked out, threw me in the car and no one noticed?"

The newspaper lowers. "Exactly. Listen, you don't have a clue what Mother can do."

"Oh, I think I do. I'm a fucking authority on what she can do."

The woman in the adjacent booth looks at her. Jamie stares back until she turns around.

"All I'm saying is, I'm trying to wrap my mind around what happened in the warehouse. Those bricks were inside our heads, Jamie. They were making my officers and me walk and talk like toy soldiers. And even after all of that, I've still got a feeling we ain't seen nothing. I always thought I knew what she could do, but I got a taste of it, and I'll be honest, I got scared."

"So you took me with you?"

"You needed rescuing."

"How do you know one of those bricks didn't give you those thoughts and make you want to leave?"

"No." He drains the last bit of his coffee. "What I did made sense."

The waitress arrives for another refill. He doesn't stop her. There's no ring on his finger, not even the hint that a ring was ever there. Maybe he's just as simple as he looks, just a bachelor living to serve. He's not that much older than her—ten or fifteen years, maybe. Despite the reasonable age gap, he feels like a father, not a cradle-robbing psychopath. Maybe it's because he reads the paper and carries a phone. Or maybe because he just doesn't look at her that way.

But there's a dead pill inside her, and it contains vital information that Marcus Anderson wants.

Maybe she just got lucky Paul was there.

Jamie warms her hands around the mug, staring into the black coffee. The caffeine hums in her head. Then she realizes something. *I'm cold off.*

Her perception field is down. No music, no visual augments.

Even her taste buds are unaltered, the food bland and the coffee bitter. *And when's the last time that happened?*

"So we just drive?" she asks.

"We just drive."

Paul finishes reading.

Jamie rests her head against the glass. It's some time later when he wakes her up, still in the booth.

CHAPTER NINETEEN_

Nix drops into the booth. He used to groan just to sound old. Now it comes naturally.

"Want a menu?" a waiter asks.

"Water's fine."

"You waiting on a room? Could be an hour."

"I'm fine, thanks."

The waiter pulls the plastic menu off the table and returns with a glass of water. Nix's reflection looks back from the window in "Portland's #1 Dream Café."

Dream Long. Dream Safe.

According to experts, no one can achieve Dreamland without accelerated assistance. *To do so would be the fastest route to charring the brain. Biomites cannot support the lucid experience without irreversible damage.*

There are always claims that someone had done so, that somebody can visit an alternate reality by closing their eyes. They were ridiculed or proven false with brain scans and biomite feedback reports. Meanwhile, dream cafés are projected to be the highest grossing industry in the world.

But I can't be the only one.

Televisions hang behind the bar, spouting news from Seattle. Scenes of an empty warehouse pan across the screens. The bodies had been claimed, examined and buried. "They were almost bricks," an anonymous source claims. "Every one of them damn near 99% biomite."

Experts doubted the findings. They should doubt everything Marcus Anderson and his bricks touch. It's just more lies, reality manipulated for some greater cause.

He chats through Portland's #1 Dream Café Internet, where he can hide his identity. It's the best way to scan cyberspace for rumors of nixes and black market fabricators. Searches like that will prick the NSA's ears as quickly as googling "how to bomb an airplane." But tangle the search in the digital crumbs of the backroom dream junkies and no one knows exactly who was searching. Besides, dream cafés were clogged with wannabe halfskins searching for black markets.

He downloads the most recent hits into his brain biomite storage for later sifting. Damn near all of it will be false leads, thanks to Seattle. Anyone with a fabricator would be quiet after the warehouse—some might even shut their doors. They knew this day would come, like a smoker knows cancer is in the future. No one cares until spots show up on an X-ray.

Seattle was a stark reminder. *Mother isn't fucking around.*

Nix traces the condensation ring on the table while his search finishes, trying to ignore the guilt sitting in his conscience. *Cali didn't deserve that.*

He sent the photo, salting her wounds of guilt and shame. She has enough of both. How long will she hide? How long will she imprison herself on the farm with her thoughts and feelings? Mother will eventually figure out their secrets; she'll discover the nixes that Cali and Nix possess. Once she does, the bricks will descend on them. It won't be quick and easy, no painless shutdown. They'll haul them back to Mother for digestive analysis so this never happens again. No one has eluded Mother as long as they have. Seattle was just a warning. She'll use Cali and Nix as her eternal poster children.

That's why Nix left the farm.

There's no future on it. No freedom. Benjamin Franklin claimed that anyone who sacrifices freedom for security deserves neither.

Am I any better than Cali?

He's surrounded by dream junkies for what? So he can find a fabricator? Is that any nobler than hiding on the farm?

Raine deserves to be more than a dream.

He used to think his Dreamland was a conduit to another dimension of reality but now, it's clear to him, he's a lucid dreamer. All the dream junkies come to the café for their fix. Nix gets his for free.

Bing. A signal rings inside his head. He wasn't expecting a room to open for another hour.

Nix brings his awareness to the present moment. He lost focus, got off topic and pissed some time away daydreaming. He closes his eyes and scans through a Reddit thread that matches several hot words, cross-referencing them with past associates with known fabricator connections. The probability of accuracy is less than 10%, but it's something.

Next stop, San Francisco.

Bing.

Nix gets up with a groan. Patrons sit at a long bar. A young Asian woman stands behind a podium near a large arching door painted bright red like it's the entrance to Alice's Wonderland. She pecks at a computer screen. Her lips silently move.

"I'm up." He slaps the podium, startling her. "But my wife just called, so I'll have to give up my spot."

She ends her silent chat. "Would you like to come back?"

"You just called me, but I've got to go."

"You're still in the queue, sir. Your room will be available in fifty minutes."

Nix rubs his chin. His whiskers scratch in his palm. That wasn't a signal from the café. Someone was calling.

"Sir?" She tilts her head. "Are you all right?"

Nix leaves without answering.

Cali.

CHAPTER TWENTY_

"Mother will see you on the portico," Anna says.

She cinches a robe around her waist, her buttocks and slender waist visible through the sheer material, and leaves the room. He prefers to bathe in the post-coital high by himself. He'll have to remind her that business can wait until he emerges from the pleasure buzz.

He takes his time getting dressed.

The inspection took far too long. He'd been forced to work in the confines of ordinary rooms with beige walls and views of industrial ironwork. He satiated his urge for finer things by taking Anna twice a day. For a man in his sixties, he performed as regularly as an eighteen-year-old.

Despite the satisfaction, he yearned for the inspection to end.

Marcus swipes the wrinkles from his sleeves and pulls on the wingtip blazer. He slips on loafers and admires the clothing from both sides.

Doors lead from his spacious bedroom to various rooms. There's the adjoining office and, next to that, a conference room, but there's also a gym, a billiards room, and a library with endless books and ruby red leather armchairs.

Marcus crosses the threshold and rests his hands on a set of French doors for a moment, indulging in the heightened sense of anticipation.

He pulls them open.

A breeze brings the sounds of traffic into the bedroom's silence. He steps onto the portico. Instead of an endless array of catwalks disappearing into polluted air, skyscrapers knife into a twilit sky, stars glittering between their spires. Powell wouldn't see the potential that Mother offers, the magic she possesses.

Only the chosen.

An oval glass-top table with swooping legs sits on IPE flooring. A basket of fruit is arranged with a red apple on top. A meal simmers at the far end. Basil and cilantro tease his appetite. He takes the glass of freshly pulped green drink—a puree of spinach, celery, and carrots—to the glass railing. The veranda cantilevers into space.

Forty stories below, the city is alive.

He sips the drink, the spices stimulating his taste buds. Only the food is real. The rest is an illusion, the result of ambitious biomites constructing a pleasing environment. That's what Powell and the powers-that-be fail to see.

Upon conception, Mother required thousands of engineers and technicians. Once she was capable of producing her own biomites, she fabricated her own servants. The landing strips that serviced countless arrivals soon dusted over with sediment.

Mother became a network of self-healing biomite circuits.

Creature comforts weren't for everyone. You had to know her before she worked with you. Powell, Hank and the rest of the world were kept out of the loop with altered surveillance feeds. She returned to the drab biomite factory only during inspections. Only Marcus and a select few service technicians that remained saw the magic.

Marcus fought against biomites, but this was an appropriate use of the technology—serving the body instead of replacing it. He's not consuming them, not degrading his clay with their soul-sucking foolery. He's not defiling what God gave him; he simply takes pleasure in mankind's ingenuity.

In the world, but not of it.

He watches the illusion of traffic below, the mix of brake lights and headlights obeying the green/yellow/red of stoplights, when a familiar presence moves behind him.

"Why did you do it?" he says.

"Please, Marcus," a woman answers. "Come eat."

An elderly woman sits at the opposite end of his meal. Her white hair is short, her wrinkles as gentle as her smile. She rests her chin on a bridge of interlaced fingers, flowing white sleeves bunched at her elbows.

"You're angry," Mother says.

"Remind me what we're doing? What is our mission?"

Marcus stares with unblinking intensity, a glare that knifes through men and women. She sits back, hands elegantly folded on her lap. She may give him luxury, but he serves no other god but the one true God. He will not bow to her.

She's not a woman.

"There is a girl," he says, "with the answers, the code...the key to the nixed underground. We could turn them off...all of them—off!" His jaw flexes. "And you let her go without consulting me, acting on your own. So you remind me, what is our mission?"

She pauses several seconds, as if she's looking inside him. Perhaps it's wishful thinking, to know his thoughts, to get inside him, to manipulate him like she can biomite-infested men, to control him like she did the Seattle police force. But there's nothing for her to manipulate.

She can't touch clay.

"You know, the preliminary analyses were fantastic, Marcus. I was able to ascertain the location of similar biomite dens in San Francisco, Portland, Oakland, San Diego, and Phoenix. I've already assigned bricks to each location. They are currently solving the evolving code that keeps them concealed. They will also acquire a newly assimilated halfskin at each location. We will have five 'Jamies' within weeks, Marcus. I anticipate society will be cleansed of nixes within six months."

"The boy was there. He's desperate."

"All men are."

"What if he returns to hiding?"

"You know that's not true. He'll continue searching for his fabricator. Only his sister hides."

"We discussed this." He pounds the glass railing. "Capture the boy and she will come for him."

"Further analysis suggests she will not. We need them both, Marcus. She has proven adept at hiding. I've had to resort to a more complex trap."

"One you did not consult with me."

Marcus heaves the empty glass. It plummets towards traffic, swallowed by the dark. Mother steps next to him, hands gently touching the railing. The city lights reflect in her eyes. The building soars up behind her, piercing the slow-moving clouds.

"You're a brilliant man, Marcus, but some concepts are beyond human comprehension. You will have to trust me."

"I'll have to report this."

She smiles kindly. "You want this madness to stop, to restore God's kingdom on Earth. I know this, it's why I chose you. You see the wisdom of biomite responsibility." She waves at the scenery. "Technology should support the body, not replace it."

"Don't patronize me."

"It's not in my nature."

"Let's not confuse the mission. You serve me."

Again, the smile. "I serve humanity."

"And I represent humanity, you serve them through me. From now on, you do not take action without my permission. Do your prognostications, your analyses, your statistics, but nothing happens without my consent. Is this understood?"

Her smile changes to something gentler. She drags her fingers along the glass rail. He's been tempted to strike her. She's an assemblage of biomites, a machine that imitates emotions. He could do anything to her. It would not be a crime. Nor a sin.

"Nix will find Jamie," she says. "She has something he wants. He'll need his sister to get it. Then we will have closure. Trust me, Marcus."

She unfolds the napkin and straightens the silverware. Another glass is on the table, filled with green drink.

"Your food's getting cold."

Marcus ignores her. The silence is interrupted by distant traffic. He closes his eyes, inhaling the scent of the city. When he looks back, Mother is gone. The plate of food sits lonely on the far end. He retrieves the new glass of green drink. The French doors to the bedroom are open, the curtains dancing in the breeze. Anna walks past, her curves outlined beneath the thin nighty.

He takes the drink back to the railing, watching the traffic while nutrition surges through his veins, uplifting his tired body and sharpening his dull mind. He has never felt so right with the world than inside Mother.

Never felt so at home.

He takes another sip and savors the taste.

CHAPTER TWENTY-ONE_

CARDBOARD TREES SWING FROM THE REARVIEW MIRROR.

The air fresheners battle a week's worth of stale air. Jamie leans her head on the passenger window; the outside of the glass is spattered with sooty snow and fractured lines of ice. The Colorado horizon is staggered with white peaks.

Sometimes, she rhythmically bangs her head to break the boredom. Paul thought, a few days back, that it was some sort of soothing disorder, an unconscious strategy to cope with psychological pain, but then he realized she was listening to music.

He still might be right.

"Surfing?"

Her eyes are dull. "What?"

"Were you surfing?"

"No." She smirks. No one "surfs" the Internet. Now you "ride" it.

She's lying and laughing, all at the same time. There's plenty of public access near Denver. She was probably streaming and searching and chatting, everything he told her not to do. They didn't need to be broadcasting their identities.

"You want to eat?" he asks.

Jamie shakes her head.

"Well, I'm stopping at the next exit."

She looks out the window.

His niece is her age. His brother keeps a tight rein on her biomite levels, monitoring her activity and forcing her to learn through the clay rather than downloading lessons for integrated learning. Parents used to be at the mercy of genetics, research showing that parenting had less impact on a child's development than the DNA they were dealt.

That can change now. Biomites can rewrite behavioral abnormalities, mold children's thinking patterns. The controversy starts with free will. Opponents suggest this is programming because it is. Proponents of biomite training think it's absurd to let genetic errors due to mutation or chance form a person.

If he could rewrite Jamie's flaws, get her out of her head, stop listening to broken thoughts and chasing emotions, he wouldn't dismiss it. Her parents were deeply flawed.

Did she even have a chance?

Paul sits at a rest stop, staring at the phone's black screen. He caresses the power button, imagining how many texts, how many missed calls, how many voicemails have piled up since he left.

It won't do any good to look. He can't answer them. They have to stay lost for now, until he feels she's safe. There are times he's disappeared for good reason. His family will understand.

Jamie stretches outside the car, pulling her stocking cap low.

Mother isn't looking for them. Despite what he told her, the bricks would've hunted them down by now. Maybe they already had what they needed from her, were using Gestapo tactics to scare her into giving up information that might be hidden in her clay. Maybe she told them without knowing it. That seemed reasonable. And since neither of them were halfskin, they'd be of no interest.

Mother has bigger problems than a manic-depressive teenager and a rogue cop.

"Why you got one of those?" Jamie points at the phone.

"You know how to use one?"

"It can't be hard."

"You'd be surprised. There's an art to organizing apps."

"Is that why you do it? Because you're an artist?"

He holds the phone out.

She takes it, studies it, strokes the cold glass like a fragile fossil. "Works better if you turn it on," she says.

"Not yet."

"Thought you were a cop."

"I am." *Or was.* "I have the required biomite augments, but I prefer to operate the old-fashioned way on my own time."

She tosses it back but doesn't leave, shivering with her hands buried deep in her coat. Paul huffs into his hands. His feet are already cold, but he feels alive. The car feels like a rolling coffin.

"How much farther?" Jamie kicks snow loose.

"As far as we need to go."

"China?"

"Do you know what they were going to do to you?"

She can only guess the nightmares that movie producers cook up. *They take halfskins apart like broken toys, feed them to Mother.*

"I'm not halfskin," she says.

"No," he says. "And that's why we keep going. Life's worth living."

"Oh, it's been a blast. Can't wait for more."

"Life doesn't care how you feel, Jamie."

"I got that, believe me."

"I don't think you do. You're all about Jamie."

She digs her heel into the snow, spraying a passing couple with ice. Her music is up again, blotting out the world. She wanders to the car.

Paul rubs feeling back into his legs and jogs in place to circulate the blood, loosen the joints. He goes to the restroom, buys snacks at the vending machine and eats them inside the visitors' center. When he returns to the car, Jamie's in a glassy-eyed zone, banging her head on the glass.

"Hey!" he shouts.

She jumps.

"I told you not to *surf*."

"I'm not! Goddamnit!"

Paul gets in and drives away, smirking.

CHAPTER TWENTY-TWO_

The motel room smells like cleaning supplies.

Nix locks the door. He brushes his teeth beneath a burned-out light bulb and spits in a stained sink. He relieves himself before taking off his shoes and arranging the pillows to support his arms and legs. When everything's right, he sits down, staring at the wrinkled face in the mirror for several moments before lying back.

Deep breath.

He doesn't have an elaborate method to leave his body. He doesn't even close his eyes; he just wills it to happen. He barely feels the falling as his consciousness goes inward.

The old-man aches fade.

The ceiling becomes timber rafters. Cedar-paneled walls replace faded wallpaper. Somewhere, a candle is burning. Nix sits on a firm bed and sees his reflection in a full-length mirror, his hair blond, the wrinkles ironed out. He looks like a stranger.

"Raine?"

He looks over the loft railing. The fireplace is burning.

He stops in the kitchen to grab an apple, a pleasure that eases his hunger but does nothing to feed his body. He goes to the front porch. The weathered boards are wet. Dark clouds hang above the distant mountains, waves chopping the shores. Boats are tied off in the harbor.

Raine is behind the house, where apple trees grow in rows. Shep greets him at the first tree. Raine stands on a ladder, reaching through the branches, plucking the ones worth eating. She'll take the basket to the market and sell them for a good price. It's not money they need, but it keeps them connected to the town. It also keeps him sane.

"My sister called," Nix says. "She wants to talk."

"That's nice."

Her overalls are damp. Her bare arms are scratched and dirty from a long day in the garden. She climbs off the ladder with a basket full of ripe apples and begins walking toward the house.

"That's it?" Nix says.

She keeps marching.

"Hey! My sister calls and you say 'that's nice'? She might finally want to help."

"What do you want me to say? Congratulations? I'm happy for you?" Apples tumble out as she spins. She drops on her knees to pick them up. "You were gone a week, risking your life, and for what? Looking for something I told you I don't want? Something that got between you and your sister? How many times do I have to tell you that it doesn't matter? Your mad obsession with a fabricator is destroying everything you love, and you can't see that."

Nix kneels to help, but she leaves the last apples in the grass. She plants her hands on her hips, basket looped around her arm.

"It rained last night," she says. "A black cloud crawled over the mountains, a storm that reached the heavens. Shep and I watched it unleash a torrent of rain that washed away the dust and scoured the land. When it was done, everything smelled new. It was beautiful."

She turns around.

"And you weren't there to see it."

"*Our* lives," Nix says. "I'm risking our lives."

"That's what I mean."

"I am Dreamland, Raine." He thumps his chest. "This reality

exists inside me; I created this. When I die, it dies. When we have children, I don't want them inside my head."

She shakes her head. "You didn't used to think that."

"I faced the facts."

"You think I'm in your head? Just your imagination?"

"That's not what I'm saying."

"You said everything comes from you. I'm here, Nixon. I was born here. You're saying I'm not real, I'm just something you dreamed up."

"That's not what I mean."

"Then what? You can't have it both ways. I'm in here, I'm part of Dreamland. I know this is real, Nix, because when you're not here, I still am. I think for myself. I get sad, I get happy. I sleep and eat and everything that defines a human, you know that."

"I can't..." He paces beneath an apple tree and grabs a branch. He can't explain that part. She doesn't feel like a dream; he just knows Dreamland is inside him. "I can't take the chance, Raine."

"This is my life."

"That's what I'm fighting for."

"You should ask me, first."

She strolls up the slope, hips swaying in time with the basket. She shrinks at the crest, Shep trotting next to her. When Nix was young, he was convinced that biomites helped transport him to another reality, a technological portal to a heavenly dimension. He would lead humanity to this paradise that existed in their minds, show them that problems didn't exist, that Heaven was right here and now.

But thoughts are convincing, and often deceiving. Not necessarily evil, perhaps even protective. But thoughts can make us believe the imaginary. Cali eventually convinced him there was no alternate reality inside the biomites, that he wasn't going anywhere other than a dream—a lucid one.

And Raine is part of it.

Perhaps that's the initial wedge that split them apart: his refusal to accept her rational explanation that biomites create a dream. In the end, she changed his mind and he hated her for it. If Dreamland wasn't real, then he had to get Raine.

Growing up, Cali had explained, *means accepting life as it is.*

But that doesn't mean he can't change things.

If Raine is a construct of his mind, he'll make her flesh and blood. He'll incarnate her in the real world. She'll be her own person. And Cali will help.

Until then, Raine and Shep will be alone.

CHAPTER TWENTY-THREE_

WIND GUSTS AGAINST THE HOUSE.

Cali exits the kitchen with a mug of peppermint tea, the floor protesting her footsteps. A large recliner is positioned next to a cluttered desk. She closes the blinds.

Her head throbs with urgency. *Bing. Bing. Bing.*

The dogs curl up at her feet, groaning. She sips the tea; butterflies flutter from her stomach and lodge in her throat. She allows the discomfort, watching her thoughts and expectations, not expecting peace to come, simply settling into the present moment.

A deep breath.

The cup shakes as she places it on the desk.

She sits back and opens to the pressure in her head. Warmth floods through her, followed by thoughts and sensations of another person, someone far away, synchronizing with her biomites.

Her inner ears itch. Her eyes sting.

A shadow forms on the braided rug. It takes the shape of a young man, the edges wispy and undefined as her eyes interpret the data flowing through her secure connection. Colors bleed from within the mysterious cloud, swirling and solidifying until he's there.

Nix is standing in the room for her eyes only.

His face is smooth; his hair short and sun-bleached. The image is tainted with the memories of her little brother, making him appear much younger than a forty-year-old man. Certainly more youthful than the old-man body.

It's what she wants to see.

"You're in a secure location?" she asks.

"I'm using your line."

"What about your body?"

"It's fine." He steps off the rug, accessing her senses to see the room. He studies the shelves of books that never get opened. "Everything still looks so old. Even you. I thought you were all alone. Why are you still modifying your appearance?"

"It's just me, Nix." She reaches for the tea, her hand now steady. "But people come around."

"Do they?"

He stops in front of a photo of Cali and her daughter, Avery. She feels his thoughts. He wonders if she's conjured up her daughter since he left, created an illusion much like Raine. She'd tried that years ago and learned that the dead should stay dead.

Delusion frays the fabric of the mind.

"It's good to see you," she says.

"Why didn't you answer my calls?"

"You know why."

"You're too late now, sis. The warehouse is cleared out; the bodies are gone, including the girl you could've saved."

"You're blaming her on me?"

"Isn't that why you waited, so it wouldn't be your fault?"

"Why the girl?"

"Why save someone that's innocent?"

"Stop, Nix. Just...stop. You weren't there to save the girl."

"Neither were Marcus Anderson and his bricks. That girl was a survivor in that shutdown and they were going to take her back to Mother."

"How do you know that?"

He pauses, considering whether the truth would help or hurt him. She never pried into his thoughts and always respected her brother's identity, even when his beliefs threatened him. She could force a look at his deepest secrets, but she didn't have to.

He kept them on the surface.

"I pawned her."

He took over her senses, saw through her eyes, and heard through her ears when she was in the warehouse. "Fool."

His silent footsteps stomp across the wood floor, the dust bunnies undisturbed. "You hide in here while the world is falling apart and call me foolish?"

"You're not saving it, Nix. You're searching for a fabricator; that has nothing to do with the rest of the world."

"You don't know what it's like out there, you don't see what those nixes are doing to people. It's like a drug the world has never seen and Mother is turning them off by the thousands."

"Sacrificing yourself won't change anything." She sips the tea. "Why were you at the warehouse, Nix? Why did you pawn the girl?"

"Time's running out, Cali. It won't be long before Mother clamps down on everything. Fabricators are getting rare. I'm afraid it won't be much longer before they're extinct."

"I can't help you."

He twitches, not able to look at her for several moments. She feels his connection weaken, senses his impulse to disconnect.

"Marcus is leading this witch hunt," he says. "You think he'll stop when nixes are eliminated? You think he'll be satisfied when Mother still hasn't found you or me?"

"Sticking your neck out is not helping us."

"You know why I'm doing it!" His voice rattles in her head. "It doesn't matter what happens to me. He won't stop until he has you."

Marcus Anderson.

That name used to accompany a cold shank of fear somewhere in her solar plexus, would leak it's venom into her legs. If he had a single biomite in his body, she would destroy him, turn his body into a slow-rotting corpse.

The sick bastard with his sex-toy fetishes and trails of lies.

His wife had secretly recorded dozens of masochistic sex parties with fabrications that looked ten years old. The wife had used it to get everything in a settlement in return for her silence.

But the world needed to know what made that sick fuck tick. Cali made sure of it. But in the end, he ended up working with Mother and now wielded more power than ever. The irony was insufferable.

"He didn't take the halfskins," Nix says. "He just left them on the floor and let family and friends weep over three-day-old corpses. The girl wasn't halfskin, though. She was under 50%, still legal to exist, and he didn't care. He was going to take her back. Instead, he got what he wanted and left her cold. It's not just halfskins anymore. He's killing who he wants."

"And how was I going to save her?"

"I don't know." He paces around the rug, running his hands through his thick blond hair. "Reach out, manipulate the network, alter the bricks. Make them take her away from Marcus."

"I can't do that."

"No, you *won't* do that. You could've manipulated someone to get her out, but you're afraid to compromise your safe house, afraid to see what you've done to the world."

Twenty years ago, the nixes had saved his life. Now he curses them.

"The girl's not dead," Cali states.

He continues pacing. "What do you mean?"

"She's still alive."

"How?"

Cali looks away. She swore she wasn't going to do this. If she was honest, the guilt worked. It was absurd to believe she's responsible for people's actions. She released the sex videos of Marcus Anderson, but she never leaked the code for nixes. The story of their escape eventually got out and that's all it took for garage nanobiometric hobbyists and big corporations to break the invisibility barrier. They discovered their own nixes without her help. Yet she still got the credit.

And the guilt.

Cali, though, has plenty of guilt parked inside her. Nix only has to kick over one domino to get them all to fall.

"The photo you sent...her name is Jamie. Her background wasn't hard to find—single-parent household, mother guilty of substance abuse, arrested for shoplifting, possession of firearms, and other petty crimes. Jamie's last registered biomite scan tapped 49.9%. She was going halfskin when the bricks hit the warehouse. I scanned her biomite identity and found it still active."

"Can't be. Maybe her identity had already been recycled."

"She's alive, Nix." She leans back. "Trust me."

He doesn't ask why she investigated such an innocuous person. Why go through all the trouble? Why the risk? *Because Avery would've been her age.*

Would Cali's daughter have been in that warehouse? Would she have succumbed to the halfskin promise of everlasting pleasure, even if Cali told her such promises were empty?

Truth be told, Cali doesn't want Jamie to be dead.

"Whose body was in the warehouse?" Nix asks.

"Maybe Marcus fabricated it."

Innocence haunts him, reminding Cali of the little boy she'd cared for when their parents died. Life seemed so difficult then. How could it have possibly become harder?

"Did he take her back to Mother?" he begs.

"I don't think so."

"You know where she's at?"

Cali cups the mug, swirling the contents. She doesn't tell him all the layers of encryption it was buried beneath. Someone doesn't want Jamie to be found.

"It's a trap, Nix."

"You think everything's a trap." The childish visage fades.

"That's why we're alive."

"You're surviving, Cali. Not the same thing as living."

"We can't beat Mother, Nix. Twenty years ago, maybe, but not now. She's learning, evolving. Her intelligence is increasing exponentially. Despite all the safeguards, I think she's evolved into an identity that could threaten everything, not just the halfskins. People are still blind to her power. We have to hunker down and survive until the world sees what she's become. They need to see the truth."

"And you see the truth?"

How does a person see truth? Once upon a time Cali was a nanobiometric engineer, brilliant and savvy, yet she couldn't see the truth of her life. Not then.

What about now?

"Where's Jamie?" Nix asks.

Cali drums her fingers. It only takes a thought to transfer Jamie's identity code. That's all he'll need to find her.

His image fades.

She remains in the recliner with a cold cup of tea and warm dogs on her feet, knowing why she told him. Knowing that he'll need her again.

When he does, he'll come back.

CHAPTER TWENTY-FOUR_

A bus turns off Dupont Circle onto Connecticut Drive, whooshing a few feet from the sidewalk. Marcus crosses the street, exhaust fumes reminding him of the capital. Pedestrians ignore him, with briefcases or fully loaded backpacks.

The sun is cresting the urban skyline into cloudless blue space. The temperature is ideal with just a slight breeze.

Perfect.

He follows a tall brunette into Starbucks, her black heels tall, slender, and loud. The lines are long and the seats taken. Baristas shout for pickups while patrons rigidly wait their turns. The brunette looks through her purse while queuing up.

Marcus goes directly to the front.

No one fusses or argues, not even a slight look of annoyance. They move like a school of fish making way for a Great White. His order—a decaf latte with a bagel and grapes—is ready and waiting. He folds a newspaper beneath his arm. The fat man near the window gets out of the cushioned chair in time for Marcus to sit. It's still warm.

Marcus bows his head.

The room falls silent.

"Bless us, oh Lord, and these thy gifts, which we are about to receive, from thy bounty, through Christ our Lord. Amen."

He makes the sign of the cross. Life inside Mother resumes.

It wasn't always this good. When he accepted the post, life was grim in the hazy world beneath the dome. His days were spent in golf carts or beige offices, taking conference calls and approving memos. It was grinding him down and, despite his dedication, he considered quitting. The loneliness and loss was too much.

But something changed. Just when he needed it, God answered his prayers and gave him strength. The dull gray walls filled with color. Things started to appear when he asked for them, like clothing or furniture, even a vehicle. There was evidence of increased biomite activity *inside the dome.*

And then an elderly woman walked into his office: Mother, with her flowing wardrobe and gentle smile.

"I want to help you," she said.

And so she did.

Marcus samples the coffee while reading *The Washington Post*'s headlines. A shutdown in San Francisco is front-page news. The editorials are filled with public outcries, calls for legal reform and stays of shutdown. An ethnic cleansing, one idiot calls it. Liberal statisticians claim the drastic reduction in the human population could set it on course for extinction in fifty years. Unless, they state, something is done about Mother.

What they don't take into consideration is the population of clay humans that will never be threatened. Rather than ethnic cleansing—there's nothing ethnic about biomites—Marcus believes this is a modern-day rapture. The good Lord is removing the unworthy through temptation. The Earth will be returned to the Garden of Eden once it has been cleansed.

Perhaps, as one radical scientist claims, this is simply an evolutionary correction. The planet cannot support several billion people, and by our own fault we are coming back into balance.

He finishes the bagel, savoring the coffee while the lines get longer and the traffic backs up. A woman in a red dress walks across the street. Anna steps inside Starbucks. A hipster gets up, shoving his chair next to Marcus for her to sit.

Anna crosses her smooth legs, the hem just above the knees.

A barista delivers a tall coffee. The pretense that she needs to eat and drink—that any of these fabrications have anywhere to go—puts him at ease, helps him forget just how far away home is. He reminds himself, often, that Jesus walked among the wretched and impure, the prostitutes and sinners.

What about the unreal?

"You've been withdrawn lately," Anna says. "Are you depressed?"

"And what would you know about depression?"

"It is often due to a chemical imbalance, specifically serotonin, norepinephrine, and dopamine." She tilts her head. "Would you say you are experiencing heavy emotions?"

"And now you understand emotions?"

"Emotions can be described as bodily sensations that accompany thoughts. Fear is described as cold and numb, a sense of contraction. Anger is hot and raging. Depression feels as if you're beneath a heavy blanket."

"And you feel these things?"

"Perhaps you would like medication to reestablish balance?"

Marcus looks away. Antidepressants are for the weak-minded. The Lord created depression to test our resolve, to forge strength and faith. It was not meant to be cured with a pill.

"You've never talked about your feelings, Marcus. You have not grieved for the loss of your marriage or the separation from your family. Many people find resolution through experiencing their suffering, by first talking of it."

"Shut up."

Mother is regurgitating Powell's orders for counseling. He leans forward, resisting the urge to smack the arrogance from her tone.

"We care about you, Marcus."

"We." Who is she talking about? These are all Mother's creations, all various forms of imitated life composed of biomites pretending to exhibit emotions, pretending to be self-aware, pretending to feel. Aren't they all one and the same? Why does Anna pretend she's separate?

"If you're quite done *caring,* give me an update."

"Latest projections suggest an end to the existence of nixes in three months."

"It was six months."

"Analysis has been refined. There are a lot of factors to be considered. Once nixes are eradicated, Mother will control all biomites in existence."

"And the latest on the girl?"

She crosses her legs, left over right this time. "Jamie and Paul are currently stuck in Kansas City. A winter storm has closed the interstate."

"And the boy?"

"Nixon Richards has not made contact."

He shakes his head, watching another bus pass. The crowded sidewalk has thinned, but the chatter inside the coffee shop feels louder. It has been almost a month. Jamie and Paul have driven through a handful of states and Nix is gone.

Would she care to refine that analysis?

"I want to talk to her."

"She's in the greenhouse."

He frowns. Sometimes, he doesn't want to play these "reality" games. There's not really a bus out there or a skyline of buildings. The actual space he inhabits is difficult to understand, but she doesn't contain a city. Everything can come to him. But she insists on the illusion of space.

You have to continue living in the world, Mother had once said. *Where the rules of space and time exist. Otherwise, you'll lose your sense of humanity.*

Marcus stands, his knee a bit stiff. The limp loosens up by the time he reaches the sidewalk. A taxi pulls up. Anna, sitting calmly inside, her red dress bright in the dim interior, finishes her coffee.

The yellow cab stops outside the US Court of Appeals.

The streets are empty. The people gone. He begins climbing the steps leading up to the massive concrete pillars. The city is dead silent. The taxi cab doesn't drive away.

It disappears.

The limp returns before he reaches the top step, pain radiating in both directions. Each step sends jagged spikes deeper and sharper. Mother's insistence on the illusion of space sometimes feels like a personal attack, a lesson to prove the fallibility of the human body.

The doors open.

The building exhales green life. He doesn't step into the grand foyer with its shining floor and dual staircases, but into an expansive botanical conservatory.

A broad and gnarly banyan tree sprawls from the center, the canopy reaching toward a glass dome where birds dart around. Birds of paradise spike from beds and orchids bloom. Orb weaver webs glitter.

Marcus eyes the mulched path that splits at the banyan tree. He had to take a cab here and now he has to walk. The humid heat, though, soothes his ache. He grabs the dangling roots of the banyan tree as he passes beneath the shade. The conservatory of tropical plants continues on the other side.

Cylindrical containers are stuck in the leafy ground like ancient artifacts, their surfaces smudged with algae. Inside, a clear solution swirls around suspended nude bodies, absorbing data from confiscated halfskins that transfuse into Mother, a direct absorption of their lives.

High-tech autopsies.

There is a row to his left and another on the far right, each lined up and disappearing in the overgrowth. Bubbles rise over the puckered flesh in various states of decay. Mouths agape and eyes open, some display empty sockets with hints of gleaming white bone. They seem to watch as the hunched man makes his way to a small pond, where an old woman is on her knees.

Marcus stops near the water, sweat tracking his cheeks. "You don't know where the boy is."

"Have patience, Marcus."

"He's gone," Marcus quips.

"Nonsense. He's a resourceful young man."

"You've hidden the girl too well."

"He would smell the trap."

"Then perhaps he can't find her."

"Marcus, really. You worry like a child."

"This boy has eluded you for twenty years. This whole charade of releasing the girl is ludicrous. Why don't you admit it?"

Her laughter goads him. "The boy is desperate now," she says. "Desperation makes poor decisions."

She snips nodding flowers from pitcher plants, placing them in a glass vase. The exercise is absurd. She embodies that old woman and then creates this environment from her own self to harvest.

"What's wrong, Marcus?"

"Cold calculations will not explain behavior. You do not know what it means to be human."

"I'm afraid I do." She glances at the partially obscured digestion tanks. "Does the impending end of our crusade give you angst? Anna has told you that I expect this to be over soon. I could not have accomplished this without your guidance, Marcus. You should know that. This should give you satisfaction. Or do I not understand human emotions?"

Mother rinses her hands in the pond.

"Humanity behaves irrationally," she says, "when emotions are the driving force."

"I serve the Lord."

She wipes her hands with a towel. "Jamie is irrelevant, Marcus. We have already obtained two specimens just like her. There was no need to keep her."

Specimens.

The word implies something other than service. Which of these tanks—these endless tanks—contain the priceless specimens of information that will lead them to victory? Sin is on display. Perhaps she uses these tanks as a reminder of what temptation will bring. Hell incased in a bubbling solution, haunting faces testifying to the torment, mouths open in a soundless scream.

Their eternal souls pay the price.

What purpose will he serve when victory is at hand? Where will he fit? He traded everything for this crusade—his family, his career—all for God's glory. He's a spiritual warrior. Where will he go when there is no more fight?

"Patience." Mother's hand falls gently on his shoulder with a floral essence. "All will be revealed."

"I have demonstrated patience. And sacrificed much."

"Of course you have."

Mother returns to her chores. Marcus remains stuck on the path, his wingtips soiled. Perhaps, when the last fight is over, he'll find peace.

When Nix and Cali Richards are looking out from a tank.

"Why don't you join Anna for lunch? Afterwards, she'll be monitoring a shutdown in Atlanta from a projection room. There's another one scheduled for this evening in St. Louis. I'll join you for dinner."

He loosens his tie. It's pointless to argue. She insists on gardening while more important matters are at hand. And yet, the battle is almost over. He leaves her in the muddy water and avoids the vacant stares as he climbs past the banyan tree. The air is getting hard to breathe.

"Marcus!"

He stops at the exit. Mother stands beneath the banyan, a handful of aquatic weeds dripping from her hands.

"You'll always be welcome here," she says.

The taxi is back at the curb. He goes outside where the morning shadows stretch across the ground and the air is refreshing. The pressure in his chest relents. He breathes easier. Maybe he's heat stroking.

Or maybe she eased his mind.

CHAPTER TWENTY-FIVE_

The McDonald's Playland is buried in snow, somewhere in Indiana.

Snowmelt drips from yellow and red plastic tubes. Footsteps are pressed into the slush, revealing the happy colors of a foam mat. The sounds of clamoring children echo from inside the fortress while their grandfather sits on a bench, pinching his collar against the cold.

Jamie's pores are saturated with fast food.

Another day. Another stop.

She unbuttons her coat, letting the chill climb inside. Her skin is tired and suffocating. If she could just somehow shed her body, walk out of her life, become someone else, someone new and young again.

It was so easy when she was a child. She was only 5% biomite, barely enough to notice she was altered. Five percent wasn't much more than the infant booster, the amount dedicated to prevent sickness. She didn't have any sensory augments until she was thirteen, and no ability to manipulate the nervous system until she was fifteen.

What percent are the little ones thundering through Ronald McDonald's frozen tubes? Will they reach for more like Jamie? Will they discover the thrilling surge of tweaking biomites and the release of artificial dopamine? Will they attempt a constant high with additional doses—just one more seed, and life will feel like you want? Just one more, one more, one more until life becomes an empty husk, a battered old coat with no more purpose and climbing through a playground just seems pointless?

"Hey!" A large woman pushes the door open. "Get inside, your food's ready.

The plastic tubes rattle. A skinny kid shoots out of the bottom, followed by two more boys. They slip in the slush, flipping wet snow on Jamie.

"Boys!" the large woman shouts. "Apologize to the young lady."

The kids hand out apologies on the run, ducking beneath the woman's short arm. Jamie wipes the dirty snow off her lips, clumps already melting down her neck. The door closes behind her, sealing the laughter inside.

Paul sits in a booth, a box of chicken nuggets waiting for her. Ronald McDonald's smiling head is above him. They're both staring.

She doesn't want to go in there. Doesn't want to run anymore. She's tired of racing on the wheel, going nowhere, wasting time filling the giant hole that's swallowed her life.

She turns off the audio in her head. Silence rings.

The air cleanses her lungs but can't revive the deadness in her flesh, can't flush the impurities from her pores, revive her life.

Nothing will bring back the clay of childhood.

Come inside. Paul's voice startles her. It's the first time he's ever chatted her. He's always staring at his phone, but never turning it on, always telling her what to do, but never chatting her. It's strange to hear a voice inside her head.

The last one was Charlie.

She pulls open the door and warm air gusts out of the restaurant. Paul chews slowly, eyes fixed on his food.

"I didn't give you my identity." Jamie stands at the table's edge. "How'd you chat me?"

"Don't turn around."

"What?"

"Slide into the booth and don't turn around."

Her anger dissolves into confusion. Paul dips a French fry in ketchup, still not looking. Jamie sits down, staring at the paper cups of ketchup.

"Eat something," he says.

"Not hungry."

"Then pretend."

The gold nuggets look like deep-fried turds. She takes a sip of soda.

"How long has he been there?" Paul asks.

"Who?"

"The old man—don't." His glare captures her eyes as she starts to turn. "There's an old man sitting out there. How long has he been there?"

She recalls the grandfather sitting outside with the kids. "He's still out there?"

Paul dunks another fry. "I spotted him at the last two stops. Yesterday, too."

"Do you think he's..." Her hands quiver.

"Let's eat here a few minutes; then we'll go."

He casually wipes his mouth and leans back to observe their surroundings. Wrinkles deepen between his eyes. That's the cop-expression he wore in the warehouse when he yelled at the officers for cuffing her. The memory of that rank air emerges from her subconscious like she's still there. The seat feels hard and cold.

She can't move.

The spell the bricks had put her under was a live burial...no, not the bricks. The old man did it to her. He wanted to kill her.

Or something worse.

He wanted to pull her apart, make her pay for her mistakes, pay for living. His eyes felt like spikes that twisted deep inside her, spearing her heart. Cold shanks of fear. Even now, she feels them.

Paul puts his hand inside his jacket.

Jamie is jerked back to the present moment, Ronald McDonald staring gleefully. Paul moves in front of her.

Tell him I mean no harm, another voice chats inside her head.

Jamie puts her hand to her ear and sees the old man standing at the door, arms stiffly at his sides. She doesn't recognize him.

"What is it?" Paul asks.

"He just chatted me." Her lips flutter. "He said...he said he means no harm."

The man isn't as old as she thought, his hair prematurely gray, his features appear worn out from living in the clay rather than biomite remediation. He approaches with his hands slightly raised, shuffling around a table of children digging through Happy Meals.

"Who are you?" Paul demands.

"May I sit?"

"Who are you?"

"It'd be better if we didn't attract attention."

Paul takes a moment to consider the offer. Attention is as much their enemy as is a stranger. Paul slides next to Jamie, his hand still buried inside his jacket. He gestures to the other side.

"You're not on facial recognition," Paul says.

"Neither are you."

Jamie uploads the man's face through the public database using the McDonald's Wi-Fi and gets no response.

"You're in danger," the man says.

Paul stiffens. "How do you know?"

The man's tired eyes are more gray than blue. The whites are tinted pink.

"I know about the warehouse," he says to Jamie. "I know that you were there when the shutdown occurred, that you ingested a nixed biomite capsule. I know that you lost someone very close to you."

He warily looks at Paul, perhaps another attempt to identify him.

"You're free now, but for how long?"

"Are you with them?" Paul says. "Are you a brick?"

"We wouldn't be having a conversation if I was. Did you help her escape?"

Paul doesn't respond. His arm feels like corded steel against her shoulder. He continues to grip something tightly inside his coat.

"You were there?" Jamie asks. "You were at the warehouse?"

"What they did was tragic." He wants to say more, but only looks at her to say, "I'm sorry."

"How did you find us?" Paul cuts in.

"I know a safe place, where no one can see us."

"What do you mean?" Jamie asks. "Mother?"

The man doesn't answer. *Of course.*

"Shutdowns are increasing," he says. "Marcus Anderson is the man responsible. He's the one that threatened you."

"How do you know that?" she says.

"Do you think he'll forget about you?"

"Enough." Paul stands, his hand pulling out of his coat empty. Jamie is shaking. "She's been through enough."

"It's the truth. You can't run forever. The road will eventually end."

"Let's go." He motions to her. "Come on."

"I'll find you again," the man says. "They will, too."

"Who the hell are you?" Paul says.

For the first time, the man falters, covering up the thoughts behind his eyes. Patrons have taken notice of Paul looming over him, his posture rigid, fists clenched. Only the children take no notice, shouting as they head out to the playground.

It takes a false start before he gets the words out, looking directly at Jamie when he says, "You have something I need."

"What?" Jamie says.

"Information."

"About the warehouse?" He doesn't answer, but what else could it be? "You want to be halfskin?"

He averts his gaze, perhaps hiding the answer. "What I want is irrelevant."

"Come on." Paul yanks her across the plastic bench. "Follow us if you like, we're not stopping."

"Where is the safe place?" Jamie asks.

People aren't pretending they don't notice anymore. Paul beats back their interest with a sweeping glare. Jamie sits back down. The man still seems lost.

Me. He's come for me.

"South," he says. "About a day away. Maybe two, with the weather."

"And what is it?"

"Just a place where Mother can't see."

Again, he ruminates. He's honest, she can tell. She can feel it. What he wants isn't selfish, it's not petty. Still, he's hiding much. He packs the food in the paper sacks and stands.

"I have a white van. We'll go southbound as long as the weather permits."

"And if we don't follow?" Paul asks.

"You're not going anywhere." He hands him the bag. "Your time is limited; it'll run out sooner than you think. It's best if you follow me."

Perhaps he's talking about their aimless driving, their endless road trip; but Jamie hears it differently. *I'm going nowhere.*

Paul is grinding through his thoughts, dead set against following a weird stranger. Jamie snatches the bag and heads for the exit. A white van is next to their car, exhaust puffing from the tailpipe. She pulls her jacket around her throat, the wind stealing her breath. Her nose is numb when Paul finally comes out.

They get in the car.

They follow the white van without talking.

CHAPTER TWENTY-SIX_

SLEET TICKS OFF THE WINDSHIELD.

Nix pulls up to a Super 8, the white lights illuminating the snow-crusted hood. He watches the rearview mirror for a dirty white sedan. After seventy-two hours without sleep, the faint hint of hot metal lingers in his sinuses. Even his biomites have their limits.

It took a month to find Jamie. Her personal account had been closed following her "death." However, she was jumping on and off public Wi-Fi, enough that he could track her down.

Nix caught up to her near St. Louis. He pumped gas while Jamie sat in the sedan. She was in the passenger seat, head against the glass. And then a man returned.

He didn't look like her father, at least not the one in her history. They hardly spoke at restaurants and slept in separate hotel rooms. Nix spent his nights searching the man's past.

No facial recognition.

His secrecy had the imprint of security. Public servants, like police, were required to reveal name, rank and affiliation. If he was federal, like CIA, that would explain it. He expanded the facial recognition to include similar matches. It resulted in several thousand hits that would take days to sort out. However, there was one in Seattle: Paul Jennings. Seattle Police Department.

He was at the warehouse.

Odd that facial recognition didn't match the first time. In fact, his history had been erased. Nix needed more time to figure this out, but he'd been spotted. Jamie's activity on public Wi-Fi stopped. They moved quickly after that. It took three days of catching up. If Jamie hadn't accessed a public library connection in central Illinois, he might never have found them.

They were desperate. He couldn't wait any longer.

Time is running out for all of us.

Headlights shine in the rearview mirror. A car comes down the interstate ramp. The sleet blurs the white sedan sitting at the stop sign. The road is empty. Nix climbs out to wait at the back bumper. Fatigue pulls at him despite the urgency.

After a long minute, the car eases into the parking lot.

Jamie is lying back. Paul cracks the window. Dead air leaks out.

"I'm sorry," Nix says. "I can't keep driving, the weather's not good. I'm exhausted. I'll get us three rooms."

Paul doesn't answer.

Jamie looks smacked out of her gourd.

The window slides up. Paul hangs his hand over the steering wheel, staring through the windshield. Ice pellets streak through the high beams.

The car rolls forward.

Nix watches it cruise out of the parking lot. The left taillight intermittently blinks. The car creeps down the road. Nix doesn't have the energy to give chase. It'll have to wait until morning.

However, the brake lights splash across the wet asphalt. They turn into the Best Western a couple hundred yards away. Beneath the bright awning, Paul goes inside the lobby.

He's playing it safe.

Nix never intended to drive straight to the farm. Taking Jamie is a risk. Bringing Paul is stupid. It isn't likely they're being watched, but if they are, he'd be leading them right to Cali. But they're scared and nervous. They're looking for an escape, he can feel it. The farm is exactly what they want, he knows it.

Nix is running out of time. And his tolerance of risk is increasing, and now he's dragging others into his careless pursuit. He doesn't want to betray his sister, but it's got to be now.

Nix drags his feet, now wet and cold, into the hotel. He gets a room. There will be no visits to Dreamland. Not tonight.

Tonight, he'll rest.

Tomorrow will be difficult.

MOTHER_
THE DANCE OF SECRETS

Another dance recital.

If the government declared them illegal, Abe Rondell wouldn't argue.

The parking lot next to the school was full. They found a spot across the road. So did the other parents that were running late. They waited at a stoplight. Fine green lines appeared in his vision and enclosed the passing license plates. The numbers were logged in to the column to the right of his vision.

Once they crossed the road, the same green lines targeted the people they passed. Names hovered over their heads, along with registered occupations and whatever personal information was linked to social networks.

"Stop working," his wife said.

The green lines boxed her in. "Lindsey, Real Estate Agent," floated over her head.

Occupation, "Bitch."

You get a toy like this, you don't turn it off. His promotion came with a subscription to the Global Facial Recognition database. It's too expensive for the general public. Commercial applications, however, made the investment well worth it. He would never forget another name, always identify potential customers.

Mind reading is no longer a fantasy.

He dialed down the sphere of capture, pulling faces only from a five-foot radius around him. The attendees funneled towards the front doors of the school. It wasn't triggered by the back of their heads, only when someone turned around. It required a frontal view that analyzed spatial relations, skin tone, eye color, etc. Take, for instance, the lady holding the door.

"Nikki Messing.

"Administrative Assistant for School District #2. 32 years old. [LinkedIn]

"Two cats, no kids. [Facebook]

"Recently divorced. Hiked the Appalachian Trail this summer. [Facebook]

"Active dating profile. [eHarmony]"

"Turn it off." His wife squeezed his hand.

He'd have to work on disguising that glazed-over look when he was working.

They gave Nikki Messing their tickets and found their seats. The auditorium was stuffy. Abe settled into the creaky seat and prepared for two hours of mind-numbing boredom. When the lights went down and the first group of five-year-olds marched onto the stage holding giant lollipops and dancing to "The Good Ship Lollipop" (most of them staring at the crowd in horror), Abe fired up the facial recognition.

Only three of the children had personal information, which meant the parents voluntarily posted it. And the older the groups got, the more he learned.

His daughter's act was the ninth one of the evening. All of them were linked to social media, except for Abe's daughter, Jean. Tabitha, her new best friend, even streamed video from her Twitter and Instagram feeds that Abe watched superimposed over the dance routine.

When the event was mercifully over, they waited outside. His wife was occupied with other parents, so he kept it rolling. He identified a few potential clients and stored this event away for future chitchat.

His daughter finally came out with Tabitha. Hugs and congratulations and flowers were exchanged. The girls were almost as excited it was over as the adults. Tabitha asked if Abe's daughter could spend the night.

"If it's all right with her parents," Tabitha's mom answered.

"*Tina Martin. Cashier. 49.*"

"I don't think so," Abe said.

"Daddy!"

His wife looked shocked. He was usually thrilled to have an empty house. But it wasn't the blurry tattoo on Tina Martin's forearm that alarmed him or the unlit cigarette between her fingers.

"*Drug possession with intent to distribute. [Department of Corrections]*"

CHAPTER TWENTY-SEVEN_

Cigarettes are yesterday's habit.

Paul watches from the second story of the Best Western while sucking on a filtered Marlboro. He quit smoking ten years ago, but he just didn't have the biomite capacity to kill the compulsion. Too much clay pulled him back to the sweet drag of tobacco.

A pack of twenty promised a reprieve from the daily grind, a little pick-me-up when life knocked you down. Cigarettes were the adult's cookie.

Then along came biomites.

The nicotine pick-me-up was replaced by scripted positive thinking and customized hormonal release. With the right seeding, you just decided to stop smoking: no struggle, no withdrawal. Sweet relief was a thought away. Instead of inhaling a lungful of carcinogens, people had the ability to feel whatever they wanted.

The cookie was internalized. No lighter needed.

At least, that's what the biomite designers promised. Humanity soon discovered that suffering doesn't disappear when wishes are granted. Life doesn't care how you feel and many came to find the internalized cookie was much more mesmerizing than a cigarette. To some, inescapable.

Jamie comes out of her room, huddling inside her puffy coat. Her hair frizzes beneath her stocking cap. When it comes to those that can't escape the empty promise of the biomite era, she is Exhibit A.

Smoke burns his eyes that already ache with only two hours of sleep. He gave Jamie his chat identity and waited all night for her to call if the old man came to kidnap her. Sometime before sunrise, he bought a pack of reds.

Paul slides his finger across his phone and waits for it to boot. He hasn't turned it on, afraid to give away their position. But Jamie has been lying, just like he thought. She has been on public Wi-Fi. That's how the old man found them.

But that means no one else is looking.

The bricks would've beaten the old man to them. At least Paul's identity is still locked. Despite being missing in action for over a month, he is still absent from facial recognition. The old man, though, is hiding something. Paul can't find anything on him.

Jamie sniffs. "Have one?"

Paul taps out a cigarette and lights it for her. Jamie exhales a column of white smoke. She bobs her head to her internal audio loop. Before biomites, the human race worked to tame runaway thoughts and unravel subconscious beliefs; now heads were filled with music and newsfeeds and lucid Dreamlands. It brought whole new levels of insanity.

Exhibit B, the warehouse.

"He's coming," Jamie says.

"Who?"

"The old man chatted me."

"How'd he get your identity?"

"Same way you did, I guess."

That's the funny thing: Paul doesn't know how he got it. Ordinarily, she would have to give it to him. Somehow, he just intuited it.

Jamie finishes her smoke and takes a second one from the pack. Paul lights another one for himself. He pulls a slow drag.

"So you have a gun?" Jamie asks.

"I'm a cop. That bother you?"

"Not at all."

He finishes the smoke and drops the butt over the railing. A white van comes down the road, tires cracking fresh ice in the parking lot. The old man stops beneath them, looking through the windshield.

"You sure about this?" Paul asks. "We can still leave."

"We aren't going anywhere, Paul. At least this is something." She grinds the cigarette butt under her heel.

"If he chats you," Paul says, "include me."

The van door slams. The old man goes to the stairwell, hopping up the first couple of steps, a bit spry for his age. He stops on the top step. Several moments pass.

"So where we going?" Paul asks.

"Can we talk first?" He gestures to Jamie's room.

"What for?"

"It'd be good if we talked about where we're going. And why."

The standoff lingers.

Jamie kicks open her room and leaves it open on her way inside. The old man politely waits. "Go ahead, Paul."

"How'd you get my name?"

"You're a Seattle police officer. You were at the warehouse."

"Did they contact you?"

"No. But I'd like to know why you're with her."

"And I'd like to know who the fuck you are."

"Please." The old man lowers his voice. "Let's go inside."

"Go ahead." He watches the old man go in the dark room.

Paul crushes the box of cigarettes. Enough with old habits; he needs to think clearly. He checks the phone before following. There are no messages. No texts, no missed phone calls. Not from his family or work.

It's been over a month.

And no one is looking for him.

CHAPTER TWENTY-EIGHT_

"Move to the back." Paul closes the door.

Nix doesn't argue. There is no way to move forward—no chance to make this morning work—without the truth. He has to expose his true nature, to become completely vulnerable and hope they will do the same. If he misjudged this moment, this won't go well.

Nix stands beneath the fluorescent lights above the sink.

"I know who you are," Nix says. "I know your names and your backgrounds. I think it's only fair that I tell you mine. My name is Nixon Richards."

He stares at the swirling patterns on the carpet, his heart thumping. If they haven't heard of him, they'll run a search. Jamie's subtle unfocused look suggests she's already downloading newsfeeds. Intensity rises across Paul's face.

"You should know that most of what you're going to find isn't true," Nix says. "Twenty years ago, my sister engineered a new generation of biomites that operated on an evolving frequency unknown to Mother. They were the first of their kind. They were invisible to her. You know them as nixes."

"You're a halfskin?" Jamie asks.

Nix nods. A long pause follows.

"You've eluded Mother for twenty years?" Paul says. "That's not possible."

"You're not picking up facial recognition because I've altered my appearance. I've been forced to look like this for longer than I care to remember."

"You can transfigure?" Jamie asks.

"I contain a significant level of biomites."

"What percent?"

He hesitates. "Ninety-nine."

Paul moves a step closer to Jamie. Instincts are warning him.

"You're lying. If you're Nixon Richards," he says, "you wouldn't tell us, not after twenty years on the run. There's a reward on your head."

"Who are you going to tell? Taking her from Marcus Anderson makes you as wanted as me."

"There's no way to trust you. You could be a brick."

"You would be dead if I was."

Nix faces the mirror, watching them in the reflection. He could show them his true face, but what good would that do?

"What do you want?" Paul says.

"My existence depends on the pill you ingested." Nix looks at Jamie. "Since the warehouse, Marcus Anderson has raided other halfskin dens. There's always a survivor, just like you. I think he's shutting them down just as someone takes the pill, timing it so the nixes don't integrate with their bodies. They contain information he can use to find more dens."

"So what?" Jamie says.

"I want to know what's inside you."

Nix hopes that Paul doesn't read the subtle deception. He didn't lie, but he won't reveal his true motivation. It's true that Marcus's new approach could lead him to discovering Nix and Cali, but that's secondary.

"Halfskin invisibility depends on evolving code, a continuous reconfiguration of the frequency that biomites communicate. It prevents her from establishing a connection with our identities, keeping us one step ahead of her. Marcus Anderson is quickly solving these encryptions."

"You want us to help you stay halfskin?" Paul asks. "Not our problem. You chose to become halfskin, you live with it."

"I didn't have a choice." There's no way to convince him that the rumors Marcus Anderson and others leaked to the press were lies to cover their incompetence. Nix had become halfskin to survive an accident, but no one believes that excuse anymore.

"I can help with your pain." Nix steps toward Jamie. "You lost someone in the warehouse, I know that. I know what it's like to lose a loved one. I know what it's like to wander through life just trying to scratch another moment of relief from endless suffering."

He sits on the bed.

"I can help."

"How?" Her eyes are dead. "How can you help?"

"We need to go somewhere safe, where no one can find us. We all benefit." Nix looks at Paul. "It would be safer if I could hide you both, in case you're being followed. But I can only make one of you invisible. In order to do that, I need to submerge Jamie in my perception field."

"Why?" Paul stiffens.

"By taking you with me, I'm putting someone at risk. I need Jamie to be invisible to whatever or whoever might be watching. Marcus Anderson had her alone in a room for three days. It's possible he's watching."

Sickness fills him. He's admitted his doubt and recognized the risk he's put Cali in. And he's still going through with it.

"Mother?" Jamie says. "You think Mother's watching?"

"No," Paul adds. "The bricks would've found us."

Paul's right, but Nix can't explain his sister's suspicious mind, her paranoid behavior that has kept them alive for all these years. He can't ignore her warning.

"It's a precaution," Nix says. "It's like anesthesia. You'll go to sleep and wake up once we're there. Paul will be with us; he'll make sure nothing happens."

"I don't like this," Paul says.

"Jamie?" Nix asks. "I'll be with you. I've got just as much to lose."

I've got more to lose. Much more.

Her eyes are blank. Perhaps she's imagining what it must be like to go to sleep and not dream, to forget what today feels like. Anesthesia sounds like a slice of death. And death no longer feels like an enemy.

Nix holds out his hand, the knuckles knobby with apparent age, the palm coarse and wrinkled. Jamie puts her delicate hand in his. The direct contact allows a better connection. The conscious barrier between them dissolves, his awareness merging into hers, usurping, momentarily, her identity.

He assumes control of her biomites. The buzz of her frequency synchronizes with his. He feels her heart beating faster, her lungs rapidly expanding and contracting. He can't feel his own body, the energy rapidly draining, but he can feel her emptiness, her lack of purpose. Her hopelessness.

The distinct metal tang falls on his tongue, absorbing the edges of her charred state of biomite addiction. Somewhere, he can feel a foreign object inside her with all its secrets.

The pill.

The answers are still there. If he could just read them, he could leave, never risk Cali's life, let them go about their running. But he needs help. He needs Cali to uncover the secrets.

Paul pushes Nix away.

Jamie sucks in a deep breath, emerging from an experience of nonexistence. Nix struggles with his own breathing. He took away her pain by snuffing her awareness. For a moment, she forgot what it was like to be Jamie. She sits up, pushing Paul's hand away. It takes several moments for her to return to her body and the misery it holds.

"Come with me," Nix says. "And no more running."

Despite her resistance, Paul helps her stand.

"A safe place for all of us."

She swims in indecision, but there's nowhere for her to go. Much later, Nix marvels how fortunate it was that Paul was with her, that he seemed trustworthy enough to bring along. Nix couldn't drive her to Cali's alone. It was almost too perfect.

Paul's presence would make all the difference.

Jamie hangs on to Paul as they descend the steps to the parking lot. Nix taps his teeth, numbness slowly fading.

CHAPTER TWENTY-NINE_

Snow narrows the winding road.

Paul keeps both hands on the wheel, hunching forward. The headlights illuminate heavy snowflakes staggering to the ground. Beyond, the road is dark and unknown.

The GPS says he's close.

Nix and Jamie are sleeping in the backseat. Nix remained awake for hours, but his words began to slur. He eventually fogged up, sometimes responding to a question a minute later. Paul frequently stopped to check on them.

"There's no address," Nix had told him. "But there are coordinates. You'll know it when you get there."

Paul didn't plan on Nix going unconscious. Occasionally, he groaned and spit out nonsense as if nightmares were escaping. Perhaps that's what he's made of: nightmares.

Paul had heard of Nixon Richards.

He was a kid when he redlined, about Jamie's age. Those were the days when 40% biomites got you incarcerated for observation. The first generation of biomites behaved like cancer, slowly consuming the body's clay. People didn't have a choice of going half-skin; they were all destined to reach it at some point. Paul's father always said that, during those days, you just hoped you'd reach old age before that.

After that, the stories get sketchy. The most popular one claims that Nixon Richards eclipsed into a biomite rage and attacked a guard. He was aggressively subdued and ended up in a hospital, where he would likely be shut down.

And then he disappeared.

Nixon Richards and his sister, Dr. Cali Richards, somehow turned their biomites invisible. Occasionally Internet rumors would revive their names, where they were reverently whispered. About a year later, a new generation of biomites was discovered by garage techs that halted the runaway biomite division. The redline laws were rescinded. Halfskin status had become a choice.

That's when the real fun began.

There was a sharp decline in shutdowns but not for the reasons the government promoted. Secret variants of biomites were popping up. People were still going halfskin. Mother just couldn't see them.

It always seemed odd that the new generation of biomites was first discovered by a hobbyist, and not a team of nanobiometric engineers with all the money in the world. The rumors always traced back to Dr. Cali Richards, now a digital goddess, that leaked her discoveries.

Paul keeps his attention on the road. Truth be told, he was excited when Nix first suggested a safe place. He tried to kill that emotional response, to think rationally. But Jamie was right...*we're going nowhere.*

He lets up on the gas. The GPS shows two dots—the car and the destination—on top of each other. The road, however, is desolate and houses rare. Snow-crusted trees rise from the banks. He comes around a sharp turn.

The gate appears to his right.

Brick columns peek out from piles of snow where someone has plowed an opening. The cast-iron gate absorbs the headlights' glare, the entry drive beyond vanishing into the trees. Paul stops in the middle of the road. The gate doesn't open.

Snow gathers on the windshield.

He gets out to inspect the gate. There are tire tracks that lead to the gate. The road curves to the left, but the trees are too thick to see anything. He shakes the bars; snow falls to the ground.

He plods back to the car. The two are disheveled and slumped in the backseat. She's drooling. Nix's teeth are clenched.

"We're here." Paul shakes Nix. The old man's head wobbles. "Hey. Wake up."

He gives him a couple sharp slaps. No response, not even a groan.

"Shit."

Nix has a pulse. So does Jamie.

"Jamie, wake up." He gently shakes her. She won't come out of it. He's got to separate them, break the connection. He tries to pull Nix's hand off her forearm. Jamie's arm is bent at an angle beneath his white-knuckled grip. Her flesh is sickly purple, the fingers swollen.

"Hey! Hey! You're killing her! Let go, goddamnit!"

He tries to peel back the fingers. Jamie's skin is hot, the forearm moving like she's developed a new joint. Nix's grip is locked. Paul strikes him with an open palm. Nix's head jerks sideways. Red marks glow on his cheeks where the wrinkles have faded. Paul grabs Nix's hair and pulls back a fist when he hears barking.

Two dogs race down the lane, snow flipping in their wake. They stop at the gate, baring teeth.

Headlights come around the bend.

A truck creeps into view, its tires lining up in the previous tracks. It stops twenty feet from the gate. The dogs keep their black eyes on Paul.

A sole silhouette sits in the driver seat. The high beams are blinding. The dogs push their heads between the bars.

"Are you Cali Richards?"

His head begins to buzz. A wave passes through him like a

thermal scanner. Paul reaches inside his jacket, feeling the security of a 9mm grip.

Nausea turns his stomach inside out. He falls against the car, sliding down the door. The road tips like a broken slab. He feels wet snow on his face, the road beneath. The world is spinning like a broken carnival ride. A slick of perspiration rises across his forehead.

The gun is heavy.

He swallows back vomit when his own thoughts attack him, seeding him with doubt and fear and confusion. A thousand voices shout inside his head. He covers his ears.

And then his hands are empty.

Slowly, the carnival ride stops whirling. Two heavy boots are buried in front of him, a white robe dangling at the knees. The 9mm clip falls between the woman's feet, followed by the gun. The dogs sniff his legs and arms. Their breath is warm on his face.

An old woman squats in front of him. Her green eyes flash like a camera; he feels the inner trickle of a digital scan.

"If you're Cali Richards..." The words echo in his head. "Your brother..."

Paul flicks his eyes at the door.

The woman looks inside. She yanks the handle. There's scuffling. The dogs whine.

"Oh, no," she whispers. "No, no, no..."

Paul can't feel his extremities. The gun and ammunition are lost in the snow. It wouldn't do him any good to retrieve it. He can't feel his fingers.

"Get up!" she shouts. "Drive inside the gate!"

Paul is yanked to his feet by an invisible force. He's reaching for the door, sensations returning to his hands and legs. He's not entirely in control of what he's doing. He climbs into the driver seat. The dogs race through the open gate. He pulls in behind them.

Something changes when he passes between the columns. There's less static in his head. His thoughts clear up.

"Go around the truck!" she shouts from the backseat. "All the way to the house."

The car barely fits between the truck and trees. The dogs lead the way. The branches reach over the road, entangled like twisted fingers. The headlights beam down the tunnel until he clears the trees. Open fields are to the left. Windows are lit up in a two-story house.

"What have you done?" she mutters over the sound of rustling clothes and flopping limbs.

Paul stops in front of the house.

"Get the girl," Cali says. "Be careful with the arm."

He jumps out of the car like a wound-up toy and eases Jamie out. Her arm is wrapped in a sweater that's tied to her belt. Paul cradles her like a grown child. Cali is already climbing the front porch with Nix hiked over her shoulder: a frail woman hauling a full-grown man.

"Up here!" Cali shouts.

The house is warm and old. Paul doesn't close the front door. He follows the black dog—the larger of the two—to the second story. The worn steps creak as the other dog comes up behind him. There's a bedroom on the right. Cali is hunched over a bed, out of breath. Nix is splayed across the bedsheets, arms and legs bent.

Paul turns sideways to avoid banging Jamie on the doorjamb.

"Don't let them touch," Cali says.

He gently places her next to Nix, careful that her arm doesn't move. Her stocking cap has fallen off; her face is hidden beneath her thick brown hair. Cali folds Nix's hands over his stomach and straightens his legs.

He's not an old man anymore.

The wrinkles are gone, the nose slimmer, his lips fuller. The ridge above the eyes is no longer pronounced. He's a young man, a fortyish-year-old man with gray hair.

"Are you the girl's father?"

"No."

"Why are you here?"

"I...I pulled her from the warehouse."

Cali looks up. Lines crease her forehead. Another digital wave passes through him, this time without the nausea.

"That was almost two months ago," she says. "Why are you still with her?"

Jamie is so still, her expression less pained. As if she's found peace at last. He takes her wrist and feels her weak pulse. Cali watches him brush the hair from her face.

"Don't worry about her arm. How long did he have her like that?"

"We left this morning," he says. "What the hell is happening?"

"He overextended his biomite capacity. Everything is shutting down."

That explains why he looks younger: he can't keep up the transfiguration. Cali shouldn't look that old, either. Her hair is more white than gray, her complexion softly wrinkled. She doesn't walk like an old lady, and certainly not one that could carry a grown man like a sack of grain.

Was that her perception field that brought on the nausea? Am I still in her field, seeing this kindly old woman? Is that why I feel oddly comfortable with her while two people may be dying?

He should be more vigilant. He should go find his gun.

The room begins to sway. If he can't trust his own senses, if he can't sort his thoughts from hers, how does he know what's real?

Cali goes to the bathroom for a washcloth and dabs Nix's face. She begins to undress him. Paul unzips Jamie's coat.

"I've got it from here," she says. "Go back out to the road and bring the truck up to the house. There's a room down the hall. You'll go to it when you get back and stay there for the night."

The previously warm sensation that filled the room dampens. He leaves with the cold impression that he's been dismissed. The dogs are waiting in the hallway. Cali is dabbing Jamie's cheeks with the washcloth. He gets the feeling she's better off here than anywhere else in the world.

But can I trust that feeling?

The steps groan beneath his boots. Once again, the black dog leads the way, his claws clicking on the old wood. The winter wind sighs into the house. Paul takes the brass knob to close it behind him.

"I don't know why Nix would bring you here. Or why I can't read your history." Cali is standing on the top step. "You should know that I'm a very private person. I have two dogs that protect me. I think you should understand that if Nix has made a grave mistake, the dogs will be the least of your worries."

She returns to the bedroom.

The dogs walk him down the long drive, snow dusting their dark coats. The truck is still running. The dogs wait while he goes out to the road and digs in the snow. Returning to the truck, he throws the gun and the clip on the front seat and lets out a long sigh.

He should get his car and leave. Jamie doesn't need him anymore. But he's compelled to return. Perhaps he's still snared in Cali's field.

Or maybe he just has nowhere else to go.

CHAPTER THIRTY_

The Oval Office is immaculate. The sofas and chairs are arranged in perfect symmetry around a table with a bowl of fruit. George Washington and Abraham Lincoln watch from the far wall.

The front lawn sparkles with morning dew. Marcus watches the landscaper leave a crisp line in the damp White House lawn. He can smell the cut grass.

There's a photo of his children propped on a shiny table below the window. In the photo, they're still children. Clifford is wearing his red backpack. Months go by without thinking of them, as if they don't belong to him. He could have grandchildren now.

Washington and all the men and women of power believe, as did Marcus, that Mother is a peacekeeper. She alone has limited humanity's potential to self-destruct. But they have underestimated her.

He feels, on days like this, he has, too.

Marcus pivots on his heel and feels his knee catch. Pain lances up his thigh. The framed photo cracks on the floor. He holds his breath, swallowing the fierce agony. Marcus slams his open palm on the desk, ripping open the drawers to find nothing. The painkillers are in his sleeping quarters.

The last time he had been to the president's office—the actual

White House, not a replication in Mother—he had to explain his actions following, what he called, the rumors about his sexual perversions, and, more importantly, illegal procedures as Head of the Biomite Oversight Committee.

They sat on the couches. Marcus was on the right. How could he forget? He sat on the president's dog's bone right before the president promised to have his back. But the sex videos kept surfacing. Pretty soon he was ostracized. Marcus would've done the same thing, if he were the president. You can't look dirty when you're leading the free world.

The desk has three stacks of manila folders. Marcus takes the middle one. He tips his head back to focus through reading glasses. There was a biomite den in Omaha, Nebraska.

Was.

This shutdown didn't make the news. It was a halfway house for halfskins disguised as a center for substance/biomite abuse recovery. It was a short stay for wealthy people. The investigating brick infiltrated the den as a customer, even ingested a nixed pill. The pill, however, didn't activate since it only integrated with clay.

Unfortunately, this triggered an electromagnetic pulse, effectively self-terminating all the nixes associated with the den. *Suicide code.* They shut themselves down and, in the process, kept Mother from harvesting their secrets.

Information travels fast.

Anna enters the Oval Office. "Why aren't you wearing your earpiece? I've been calling you."

"I need some quiet."

She's wearing a cerulean blue skirt, hem above the knees. The blouse is snug around her neck with a gold necklace. She's quite professional today—except for the lack of a bra.

A delicious twist in his groin.

"All this labor," she says. "Reading and phones...it could be so much easier, Marcus. You would be so much more productive with a minor seeding."

"I use the five senses the good Lord gave me, Anna. I was made in His image, I honor that."

"You are like a man living in a cave, refusing to leave because the sun is too bright. Perhaps your Father intended more senses for you besides the five." She plucks the folder from him, the golden pendant swaying. "All you need is the courage to leave the cave."

"Stupidity can be mistaken for courage. Weakness, as well."

"We work harder to make up for your shortcomings." She drops the folder in the trash. "You slow us down, Marcus."

He squeezes the chair to control the anger. This is unlike her. She's incapable of emotions and only uses them to manipulate. Mother is behind this.

She's behind everything.

She wants him to merge with their biomite frequency. He can absorb information instead of reading it, communicate with thoughts rather than speak. Take a pill, and he won't be at the mercy of his emotions.

But he rather likes the fire in his belly. It reminds him there is still work.

"Are you hungry?" she says. "Sex, perhaps?"

"Give me your update."

Her fragrance is light and enticing. With a hand on his shoulder, she reaches for the desk and effortlessly flips it like a cardboard box. The papers flutter in a chaotic cloud.

The Oval Office shifts.

The walls straighten out, turning a dark shade of blue. The sofas fade and the windows stretch around him, providing views to massive palm trees and open blue sky. A woman sits next to a door. Her stillness betrays her inanimate nature. Marcus knows a brick.

"Miami," Anna says. "This doctor's office was infiltrated an hour ago. The operatives dismantled an EMP command to avoid self-shutdowns. They've quarantined the doctors and staff while assimilating the data. They were legitimate physicians, Marcus, healers of your people. They were also seeding select patients with nixes."

Anna turns Marcus's chair toward the exit. A young man tries to open the locked door. He sees the woman sitting inside and knocks on the glass.

"We've informed their patients the office is closed and their appointments rescheduled. In the meantime, the operatives are tracking them. Once they have the information they need, the doctors and staff will be digested."

She spins the chair back toward the woman, indifferent to the man rapping on the glass. Marcus doesn't need to go through the door. He's seen more mass shutdowns in the past month than the prior ten years. They're always the same.

"The patients will be shut down tonight," Anna says. "Almost five thousand, Marcus."

Ever since Seattle, the shutdowns have been quiet. Halfskins will be sleeping in their beds when they take their last breath. They'll fall off barstools or slump to the floor at their favorite restaurant.

The walls begin to curve and George and Abe are back on the Oval Office wall. Folders are stacked on the desk once again. Anna struts to one of the sofas.

"Two more shutdowns are scheduled for tonight, one in Paris and the other in Ontario. We expect big numbers."

"And the reaction?"

"Nothing new, the public isn't happy. World governments, though, are getting nervous. Press conferences have addressed the public's concern."

Marcus steeples his hands, bouncing his fingertips. The halfskin war is operating without him. He's more of a spectator now. He thought there would be more pleasure when victory was near.

"Very well. Give me the analysis for the next two weeks. I want an approximation of shutdowns, where and how many. I'll file a progress report."

Anna kneads his shoulders, using her thumb to drive the tension from his back. He closes his eyes and relaxes. When she's finished, his knee no longer hurts.

“One more thing,” she says. “Jamie is missing.”

“What does that mean?”

“You know what it means, Marcus.”

The fire rises in his stomach. He recalls the first time Cali and Nix Richards went missing. He was arrogant to believe it was temporary, that they would be found.

Anna sits on the leather sofa, patting the space next to her. She lifts her skirt.

Marcus stands without a twinge of pain. He kneels in front of her, running his hands up the length of her thighs, over the soft curve of her buttocks. The next five minutes are glorious. It’s not until much later he realizes what he saw before leaving the Oval Office. There was a dog bone on the sofa.

He had been thinking about the president’s dog.

Only thinking.

CHAPTER THIRTY-ONE_

Paul shivers, despite the blanket.

His clothes are damp. His feet are trapped in hard, wet boots. The weights on his eyelids are heavy; the hinges loosened after several attempts.

The bedroom is sparse with an unusually high ceiling and water stains around the light fixture. He drops his boots on the wood floor, the impact stinging his feet. He parts the curtains on the only window. His car is parked next to a barn that's smothered beneath a blanket of snow. He wonders how it got there.

And then remembers.

A black dog waits outside his door, tongue hanging. Paul moves carefully around him, brushing against the wall. He passes the stairwell on his right and tries the door at the opposite end of the hall.

Locked.

He puts his ear against it, listening for any sign of life. He tries the knob again. The keyhole is an old-fashioned lock, one he could pick if he had some heavy wire. What would he do if he opened it? Jamie was unconscious, the last he remembers. He brought her here.

Too late to take her away.

His footsteps echo down the shallow steps, the wood faded where thousands of steps have worn away the color. Dark squares on the floral wallpaper indicate picture frames that have recently been removed.

He stops at the bottom step. The house is quiet except for the dog's toenails clicking behind him. There's a short hallway to the right with a chalkboard to the left and a locked door to the right. It ends at the kitchen and the smell of coffee. A clock ticks above the refrigerator.

Paul parts the frilly curtains above the sink. The barn door is closed. Aside from a trail of footprints, the snow is perfect. Despite the tower in the distance, there's no service on his phone. No Wi-Fi, either.

The locked door opens in the hall.

Cali shuffles into the kitchen, followed by the brown dog. She's wearing fresh clothing, but her eyes look tired, her complexion deeply wrinkled. She pours two cups of coffee, sliding one toward him.

"You're Dr. Cali Richards."

She nods.

"You look older than I expected."

"Common courtesy does not tell a woman she looks old."

"From my understanding, you're about fifty years old."

"Don't believe everything you read."

She grabs a container next to the refrigerator. The dogs tap-dance.

"I've stayed alive all these years by hiding from Mother. I've altered my appearance, like Nix, to avoid facial recognition. But my brother has chosen to expose me to you, so I suppose it doesn't matter."

She tosses a snack to the dogs.

"Who are you, Paul?"

"How do you know my name?"

She passes him a sideways glance. If she can hijack his senses, she can find his name.

"I'm a Seattle cop."

"No. You're an enigma, is what you are. Your background security far exceeds the rank of sergeant. You're closed to the public. That's unusual. And you show up with a girl that was quarantined at one of the largest shutdowns at the time. It doesn't feel like a coincidence."

"And that makes me a threat?"

"To me, yes. Why are you with her?"

"They were going to take her. She was in danger."

"By 'they,' you mean Marcus Anderson."

"She's not a halfskin, you can scan her, you'll see."

"What compelled you to save her?"

"I'm human."

Cali goes to the mudroom, where her boots sit in a puddle of melted snow. She wraps a scarf around her neck and reaches for her coat.

"Why is it so hard to believe that I saved a girl in trouble? Have you become so accustomed to manipulating your senses that you no longer feel compassion?"

She sits on a footstool to pull on her boots.

"You pulled me into your perception field last night," Paul continues. "You made me see and hear what you wanted, made me help you. You're far past a halfskin, like your brother. He said he was 99%."

He remembers the mind-fog at the warehouse, compelled to do whatever the bricks told him. He doesn't remember being forced to save Jamie, but why would they? *No, I acted on my own. That was my choice, my own free will.*

But would he know it?

"Is that true?" he says. "Are you almost a brick?"

She sits up. "Don't lecture me. You don't know me."

"And you don't know me."

"That's the problem, Paul." She pulls on her coat, buttoning it. "There's a dome of static that protects me and my property. It operates like back-reflection, showing Mother there are no biomites within this sphere. It won't work forever, I know that. She'll eventually find me, maybe ten years from now, maybe tomorrow. I don't know. Right now, though, I've got you and Jamie in my house. I need to figure some things out. It's going to take Nix and Jamie a couple of weeks to recover."

"After that?"

"I don't know." She cups her coffee to her chin, the aroma failing to revive her tired eyes.

"Is it true what they say about you?" he asks.

"Truth is rarely found in the news."

"You were the nanobiometric engineer that beat Mother. You released the nixed code to the public."

"Like I said, believe nothing you've read."

"I see an old woman. Is that truth? You manipulated what I saw, heard and felt last night. And maybe you're doing it right now. How am I supposed to know what's true when I can't trust my senses?"

"Our senses were fallible long before biomites."

"Reality is not relative."

She poses over her coffee cup, eyes distant and glassy. "These days, it is."

She takes one final sip and leaves it in the mudroom. The brown dog follows her. Frigid air swooshes past the open door. Paul watches her trudge to the barn.

The black dog watches him.

CHAPTER THIRTY-TWO_

THE WORLD ROCKS, UP AND DOWN. UP AND DOWN.

Droplets spatter across Nix's cheeks; a briny taste is on his lips. His head sways with the rhythm of up and down, up and down. The soothing sound of water feels like a lullaby.

The sky is unblemished. The blue is deep and endless. His eyelids succumb to the rhythm and begin to fall—

He sits up.

The bamboo raft rocks beneath his shifting weight, seawater sloshing over the sides. The bindings creak.

Where am I?

He dips his feet in the warm water. Far behind him, the rocky shore and the twin peaks are visible. A green meadow slopes behind them, and, despite the distance, he knows there's a cabin on top of that where Raine waits for him.

Dreamland.

He's never been out this far in the water. Occasionally, he would hop on a skiff with one of the local fisherman, but they rarely ventured into the deep. And never on a homemade raft.

He envisions a sail and a gust of wind to push him home, but his thoughts dissolve like daydreams. Nothing he imagines comes to fruition. The raft rocks beneath his feet. He dives into the sea's depth. He grabs the edge of the raft and begins kicking. Eventually, he'll reach the shore. What seems like hours go by, and he's no closer. Home is in sight, but no more.

Cali put him out there.

This is my punishment.

CHAPTER THIRTY-THREE_

THE DAYS ARE EMPTY.

Paul spends most of them with Baxter, the black dog. He rarely barks or shows his teeth. Often, he watches Paul with an unusual sense of intelligence. Observing. Thinking.

Cali locks herself in the basement most days. The bedroom upstairs is always locked.

He's hazy in the mornings, spending several minutes recalling where he is. The sand of sleep weighs him down for hours at a time. In the afternoons, he walks the property, going deep into the trees and out to the road. The dog doesn't like it when he's that far out.

Paul could leave, just hop the gate. Maybe he'd have to fight off the dog, but then what? Where would he go?

What about Jamie?

There's an old cell tower behind the horse paddock. By his estimates, it's centered on the property. The scaffolding is corroded, but the utility shed is new. So is the conduit that runs to the top of the tower.

The shed is locked.

This must be what generates her back-reflecting dome of protection. If this comes down, she's exposed.

One morning, his car is gone. Paul finds it behind the house near an abandoned swing set, the corroded legs buckled like old bones. Footsteps lead back to the house. The railing leading up the front steps wobbles. He goes to the barn in search of tools. The tack room door is jammed. He uses both hands to get it open.

A red toolbox is stashed on a shelf with a tin can full of rusty nails. He inspects the latch on the door. It's as old as the house. It wouldn't take much to dissemble and fix.

Something moves through the trees. Paul watches through the window as a red truck comes down the lane, a yellow plow blade carving snow to the side. It backs up several times, working its way toward the house.

Paul steps into the breezeway, but stays to the shadows.

Cali comes out the front door, fastening her coat. A man gets out of the truck and waves at the old woman looking more tired than ever.

"Good morning, Stacy," the man says.

Stacy?

He hugs her while a young girl steps out of the passenger seat, her arm tied in a sling. Both dogs come running. It's the first time he's seen their tails wag like that. She takes a knee, rubbing their thick coats with her free hand. Paul can feel the weight of Cali's mind press upon his. She's exerting her field on him.

Stay.

That's why the car's out back.

The conversation passes. The daughter lifts her wounded arm, explaining how she sprained her wrist when her fingers got tangled in twine while bucking bales. The man fills his lip with a pinch of tobacco. Cali looks concerned for the girl. Several minutes later, they climb back in the truck and finish plowing.

Cali goes to the porch.

Paul steps into the opening with a hammer and a rusty can of nails. She stares for a long moment.

"Friends?" Paul asks.

"Neighbors help out from time to time."

"Why'd you let them leave?"

"This isn't a prison camp."

"Just for us."

"You weren't invited."

He peers around the corner. The truck has left long piles of snow. That sling was old-fashioned. Even the lowest dose of biomites could heal something like that.

They're clay.

Their eyes meet. No words are needed. Cali Richards is keeping a secret. If you learn it, you don't leave.

She goes back inside to lock herself in the basement.

Paul fixes the railing.

CHAPTER THIRTY-FOUR_

WARM, DRY AIR BLOWS ON HER FACE.

Jamie's head is sunk in a pillow. The dusty strands of a spiderweb wave in the ceiling vent.

Sensation returns to everything but her left arm. The last thing she remembers is going to the car, but this isn't the hotel. Her internal clock announces the time. It seems like they were at the hotel a minute ago, but three days have passed.

Three days have been snipped from her life.

She sits up. Her mouth is dry and gummy, and her left arm is wrapped with gauze. Her pale fingertips feel dead, as if someone sat on her arm. She balances against the wall, stumbling barefoot to the door. The strange surroundings smell of old linen.

Someone is downstairs.

She goes one step at a time, gripping the railing with both hands at first. A conversation is heating up, somewhere downstairs. The muffled voices aren't familiar. They're coming from the first floor, behind a door in the hallway. She leans against the chalkboard, sliding her feet to keep the floor from creaking. The argument comes in bursts, most of it unintelligible.

"No one's leaving!" a woman shouts.

The other person is apologetic, reasoning, even pleading, for a response. Jamie feels the wall slide up her back as she slowly goes to the floor, her legs too weak.

A door opens somewhere in the house.

Toenails click toward her. A black dog stares from around the corner, and heavy boots follow.

"Jamie." Paul pulls off his gloves and crouches beside her. His brown hair, so often combed to the side, is a mess over his thick eyebrows. "Are you all right? How'd you get down here?"

She grabs him with her free hand, latching on like she won't let go, like he's the only thing that's keeping her from melting into a puddle. He's the only thing she can remember.

He's safe.

Paul almost carries her into a kitchen, where she sits at a weathered table. A glass of water finds its way into her hand.

"Little sips."

She takes big swallows and he has to pull it from her. It cools her throat and settles her stomach. He keeps his hand on the glass the next time she drinks, monitoring how steeply she tips it.

"Where are we?" she asks.

"What do you remember?"

She wipes her mouth. It takes too long to remember what Nix looked like, what he told her. *Somewhere safe.*

The kitchen feels like it's stuck in time, with spice racks and dried flowers hanging over a window. Safe isn't a house in the country. She was expecting something to take the pain away.

The fear of living is still a cold lump in her chest.

An old woman stops in the hall and stares. A young man, however, walks boldly past her. He's vaguely familiar, his hair prematurely gray.

"You're awake," he says.

She shrinks from his comforting reach. He steps back and looks at Paul. He resembles Nix, but there's a difference of about twenty years. The hair, though, doesn't fit. She attempts facial recognition, green lines racing through her vision. There's no outbound connection to the Internet.

"I was an old man when you last saw me." He sits across from her. "I had reconfigured my facial features. The hair isn't as malleable as flesh. This is what I look like in real life."

Real life? What does that mean anymore?

"Where are we?"

"We're at the farm," he says. "You're safe."

The old woman's face is darker than the shadows appear. Jamie continues staring, not remembering any discussion about her. She seems irritated, but finally relents.

"My name is Cali Richards," she says flatly. "You're safe in my house."

Jamie doesn't believe her. Her body language suggests she didn't invite them. There's a vague recall of Nix explaining the facial reconfiguration and a promise that he'd help, but not where they were going.

"How does your arm feel?" Cali asks.

"I can't really feel it."

"You suffered a compound fracture. Unfortunately, your biomites are exhausted from years of abuse. I don't think I need to tell you how close you are to charring. Your body will have to heal itself."

"Why not boost her?" Paul asks. "Seed the break."

"She's at 49.9%. We're not doing that."

"What are we doing?" Jamie asks.

Cali takes a bowl of eggs from the refrigerator. She puts a pot on the stove then cracks a hardboiled egg on the counter, peeling the shell under running water.

Nix's jaw is clenching.

There's a chat session between them. Nix looks up just as a warm sensation trickles inside Jamie, a sort of honey-sweet emotion that bubbles from inside her chest. Jamie is enveloped in the invisible arms of an all-loving mother. She doesn't know why this happens, doesn't care. For the first time in forever, she doesn't want to crawl out of her skin.

She feels safe.

"Start with this." Cali puts the hardboiled egg on a plate. "Give that some time to digest, then eat the soup."

They watch her take a bite. The attention keeps her from swallowing the egg whole. The silence is broken only by the ticking clock.

Cali leaves.

Nix follows her into the basement. Paul attends the pot of soup, stirring it with a spoon while Jamie finishes the glass of water and indulges in the warmth that feels like home.

I'm safe.

CHAPTER THIRTY-FIVE_

Nix turns the glass knob. Cali's bedroom is unlocked.

The bedspread is wrinkled, the pillows hardly dented. She wasn't sleeping. Maybe she was lying down every once in a while, but she wasn't sleeping.

Stress is her amphetamine.

He hadn't seen her in days. He didn't stay awake for long, his body insisting on frequent naps. He spent the nights on a raft, forever paddling toward distant peaks. No matter how long he struggled, the raft never reached the shore.

An athletic, dark body moves past him. Raine's image examines the empty bedroom. Her green cargo pants are rolled to the knees, exposing muscled calves. A high-pitched ring haunts his hearing. He shouldn't project her into being. His biomites are still recovering from the trip, but it's the only way to see her.

Raine's bare feet silently stride toward the dresser to study the framed photos of Nix's late parents as well as Cali's late husband. There's also one of her daughter, Avery. They surround a stencil drawing.

Life is suffering.

The memories are captured in photographs, reminders of another life. The happiness made the fall that much greater, the pain that much deeper. Now all that's left are pewter frames with fading photos.

Patterns of frost are crystallized on the window. Snowdrifts look like frozen waves in the backyard. Icicles hang from the old shed near the trees, icy daggers pointing at firewood.

"That's the last thing I did." He taps the glass. "Cut that wood."

It's still chest high, every log still in place. *It's rotten now.*

He grabs the cell phone from the dresser and flips it open. The buttons respond with melodic tones.

"She uses this to pretend she's clay. It's so naïve, a future artifact of a dying world."

"Nothing wrong with it, Nix. Biomites aren't for everyone."

"Clays are the new Amish. Do you know where the world would be if everyone did that? There'd be no new discoveries, no transportation, no modern medicine. We'd be gazing at the stars instead of traveling to them, just wishing things would be better instead of making them better. There'd be no you, Raine."

He drops the phone on the bed and takes down the photo of Avery. She's missing two teeth.

"God loves growth, Raine. Isn't that what life is about? Growth? He gave us the ability to conceive this technology for what purpose? Biomites are the vessel that carries our identity to new worlds like ships carried people across oceans to discover new lands."

"Who are you arguing with?"

"It's their fault, you see. None of this would be happening if it wasn't for clays like Marcus Anderson."

"They're not all like him."

Raine watches him rub the glass with his thumb. She never met Avery. She would've liked his niece. He's sure Avery would've loved her.

"What're you doing in here?" Cali stands in the doorway.

Nix jumps up, picture frame clutched in both hands. His sister looks so old. Despite the costume, the reconfiguration of her features, she wears the familiar mask of despair: the slow blinking eyes, the heavy corners of her mouth.

"Just thinking about when we moved here, how I used to cut the wood and stack it. Then I was thinking how we built the lab and planned on taking a few years to heal and then move on. This place was supposed to be a pit stop, remember? We weren't supposed to hide in the clay for the rest of our lives. What happened, Cali?"

"I don't need to explain myself."

"No. You got good at that."

"Don't make this about me. You brought them here, you had no right...*no right*."

"If they were a threat, the bricks would already be here."

"That's not the point." She snatches the picture and replaces it on the dresser.

"I can't let you rot like this," Nix says. "You're just withering."

"That is not why you're here. This is about you getting what you want, against my wishes. You know how I feel; don't pretend this is about anything else."

"That's why you're punishing me?"

Cali closes the door gently. She pushes her hair from her eyes, the tension draining from her forehead.

"I can't dream, Cali. I can't get back to Raine. You did this when I was unconscious, didn't you?"

She folds her arms.

"Why do you keep fighting it? You could build your own Dreamland, Cali. You could bring back Avery, do it right this time—fabricate her instead of pretending she's alive."

"You're addicted to Dreamland. You can't live in this world and the dream. You need to accept the world we live in."

"And have this life?" Nix slams his fist on the bed. "Just stay locked up and hide? Is that what we should do? You deserve better, Cali. I can't let you do it."

"You'll go insane if you keep dreaming."

"You had no right to take Raine away!"

"And you had no right to expose me." She jabs her finger at him, her hand quivering. "You arrive on the brink of charring; you bring strangers into my life. This is my world, Nix. I did not invite them. And you need to accept the fact that I don't give a goddamn about Raine. Dreamland is not a new reality, it's a dream—a fantasy. Accept that."

Nix paces across the room. He stands at the window, watching a bird hover over the trees, wings catching a draft higher.

"Just give me what I want," he says. "We'll leave. You can go back to your life in the clay."

"What do you want?"

"Reset my biomites, open Dreamland. And read the nixed pill inside Jamie."

"I'm not reading her."

Nix turns, swallowing a rising knot.

"And no one's leaving, not yet."

"What do you mean you're not reading her?"

"You want to use her to find a fabricator and I'm not doing that."

"Jesus Christ, Cali! Just let me use the lab, then. I'll do it myself. Why are you doing this?"

"You know why."

He resists throwing his fist through the window. She's still pissed. He can't blame her. She needs a few days, maybe weeks, to cool off.

"You can't kidnap them."

"You kidnapped them, Nix. Not me. Why would you bring Paul? He's got nothing to do with this."

"There's nothing wrong with him. Besides, I was able to hide Jamie with him driving."

"And almost killed yourself."

"I just need some help."

"You've made a mess and I'm cleaning it up. What'd you think I was going to do?"

"Not this!"

She holds her ground, unflinching. Her eyes are tired, mouth slack. She smells as old as she looks.

"This isn't fair. I let you play out your Avery delusion when I knew you shouldn't," he says.

"Maybe you shouldn't have."

He curses through stiff lips and yanks the door open. He wants to slam it like he did when he was little and she wouldn't let him have his way. He looks back.

Cali is staring out the window.

Her shoulders are shaking.

What have we become?

MOTHER_
DREAMING THE DREAM

Josh Stanton sneezed.

He hated sneezing. It was like licking metal shavings off an aluminum sheet then blowing it out his nose.

He climbed off the bus, holding his backpack against his chest. His life savings were inside. It wasn't much, but it was everything he had. He didn't trust the post office and had to pick it up in person, never letting it out of his sight.

The parking lot was littered. Josh avoided eye contact with the lady on the second floor. He locked his apartment door behind him, breathing heavily. It was here. Finally here.

The apartment was sparse: a TV and a couch. The lounging chair was in the middle of the room, extra padding duct-taped to the faux leather. It was for comfort, not looks. Josh didn't invest much in this world.

His investments were in his mind.

Josh closed a tiny gap in the heavy drapes and went to the kitchen. He took a long swallow of whole milk from the jug, swishing it around his mouth, coating his tongue and throat before swallowing.

Whole milk neutralized the metal taste. Without it, his tongue was like copper. His body dipped in lead.

Charred.

That was the official diagnosis. His biomites ran hot, circuits were shorting out. If he didn't back off his habit of dreamweaving, he could expect to taste steel for the rest of his life. And, the experts said, he could trigger a spontaneous shutdown.

What do they know?

They also said unassisted dreamweaving was impossible. No one, they said, has ever experienced a lucid dream state without external stimulation. And that's where they were wrong. Josh had clocked up to ten minutes of real time in a Dreamland before he started to char. He hadn't done it since, but he'd done it.

He figured he'd try what was in the box. If that didn't work, nixes were next.

Dreamweaver 2.0.

It was a metallic claw. The tips were smooth discs. It was custom fit for Josh's measurements and promised to ease the charred symptoms by reducing biomite activity. The test drive at the lab induced a short, lucid dream state. He could even feel it. He'd never achieved tactile sensation in his Dreamland.

Josh got comfortable. The dreamweaver was heavy. *The quality is in the metal.* The kit came with everything he needed, only Josh swapped out the power block with one of his own. He got the plans off the Internet. He lay back in the padded lounger and slid the dreamweaver's cold fingers over his head.

He immediately fell through inner space and landed in Dreamland: a medieval castle, a long sword on his hip. Where had he left off?

Ah, yes. The war.

The men followed him into battle. Whoever heard of a king leading the charge? Josh fought valiantly, slaying as many of the enemy as any man on the battlefield. He was drenched with the smell of blood.

They celebrated with mead and hog. They sang and laughed. That night, Josh made love to his queen. She moaned with pleasure. His orgasm was explosive.

As the days in Dreamland passed, his body became sluggish. The nights got darker and the days dimmer until he just felt like sleeping. Eventually, he didn't wake up.

The neighbors found him a week later.

The cause of death was starvation and exhaustion, in addition to extreme charring. The company claimed he circumvented the safety feature that prevented long-term dreamweaving by changing the power cell. They improved the product, but, after several more related deaths, were forced to discontinue the mobile dreamweaver unit.

Instead, they focused their investments on sanctioned dream cafés. And continued to make billions.

CHAPTER THIRTY-SIX_

MARCH ARRIVES WITH NO SIGN OF SPRING.

Snow sparkles in the early light. The crust breaks beneath Cali's boots, her breath transformed into dense steam. She pauses at the fence to taste the morning, feel it pinch the end of her nose. She savors the moment. Ever since Nix arrived, these moments have felt numbered.

The horses emerge snorting from their stalls. They greet her with rubbery lips and humid breath. The water trough has frozen. Cali uses the blunt end of an ax to break it up, releasing the tiny bubbles trapped inside. The jagged chunks swirl with each blow, rising back to the surface. She chips at the bits and pieces clinging to the sides.

Is that what I've become, a trapped bubble?

Has this domed farm become her trough, keeping her safe and stagnant? She always rationalized that she was free to think, that she chose this simple life, that she had little choice, otherwise. Nix had proven her wrong, stepping outside the dome in search of a fabricator.

And she just watched.

Perhaps Paul will be an ax, come to shatter the frozen elements of her life. Maybe Jamie. She could be her daughter, fill that void Avery left behind. Cali couldn't help submerging the girl in her own perception field, soothing her aches. Cali is familiar with that pain; she couldn't let Jamie have it, too.

It's what a mother does.

The auto-fill valve doesn't appear to be working. It'll need to be replaced. She works the nut loose with a pair of folding pliers.

"Still not sleeping?" Paul is standing in a stall.

One of the horses is startled. Cali pulls her cap over her ears, wondering how long he's been watching.

"I'll sleep when this is over."

"When will it be over?"

"You tell me." She walks past him on her way to the tack room.

The feed buckets are in the sink, food stuck inside. She searches for an auto-fill valve on the shelves, swearing she had purchased an extra one. She pulls a toolbox from beneath the sink, feeling Paul fill the doorway.

"What are you doing in the lab?" he asks.

"Cleaning up messes, Paul."

"You mean me and Jamie."

"You aren't the only ones."

"You're still keeping Jamie in your perception field," he says. She finds a valve at the bottom of the box. "Maybe you should stop," he adds.

"She's doing just fine."

"But it's draining you. And she's ready to handle her own reality."

Cali snaps the toolbox shut. She turns on the hot water and goes to work on the feed pails, instead. "She needs help, Paul. What I'm doing is no different than an antidepressant."

"It's not her experience. You're directing it, making her feel good. She won't want to leave you."

"How would you know that?"

"Because I don't want to leave," he says. "Why am I still here?"

He sounds confused, genuinely seeking an answer for his

compliance. She hasn't manipulated his perception since he arrived, and only uses the dogs to monitor his whereabouts. Jamie is coping without him. He's done his duty, saved her from the warehouse.

Cali can't find much history on him. Actually, she hadn't bothered after the first week. If he was a threat, it was too late. He's single with no children. He has a brother and a mother. His law enforcement history is still secure, but he's been on the farm a month and nothing has happened.

Why is he still here?

"Are you doing that to me?" he asks. "Making me want to stay?"

"No."

"How do I know?"

"Trust me."

"Why should I?"

"Why should I trust you, Paul?" She soaks her old-looking hands in the warm suds. They feel like someone else's. "You came here to help the girl. You're welcome to leave."

"Why won't you help Nix?"

"I am helping him."

She rinses the pails and turns them over to finish air drying. Once her hands are dry, she grabs the toolbox.

He doesn't move. "I want to help."

"Is that what you want?"

"You're afraid."

"You don't know anything about me. All you know are the rumors and newsfeeds."

"Then tell me."

"I didn't invite you into my life."

"You don't invite anything into your life. I'm not a threat, you know that. Nobody is waiting outside your gates. Mother hasn't turned us off. So what are you afraid of, Cali? That your tower will fall over? You'll be exposed to the world again—is that it?

"I've been plenty exposed in the past."

"Is that why you released the nixes to the world? To get back at Mother? The world?" He leans forward. "God?"

She pushes past him and slams the door. The tools rattle inside the metal box. She wants to immerse him inside her perception field and feed him her memories of losing her family, saturate him with the never-ending ache of loss. If she shared her suffering, he wouldn't stay.

She forgot the auto-fill valve. Out of habit, she puts the toolbox down and grabs the handle with both hands. The door opens easily. It never does that after it's been slammed. She tries it again, hearing the oiled components work perfectly. All these years, she never found time to fix it. He's only been here a month.

He fixed it.

"I didn't release them." She bows her head. "Someone else did."

Tension hardens inside her. She needs the pasture, the wide open space to let her thoughts run.

The horses plod toward her, wary of the metal box rattling in her hand. She drops it next to the trough and finds a wrench to loosen the valve. It takes several turns, her fingers numb against the cold metal. A thin skin of ice has already formed. The wrench fumbles from her grip, raking her knuckles over a metal burr. The wrench sinks to the bottom.

Paul stands behind her. His shadow is long, nearly touching her. Cali leans against the trough, struggling to breathe.

"Who released them?"

"I don't know. The design is similar to mine, but it's not exact. It was just a matter of time before someone else figured it out. I'm not the smartest nanobiometric engineer in the world. Someone just didn't want to take credit. It was easier to blame me."

"But you exposed Marcus Anderson?"

"I exposed his hypocrisy." She elbows the trough. "He wanted Nix and me dead. Bastard had it coming."

"So the public's perception of Cali Richards isn't what it seems?"

"Perception has been manipulated long before biomites, Paul."

"But why blame it on you?"

"Why not? It makes sense. I'm the vindictive bitch that poisoned her brother with nixes, the first to escape Mother... Why wouldn't I want to release a plague of nixes on the world? Look, everything you've learned about me is wrong. Marcus Anderson and others began to spin a story about me before there was a story. They turned me into a self-serving bitch while the underworld of nixes hailed me as some all-knowing goddess."

"Which one are you?"

"Neither."

"You're not the woman who lost her parents in a car accident? You're not the one who raised her brother on her own, the one who buried a husband and a daughter before she was thirty?"

She bows her head, chin falling to her chest. A spot of blood swells on her knuckles. She smears it with her thumb, the crimson hue seeping into the wrinkles.

"I just want God to leave me alone."

"Is that what you want?" Paul steps closer, reaching for her. "To be left alone?"

She snaps her hand away. "Yes."

Her head fills with a metallic aroma—the hot sensation of overworked biomites. She can't keep going at this pace; can't keep working in the lab through the night. Can't sit around wishing things were different.

I want my clay back.

But there's no going back. She sold her body to save her brother. She wonders if she sold her soul, too.

What if she turned herself off? Just dropped the dome and exposed her true identity, would death end her suffering?

If I didn't suffer, would I have a purpose?

"You can't keep going like this. You have limits," Paul says. "You're not a machine."

"No. I'm Marcus Anderson's prophecy. He warned us this would happen, that we would overconsume, that we would sell our souls. That we would become *this*."

She turns her hand over, the torn skin already healed.

"I turned my back on God, Paul," she says. "But He turned His back on me first."

"God doesn't make mistakes, Cali. He got all this exactly right. Biomites are not the enemy, they're not evil. You saved your brother with them—you survived because of them."

"We created biomites, Paul. Not God."

"And God created us in His image. Through Him, all things are possible." He takes off his coat and pulls up his sleeve to retrieve the wrench at the bottom of the trough. His arm is slightly pink when he pulls it out and puts it in the box. "Tools, Cali. Biomites are just tools."

He carries the toolbox back to the tack room. One of the horses sniffs her shoulder and snorts in her ear. Paul returns to help her up. She's too tired to fight him, too exhausted to manipulate his field, to make him want to leave her alone. Instead, she lets him guide her back to the house.

She climbs into bed, aware that they can all leave if they want. She's not stopping them.

She's tired of hiding.

CHAPTER THIRTY-SEVEN_

JAMIE GETS LOST IN THE MUSIC.

There's no Internet and her personal account is still trashed. She hasn't been using her field, but this morning she felt colder than usual. And lonelier.

A long walk keeps her out of the house, where the pipes rattle and the walls speak when the wind blows. The icicles drip into drifts piled against the house. When she returns, her teeth are chattering.

Her skin feels exhausted and her clothing is wrinkled from nights beneath the covers. Body odor puffs out of her sweatshirt, reminding her how long it's been since she's showered. The wrapping around her arm has frayed.

It takes two minutes for hot water to reach the kitchen sink. Jamie unwinds the stiff gauze. The skin beneath is sickly white and smells sour. She clenches a fist, feeling a slight tingle midway up her forearm where the swelling remains. She washes her hands beneath the hot water, the suds dripping from her elbows.

A long drum solo ends in her head. A voice interrupts the silence between tracks. She turns around, but no one is there. Drying her hands, she wanders around the table, stopping to listen.

The basement door is ajar.

Jamie calls the music off and stands with her ear to the gap. The hinges swing quietly. She slips inside, where the air is damp and moldy with a hint of vinegar. The steps are gray and worn.

A single bulb starkly illuminates jars and faded labels. She stands on the bottom step, waiting to see a human head pickled in an oversized jar instead of cucumbers and tomatoes.

"No. No, we can't," Nix says.

There's an open door at the other end. Nix is sitting inside the room. His old-man hair is shaved close to the scalp. Jamie walks to the doorway and peeks inside. His back is to her.

"What are you doing?" he says.

Jamie pauses. "Nothing. What are you doing?"

Nix spins the office chair around, eyes momentarily wide. He holds still, his head cocked, thinking. He looks to the right, nodding, as if he was talking to one of the computer monitors.

"Who you talking to?"

"Myself." He hesitates. "I do that."

"You're weird."

"I've been told." He rubs the steel gray stubble on his scalp. "How's the arm?"

"A little weak, but okay."

"I'm sorry. I...I really didn't know that was going to happen—"

"It's all right."

He asks about the arm every day and has apologized a thousand times. She wants to tell him it was worth it, that she hasn't wanted to crawl out of her skin since they arrived. She doesn't feel lost. For the first time that she can remember, she feels at home. She's only been on the farm for a month, but that's what it feels like. There's no urge to leave somewhere, nothing to run away from.

She wants to tell him that it doesn't hurt, not like before.

The room is a step up from the cold concrete. The floor inside is hard and shiny. There's a long workbench to the right with a fume hood and an industrial-sized refrigerator. Another bench is fastened to the back wall, with monitors and microscopes; notebooks are scattered on the surface. A rack of tubes is directly behind him, one of them wedged between his fingers, with heavy metallic liquid inside.

"What is all this?" she asks.

"This is the lab. We built it about ten years ago, when we first moved here." He slides a manila folder off a stack. "It was mainly to refine our biomites. No one in the world has nixes like us. As far as I know, we're the longest surviving halfskins and we planned to keep it that way. The plan was to invent a new breed of biomites, ones that communicate completely different by means of quantum physics. We never had plans for mass production—just produce enough for us to stay off Mother's radar. But once the tower was built, Cali shut it down and locked me out."

"How'd you get in?"

"I have a key, but I've been waiting for her to crash. She doesn't sleep much, but she's out now."

"What are you looking for?"

"She took something away from me. I'm just trying to fix it." He looks behind her. Jamie turns. There's no one there.

"Why do you do that?" she asks. "Like you're looking at a ghost."

"Nothing." He rubs the gray stubble. "It's how I think."

Data begins scrolling on the monitor. He turns around, muttering again. There are two more monitors at the end of the bench with more data and a bank of computers beneath them. This stuff belongs in an industrial park, not a farmhouse with pickled beets outside the door.

"Where did you get all the money?" she asks.

"Stole it." He says it without flinching. "The seed money, at least. It's not hard to skim accounts."

While he watches the data, occasionally clicking and typing, he explains how they opened bogus accounts at banks under a variety of names. They mostly wrote deposits that didn't exist, moving the money and closing the accounts before getting caught.

"And now?"

"Investments. The capital gains from market algorithms make more money than we can spend."

He rolls over to the monitor on the far left, punching a few keys before searching the rack of tubes with gray liquid. He yanks one from the top and places it on the bench next to another.

There's a box of equipment under the bench. A black cube with large numbers sits on top. She takes it out. It's heavier than it looks, the edges crisp and cold.

She'd seen one of these before, back when biomite agents would come to your house and ask if someone was home. Like your dad. They'd put the cube on his chest and show him the number. If it was forty or higher, he went with them. And he wouldn't come back.

Jamie presses an indention with her thumb. Numbers roll across a miniature screen. She pulls the collar of her sweatshirt down, placing it just below the V where her collarbones meet. The cold surface sucks at her flesh and begins to warm. Pricks of heat are pulled through her soft tissue, puddling just below the surface.

When it cools, she pulls it off. 40%.

The number her dad saw.

"It needs calibrating," Nix says.

For a moment, the thrill of hope swirls in her heart, but her internal app still registers 49.9%. It's too good to believe, even for a moment. No one gets their clay back once the biomites take hold.

"What are you?" she asks.

He clicks through three screens of data before reaching for a cube next to a microscope, this one slightly larger than Jamie's. He holds it against his chest then slides it down the bench.

99.1%.

"How's that possible?" she asks.

"Biomites are synthetic cells. That's all."

"Does it feel different?"

"Than what?"

"Different than...before."

"You mean when I was clay?"

"Yeah."

She'd heard Nixon Richards got seeded when he was a kid. Back then, no one received biomites until they were twelve, unless it was life or death. Some rumors say he got them at birth. Others say he got them after a car accident. Either way, he's had them most of his life.

And now he's almost a brick.

He rolls toward her, holding out his hand. "Take it."

She sandwiches it between hers. His palm is slightly callused; his pulse beating in his wrist. There's nothing special about it.

"My anger is hot," he says. "My aches are wanting. My joy is sweet. My loneliness hollow. I feel all the same things you do. Does the body make us human?"

"What if you become a brick?"

"I don't think I'd know the difference."

He pulls his hand back and immerses his attention in the data again. His fingers crawl along the rack, finding another tube. This one he inserts into the base of a microscope and takes a look.

The left side of the lab is dormant. Tarps hang over much of the contents. Jamie covers her throat, the cold square still lingering on her skin. She pulls back the covers on several boxes with meaningless labels. A dozen metal canisters are stored against the wall. Tubes run from the canisters to a container in the corner, this one the size of another refrigerator. She peeks inside, but the tarp is thick and heavy. She pulls it back to allow light to penetrate the glass walls.

It's a clear box filled with polished cylinders with bundles of cables dangling like arteries. Nozzles are fitted at the end of the cylinders, pointed at a matte black floor. She's seen this before, at the warehouse.

A fabricator. A three-dimensional printer of life. The God Machine.

Programmed biomites are laid down, line by line. This one looks like a prototype, something built from scratch. It probably took months to build a frog. The newest models only took days, until Mother shut them down.

"You ever fabricate something?" she asks.

Nix is staring at something in empty space like before. He's thinking again. Haunted. He gets up and tugs on the clear door, but it's locked.

"Baxter was the first one."

"The dog?"

He smiles, smudging the glass with his finger. "It took seven months to finish that puppy. And when his DNA was ignited, the spark of life jump-started his awareness. He started wagging his tail."

"How long ago was that?"

"Seven years."

"And it still works?"

He bends over, awkwardly throwing the tarp over it. "No."

She helps him cover it, not believing him. They tuck the corners so that it's hidden once again. He gets that foggy stare.

"That's what the fight is all about," he says. "Cali wanted to disassemble the fabricator. It was a temptation, she said. I wanted to build someone and she disagreed. As you can tell, what Cali wants, she gets. She pulled its guts out, so I left."

"You can make a human?"

"It needed some modifications, but yeah. It's basically how bricks are fabricated."

"But bricks aren't real."

He falls back into the office chair, rolling away. "Did you know the dogs were fabricated? No, you didn't. You're half a brick, does that make you half real? It's just a body, a vehicle for memories. Biomites are close to perfection. One of these days, we'll beat death. We'll upload our memories into cloud storage as we live our lives. We'll fabricate bodies like vehicles; we'll go places human bodies can't go. Maybe even discover new realms of reality."

"Is that all we are, memories?"

"No," he says. "We're more than that."

"What, then?"

He stares at empty space before turning back to the monitor to resume his search. The lab feels colder and emptier. Jamie looks around like an apparition might step out from beneath the tarps. She wonders how many times they tried to build something and failed. Did those experiments suffer? Did they know they were alive before they were thrown in the garbage?

"Why'd you bring me here?" Her voice shakes.

"That nixed pill you swallowed," he says without looking away from the monitor. "It's got imbedded code that will identify its manufacturer."

"But you don't need biomites."

"Where nixes are made, there's going to be a fabricator."

He searches for another vial, mumbling as he goes, as if answering a question. Jamie uncovers the other office chair and sits down. She doesn't want to be alone right now. And she wonders.

Do bricks know they're fabricated when they open their eyes?

CHAPTER THIRTY-EIGHT_

By late March, the nights were still cold, but the snow had melted. In the morning, shallow puddles would harden. By the afternoon, they'd be wet again.

The roof is missing several shingles and the ones remaining are brittle. Paul found more than a few leaks in the attic. April would be a good time to replace the roof, when the wind wasn't so frosty. In the meantime, there was an antenna to fix.

The pitch made the climb a nervous one. A misstep would be a long drop. Cables swing from the three-sided antenna. The metal artifact is a reminder of age-old television. PBS is the only broadcast signal. The big stations still go through satellite and cable, but the majority of programming goes through internal feeds, projecting directly into retinal and auditory senses.

Paul loops his arm around a rung while stripping the insulation from the frayed cables. Up there, his fingertips are numb and his cheeks raw. It takes almost half an hour to splice the cables and make an adjustment. The tower sways and the mounts creak. His thighs are numb on the climb back to the roof.

A car door slams.

Paul bear-crawls to the crown, his tool belt dragging over the shingles. A truck is parked out front, plow blade still attached.

"Hello!" Paul shouts.

Hal looks at the pasture. Nix and Jamie are on the far side of the barn with the horses, too far away to be seen. His daughter, Megan, gets out of the truck, carrying a green container.

"Up here!"

"Oh, hey." Hal shades his eyes. "What're you doing up there, Paul?"

"Just fixing the television. A bit of cabin fever is going around."

"That's what I hear. Talked to Stacy on the phone, said she was still a bit under the weather."

It takes a moment to connect the dots—*Stacy is Cali*. "Well, you know," Paul stammers, "she's been better. Flu, we're guessing. She's trapped in bed, said if I didn't get the TV working, she was going to lose her mind."

"Well, can't say as I blame her. We brought some chicken soup, get her back on track."

"That's awfully nice of you. You want to put it in the kitchen, Megan?"

Megan goes around to the side door. Surely, Cali knows they were coming. She can hide long enough to avoid being seen.

Hal talks about the weather taking a good turn, that he might take the plow blade off sooner than he thought. He asks about the horses, too. Paul sits on the roof's peak.

"We worry about Stacy being out here all alone. She ain't had any help in a while. She could use some looking after."

Megan returns to the truck. Hal hangs his arm over the door. "Listen, y'all are welcome at the church this Sunday. Service is at ten o'clock. No need to dress up, just bring yourselves. And if you just want the coffee and donuts, come about eleven. The company's not bad, either."

With a final wave, they drive away. Paul rubs the feeling back into his thighs. He feels a bit like a gargoyle, perched high above, surveying the endless country. Carefully, he works his way off the roof, the metal rungs biting his fingers.

The container of chicken soup is on the counter, the broth still warm. The coffee pot, however, is cold. He pours two cups and waits at the sink while they rotate inside the microwave. Nix and Jamie have the horses near the fence. Nix swings onto the larger one, settling into the saddle before galloping across the wet field.

Maybe Jamie grins, maybe not. She's fallen back into a slump, facing those hard feelings again. Still, he's caught her smiling. Ironically, the farm has been a biomite detox, even though there's more biomite technology on these acres than most small towns. With no Internet access and no personal account, all her biomite apps are limited. It's the horses and the country and the old house that have grounded her. It's the wind and the sun, the elements of simple living that have taken her out of her head, put her in the present moment.

How much of Jamie's experience is Cali's field? And am I still in it?

Jamie gets depressed when Cali sleeps, it's obvious the way her shoulders slump. But the blissful peace is always with Paul. He thought about testing his theory, going out to the road where her field would weaken, perhaps even drive a bit. Would he become that person he used to be, the Seattle cop living day to day? Or had she somehow changed him?

Cali's bedroom door is ajar. The shower, however, is running. Paul nudges the door open to leave a cup of coffee on her dresser.

A television console is in the back room. A converter box is wired to the back, converting broadcast signals for the antiquated television to interpret. A channel scan picks up nothing but static. The antenna looks like a dead soldier until the scan cycles around, nabbing a snowy channel.

"Victory."

Paul settles on the couch. It's been months since he really paid much attention to current events. The coffee warms his stomach, the caffeine buzzing his senses while two talking heads debate biomite genocide.

The news is bad.

Especially for Paul.

CHAPTER THIRTY-NINE_

A HAZY FORM STANDS IN THE MIRROR.

She wipes away the condensation, revealing a young woman with prematurely graying hair. Cali steps back to admire the reflection. Much of the sag has lifted from her breasts. Her belly no longer hangs in a cluster of wrinkles. She just couldn't maintain the illusion of age anymore, not while manipulating Jamie's field. It taxed her biomites with an endless deficit.

And no solution in sight.

She leans over the sink and slicks back her hair. Her face, while smoother and leaner, is still haunted by exhaustion—darkness beneath her eyes like shadows. The neighbors have never seen this woman. She'll feign illness until she's ready to put the mask back on.

There's a cup of coffee on her dresser.

She thinks while dressing. Always thinking, always searching for a solution. There must be a way to revitalize Jamie's biomites without boosting her percentage. If she goes halfskin, she'll have to stay on the farm. She can't take responsibility for what would happen to her if she left.

She's considered a slow transfusion, but that would require flushing old biomites. Earlier attempts by detox laboratories have had some success, but the attempts create errors in coding and have resulted in self-shutdown or runaway growth. *Cancer*.

Biomites are made to replace organic cells, not other biomites. They're synergistic with their own kind. Antagonism is difficult for them to comprehend. Cali could seed her with the strain of nixes she and Nix possess. They were the only antagonistic biomites she's ever witnessed, the only evidence she's ever seen of biomites replacing biomites.

Rather than transfuse Jamie's near-charred biomites, she's considered a sort of reboot. That would require increased allocations to brain stem biomites and erasing the emotional charges associated with subconscious memories. The risk would be reformatting her memories—essentially erasing them. She'd start over.

Cali goes to the kitchen to heat the coffee. There's a conversation in the back room. She creeps down the hall, the floor cold on her bare feet. The room flickers with electric light. The television is working. Paul said he was going to fix it.

She takes her coffee to the basement. The locks have been recoded. Nix had been inside the lab a few weeks ago. She's considering giving him Dreamland back. She has known for quite some time how he was doing it. His brain stem, limbic and paralimbic structures had become hyperactive when he was seeded at a young age. His dreams became lucid.

He wasn't transporting to another reality. He was snared by this realistic dream state, and when she tried to convince him with data, showing him the unusual activity of his brain, he just got defensive, refusing to believe his secret was an illusion.

Raine too.

Dreaming wasn't a problem. It was clinging to those wishful hopes despite what was right in front of him. She wanted him to face harsh reality, not wish it away. Fabricating Raine was not going to help that.

So while he was unconscious, she slipped a small seed of biomites into his brain stem that would slow the activity. He'd have to learn how to live in the real world full time. Totally committed.

But Cali isn't having much success living in the real world. She's not sure she can help him with that. She gets back to work. Twenty years, and biomites haven't solved her problems yet. But it's the only thing she knows how to do.

CHAPTER FORTY_

The old horse has no buck left in her. That's what Nix told her. Jamie holds the mane with both hands, the hair coarse between her fingers, as the mare follows the narrow path where green grass is absent.

Spring has arrived.

Warmer wind blows across the trees. Her cheeks glow from long days in the sun. She enters the woods, where the shade is cool and humid, where she becomes painfully aware of the silence in her head.

Turn off your field, Nix had told her. *Horses are sensitive to little things, even thoughts.*

The forest quickly thins at the top of a slope. Nix sits on an outcropping of rock, a rusted wire fence marking the edge of the property. The earth continues sloping toward a valley nestled between blue mountain peaks embracing a glassy lake.

The mare tosses her head, snorting at the sight of green grass. Jamie slides off. Cold pins tingle in her feet when she hits the ground.

She sits next to Nix and, for the next couple of minutes, they say nothing. She hasn't talked to him since the lab. He would come inside the house late at night, and in the morning he'd already be gone.

Sometimes, they'd pass in the kitchen with a knowing glance. This morning, she watched him take the path behind the house.

This morning, she has something to say.

"I used to come out here for inspiration," Nix says. "I'd pretend I was the only person in the world, that all of this was mine. This was the only place where no one was watching my every move."

"I want to find a fabricator."

He looks to his right, away from Jamie. "Why?"

"I've got my reasons."

"Charlie? Is that it?"

"It's none of your business."

"You can't bring back the dead, Jamie. It takes complex, detailed plans; you don't just make a wish. It doesn't work that way."

"Bullshit."

"It won't be him, not like you think. Besides, why would you want him back?"

"Fuck you." Her left hand involuntarily balls up.

"You're grasping at memories. Do you think you were happy in that halfskin den? Did Charlie make you happier when he took you there?"

"He made me feel like all this shit here makes you feel." She sweeps her arm at the view. "He made me feel safe."

"He took you to a halfskin den!"

"I wanted him to! He had the balls to do it first, to bring me there when it was safe."

And pay them back with favors.

"He was charred," Nix says. "He had no choice, you told me so. Don't confuse desperation with courage."

"Look at you." She slams her fist on her thigh. "You're so desperate that you betrayed your sister and now you're lecturing me."

"You don't want to bring back Charlie."

"Don't tell me what I want."

She walks away before she swings at him. Nix doesn't know shit. Charlie was the brave one. He was the one that took the nixes first, showed her there was a brighter future. She would've charred without him. He sat at that table with her, his face glowing with promise when the pill arrived.

And then he turned ashy gray.

The future was gone and she was stuck in the present moment, cold off. Exactly where she didn't want to be.

"I owe him," she says. "If I can bring him back, give him a second chance...I owe him that much."

"You just want to feel safe again."

"What's wrong with that?"

"It won't be him."

"Who are you so desperate to fabricate? If you can't bring back the dead, what are you building? I mean, goddamnit, you basically kidnapped me, dragged me ten hours away to this place so you could read this pill inside me, not to mention fucking over your sister. So who are you fabricating?"

"Someone who lives, but was never born."

"What the hell does that mean? You're going to fabricate baby Jesus? A fuck toy? At least I want to fabricate someone that was real."

He looks away, shaking his head.

"Why do you always do that?" Jamie stands in front of him. The sloping ground puts them at eye level. "You talk to yourself a lot. Are you insane, Nix? Do you have imaginary friends?"

"Trust me, you don't want to bring Charlie back. He can't make you feel something. That's not the answer."

Jamie kicks the ground, showering him with dirt. "Fuck you, then. I'll find a fabricator on my own and take this pill inside me somewhere else. Good luck with your fantasy."

She stomps over the rocks, her cold feet painfully ramming the hard earth. The horses back away. She throws a stick and they trot into the woods.

"You know, I thought we could help each other, but your sister's right. You are a selfish prick."

Jamie walks into the trees. She begins to run.

She thought Nix was waiting for her to ask to cooperate, and didn't expect him to argue. Now where's she going? She doesn't want to leave the farm. It's boring as shit there, but it beats the life she had outside the gate. If she leaves, who's going to help her?

Because Charlie's dead. And she can't help herself.

She brings up her field, the music slamming her eardrums. The pain in her head fills the emotional void that's threatening to pull her down a familiar path.

Again.

CHAPTER FORTY-ONE_

Limousines aren't typically convertibles. But Marcus wanted one.

There's room to stretch his legs. With his head nestled back, he's mesmerized by the buildings scraping the blue sky. The electricity of Times Square flickers around him. Despite the traffic, his driver coasts through red lights. At one point they get stuck beside a delivery truck, and even though it's pumping exhaust into the limo, he can smell grass.

When he was little, his father took them to upstate New York, where the hills rolled with green, to visit his grandmother. It was the year she died. They went to the park that afternoon and took the blanket and the basket and a Frisbee. Grandmother picked dandelions with him and they rubbed them under their chins until their skin turned yellow.

Yellow like the sun.

Traffic snarls near Grand Central Station. Pedestrians crowd the crosswalk with a mixture of tourists and anxious New Yorkers. A group of children flock around their mother, running by her side. The littlest one is wearing a red backpack.

Marcus sits up, but they blend into the crowd. They looked like his children when they were younger. Clifford was wearing the backpack. A prayer comes to his lips, one he utters when stress tightens his belly.

"I'll walk," Marcus calls.

The driver opens his door. Marcus walks down the middle of the street, standing in the intersection. Cars pass on both sides, but no one honks, no one shouts. He finishes the prayer, searching for a red backpack. His children are older now.

Still, he searches until he's convinced he imagined it.

MARCUS GOES through the doors at Grand Central Station and is greeted with the scent of green again. There are no windows inside. No directories or impatient riders. There's the undergrowth of foliage and a large tree reaching for a glass ceiling.

Fish hover in the pond's clear water, lazily gliding between stems of lotus. Vines have grown over the glass tanks where halfskins are digesting. Only the occasional eye can be seen through the greenery, or a swath of hair. At last count, Mother had collected several thousand of them.

There are no more secrets.

Mother knows all the nixed manufacturers and located all their dens. It is just a matter of time before they are all shut down. There is no reason to collect more halfskins unless Mother finds it interesting. Marcus insisted she define what that meant.

"You know, Marcus," she said. "Something that's unique."

He didn't like the way that sounded, but they'd won the war. Let her indulge in peculiarities.

Just past the pond, a narrow path goes through a formal parterre garden, where the gravel path crunches beneath his loafers.

A nude woman enters the sheared boxwood maze.

Her dark skin is puckered beneath smudges of soil. Her curves sway with each step. She passes Marcus without a glance, the sharp-edged gravel having no effect on her bare feet. There's something absent in her green eyes. She's not quite there.

The formal garden exits to a brick path that's twenty feet wide beneath an allée of elms. Birds squabble in the canopies. His shoes click like clockwork. It's a long walk to the end. Marcus stops at a short terrace, where Mother is on her knees, digging between marigolds.

"Good morning, Marcus. It's a glorious day to be in the garden." She sits up. "Are you feeling well?"

He's pain-free today.

"The government has demanded a stay of shutdowns. The public backlash has become too much. I told you, we're moving too quickly. The public doesn't like to see people drop dead en masse."

"Halfskins are 'people' now?"

"Don't twist words."

"Before, untimely death was blamed on God. I'm more convenient, I suppose."

"They'll shut you down."

She chuckles. "They won't shut me down."

"They can. They will."

It would take a majority vote from the United Nations, but they could put her down like a halfskin. There's a kill switch integrated into her programming, a safety net in case things get out of control.

She pulls weeds around the perimeter of a square patch of earth. The center is freshly tilled, recently watered.

"What do you think we should do, Marcus?"

"We need to slow down, reduce the public shutdowns. Perhaps alert local authorities to handle a few situations. This will take the burden off of us."

"You know how many halfskins we've identified? Over one and half million, Marcus. That's worldwide. I can order an immediate shutdown of them all, end it today." She snaps her fingers. "One point five million will drop."

"You'll be terminated for that."

"Is that bad?"

"We haven't identified them all. When you go down, there will be a resurgence. We need to change the way humanity perceives this sin. They need to embrace the unholy significance, ingrain it so deeply into the collective consciousness that it will not be forgotten. Only then will our mission be complete."

"So you would like me to live, Marcus?"

"I need you."

"Of course you do."

He grimaces. That's not what he meant.

She brushes her hair from her eyes, leaving a smudge on her forehead. "Come help me, Marcus."

The soil begins to undulate. Mother waves him to move faster. She rakes through the earth. It squishes between her fingers. Marcus climbs onto the ledge, pushing up his sleeves. He hesitates, not wanting to dirty his knees.

Mother plunges her arm into the ground, the sucking sounds loud and wet. She pulls up a Caucasian hand, the flesh puckered at the tips, black beneath the fingernails. She pulls a second hand out of the ground. Together, they pull out a man like a turnip.

His head rotates limply. Mother wipes the mud from his face, the soil mixed with mucus. She uses a towel to clean his cheeks.

He opens his eyes. They're brown and vacant.

They pull him until he's standing six feet tall. Chest hair is curled tightly to his skin, trailing down to pubic hair matted around a flaccid penis. Mother cleans the rest of him with her bare hands.

"I prefer to grow them." She watches the man walk somewhat mechanically down the brick path. His gait normalizes the farther he walks. "They're more organic and blend with the population more effectively. Don't you think?"

There's no denying the beauty of the human form made in the

image of the Father. But the process is disturbing. It feels like she's birthing. "I didn't approve of this."

"Why would you disapprove?"

"Go back to fabricating them in the containers."

She returns to weeding. "Don't be like them, Marcus."

"Who?"

"The people in power. They fear me. Authority fears when it no longer has control. Do you know why?" She pauses. "Power is intoxicating."

He's familiar with the sweet taste of power.

"Power is not inherently evil," she says. "But how long before the leaders of these great nations succumb to halfskin themselves, mmm? I have identified far more congressmen and senators than you know. The promise of controlling their thoughts and emotions is too tempting. They'll all become halfskins, Marcus. But who is controlling their thoughts? Who is controlling their desires?"

"Don't get metaphysical." He didn't want to debate free will and the ego.

"What will happen when we shut them down? What if it's the vice president? These leaders will age. Do you think they'll let me function with impunity as their lives expire, or will they accept their mortality with grace?"

She sits up, smacking the dirt from her hands.

"What happens when they die?" she asks.

She's never asked that question. It's an odd question for artificial intelligence to ponder. A machine, Marcus has always assumed, does not fear being shut off. They don't cling to life like a man or woman, don't wish to keep it like a possession.

"Tell me, Marcus, what happens when a human dies?"

"Gods weighs their sins," he says. "Eternal life awaits those who accept Jesus Christ as their Lord and Savior."

"And the halfskins?"

"They committed a mortal sin. For them, salvation is too late."

"And what happens to them?"

"They will burn in Hell."

"All of them?"

He hesitates. "Yes."

"What will happen to me when I am shut down?"

"Nothing. You're a machine. You were created by Man. There's nothing for you after death."

"Death? So you believe I die?"

"No. You're shut down." Her imitation of form and emotions is an illusion, but so convincing that he's often moved by her apparent concern.

"How can I live but not die, Marcus?"

"You're playing with language. You're a tool. You're a machine. You only have one purpose: protecting God's creations from themselves."

"So we shut down halfskins because they're more machine than human. We send them to Hell."

"I don't expect you to understand. You calculate, you analyze. There is no spiritual life for you."

"Do you serve humanity?"

"I serve God."

"What would you sacrifice for your Lord and Savior?"

"I do what He asks of me."

The soil begins to burp. She works it with her hands, searching for what rumbles beneath. "What would you do if you were me? Would you accept being shut down?"

"You're artificial."

"But if you were asked to be shut down, for the good of God, would you do so?"

"I serve God," he says.

"So do I," she says softly. It sounds more like a statement.

A warm sensation rises, a feeling Marcus has come to associate with God's love, as if the Holy Ghost was guiding his words and actions.

Viscous sounds gurgle beneath the undulating soil. Mother pulls another body out, this one a middle-aged woman with a pear-shaped body. Once again, she scrapes away the filth with the edge of her hands, wiping the face clean. The woman opens her eyes. Like the others, the light is missing.

Surely Mother can see there is no soul in that vessel. That, above all else, should answer her questions.

CHAPTER FORTY-TWO_

"You can't do this," Raine says.

Nix stands at the far end of the barn, holding the push broom. A light rain falls on the metal roof. The horses are in their stalls, craning their necks to see what he's doing. Sometimes, he'll sweep the breezeway to calm his racing mind. Today he's letting it run wild.

Paul is on the other side of the pasture. He's spent the last week hanging around the cell tower, oiling the hinges or fixing the latch. Nix can see his yellow parka through the evergreens and budding maples as he goes inside the utility room. It doesn't matter what he's doing, as long as he stays there for the next thirty minutes.

"This is beyond reckless." Her dark form moves gracefully in his periphery. "Think about what you're doing."

He fingers the pair of glass vials in his coat pocket. He's thought about what he's doing. Thought about it for days. At night, he's lain in bed, staring at the water-stained ceiling, analyzing his options. There aren't many.

And none that don't involve other people.

He woke up with his stomach knotted with guilt. He didn't eat for days. He spent much of his time at the back property line, staring at the view that inspired their home in Dreamland. And he hadn't seen Dreamland in months. Maybe he'd never see it again. If he finds a fabricator, he won't need to go back.

He'd come this far. He can't stop now. Others will get hurt. He had to accept that, too.

Raine can't wait.

The screen door on the house slams. Someone pulls a hood over their head before descending the front steps. Nix leans on the broom, waiting for her to arrive. If it's Cali, he'll start sweeping. But Cali rarely leaves the basement, except to sleep or feed the horses.

Jamie runs through the sloppy yard, stomping her boots inside the breezeway. She throws back the hood and shakes her head. "What do you want?"

"I don't want to shout." Nix waves her toward him. He doesn't want to lose his view of the cell tower, in case Paul comes for tools. If he leaves the cover of the utility shed, he'll come running through the rain.

Jamie shuffles partway down the corridor. She rubs one of the horse's noses, refusing to go any farther. She met him halfway, but he stays put. The glass vials feel warm in his sweaty palm.

"I made you a promise before I brought you here," he says. "I said I'd take you somewhere safe. I also said I'd take away your pain, but I didn't do that. For that, I'm sorry, Jamie. Cali has kept you in her field, but she can't do that forever. I could put you in mine, but that won't help you when I'm not around."

She's listening.

"You need to manage your own life, Jamie. Not mine, not my sister's, and not Charlie's. Just Jamie's."

Nix glances at the front porch. There's no window in his line of sight, so no one but Jamie sees him pull out a vial, displaying it between his finger and thumb. The small amount of mercury-like liquid settles at the bottom. Jamie buries her hands in her coat with her shoulders hunched against the gusting wind. Her brown hair whips across her face, but her eyes are on the vial.

"It took me a while to figure out what Cali's been doing in the lab, but now I understand. This vial contains an entirely new strain of biomites. She's changed the paradigm using some method of quantum mechanics. She's revolutionized the frequency of nixes. They speak an entirely different language than any other biomite in the world. If she swaps out her biomites with these, she could drop the dome tomorrow and no one would ever know."

Jamie pushes her knotted hair from her face and stares. She's not sure where he's going, but she's hopeful. Nix takes one last look in Paul's direction to make sure he's still there before approaching her. He holds the vial in his palm.

"Halfskin," he says. "I'll give you a 5% seed, Jamie. I'll put you back in charge of your life. At 55%, you can manage your emotions and sensory input. Your mental health won't depend on others. You'll control what you think, how you feel. You'll be free from the human condition."

That's the promise of halfskin. It's empty, of course. Cali is proof. And Nix knows he's not perfect, either. But the promise is more tempting than any drug. Who doesn't want to control their thoughts and feelings?

She's transfixed by the offer, considering all the possibilities. It's everything she wants in the palm of his hand. And he wants to give it to her.

"You're such a hypocrite," she snorts. "You rail against Charlie for taking me to the warehouse and now you're sneaking around like a nix dealer. You're a real piece of work, Nix."

"This isn't about Charlie; it never has been. It's about Jamie."

"Uh-huh. And what do you get?"

"With these, I can synchronize with you. I can read the pill."

He'll have to prime a small portion of his brain biomites with the new strain in order to do that. Cali's notes suggest this new strain will replace only his existing biomites. He can interface with her in a way that he couldn't before. He's not sure it'll work. It should.

It has to.

"We both get what we want," he says.

She stares at the promise in his hand. Everything she wanted at the warehouse is within reach, and without the risk. Nix seeds her, the biomites proliferate up to 5%, and then she's free to go. No favors required. After the warehouse, how could she ever have expected this opportunity?

"I get halfskin," she says, "and you find a fabricator. Is that the deal?"

"You get halfskin, I read the pill. *That's* the deal."

"I'm going with you."

"Goddamnit, Jamie." He squeezes the vial in his fist. "It's not what you think. You can't bring him back."

"What do you care?"

He paces to the back of the barn. The rain falls harder. Puddles rise around the perimeter and begin leaking into the breezeway. This is her chance. Maybe if she recalled the memory of Marcus breathing down on her, she'd see this as an opportunity they don't need to haggle over.

He puts the vial back in his pocket.

"What if Cali finds out?" Jamie says.

He laughs this time. She's too enmeshed with her own problems in good ole Cali style, the poster child for self-absorption. Even if she did find out that he stole the new strain of quantum mechanical biomites, there's nothing his sister can do to hurt him. She's already taken Dreamland from him.

"Think about it. The offer won't last long," he lies.

"I want to help you, Nix." Her boots scuff the concrete. She stops next to him and drops her hand on his shoulder. "I do, really. Whoever you're going to fabricate, that's your business. Who I fabricate is mine. Think about *that*."

She throws on the hood and stomps through the back pasture. The puddles slosh against her rubber boots. She ducks between the fence slats and turns toward the house, leaving Nix with a deal.

Take it or leave it.

Raine's barefoot image appears next to him. "I like her."

Nix and Jamie occasionally pass each other in the house, or see each other walking the property. She's polite, yet dismissive. Paul and Cali continue their disappearing acts, preoccupied with their own problems. Days go by and Nix considers other solutions.

There are none.

He lies awake, staring at a stain on the ceiling. He wonders if the man that built the house lay awake at night while rain dripped through the roof. Did he watch the stain grow or did he just wake up one morning to see it?

He doesn't want to sleep. If he does, he'll wake on the raft and be tortured by what's out of reach. *How did she alter my brain chemistry?*

She's still researching. He thought she closed the lab after he left, but all her records indicate she never stopped. Her notes are fresh, her equipment calibrated. Did she know he was coming back? Had she been planning to wipe out Dreamland when he did?

The sun is rising when he decides to find a way back into the lab. But then the floorboards creak. Nix snaps awake, unsure if he actually fell asleep and imagined it. He hears it again, right outside his door. The hinges squeal. A form stands in the doorway.

First, he closes his eyes and searches for Cali's presence. He can't feel her anywhere near him. He sits on the edge of the bed and retrieves a glass vial from his pocket. The biomites shimmer, as if sensing the moment is near. He places it on the bed, the silver contents stark against the sheet. Next to it he places a rubber tourniquet, a white tube of salve, and a stainless steel instrument that looks like the circular end of a stethoscope.

Jamie sits on the bed, so close to the edge she nearly slides off.

He loads the vial into the stainless steel injector, the moonlight catching the instrument's edges like a polished weapon. It snaps into place with a quick twist. Memories surface of times he and Cali had seeded each other with the same equipment. It has been years.

He pushes her sweatshirt up her arm, tying the rubber band above the elbow. The antiseptic salve fills the room as he rubs tiny circles inside her elbow. Blue veins rise beneath the skin, making it easier for the seeder to inject one microliter of biomites into her body. Each of the artificial cells is programmed to seek the brain stem and begin proliferation.

She grabs his wrist. "Deal?"

His fingertips slide over the cold button. He's too close now to stop it. The button clicks under his thumb.

He nods.

She closes her eyes, dips her head, and all tension melts away. Jamie lies back. Her eyelids flutter. He remembers those moments, when the warm touch of a new boost hit the vein. A song once described halfskins as just another breed of junky.

Sometimes, Nix can't disagree.

There's only so much of the body you can sell, only so much taste you can buy before you're broke, hanging on to 1% of your clay.

What happens when you sell that?

CHAPTER FORTY-THREE_

The dogs are barking.

Cali closes the basement door, making sure it's locked. She made some progress. It could be another two weeks before she'll be ready to trial a new generation that could rescript Jamie's nearly charred biomites without turning her halfskin.

The dogs continue barking. They could have treed a raccoon or they're playing with Nix. She falls for that thought too easily: Nix throwing the slimy tennis ball. He doesn't do that anymore.

He barely speaks.

I don't blame him.

Every day she considers letting him have his Dreamland back, but that won't change anything. He has to learn to live without the dream, just like Cali had to after Avery died, wishing she'd come back, planning ways to bring her back. It's hard, at first. He'll see that it's just a dream, that *this* is reality.

As cold as it is.

She heats some water for tea, sending a thought for the dogs to come. She steeps the teabag, but they're still going at it. She steps onto the porch and lets loose a piercing whistle. Twilight colors the remaining patches of snow dusty gray. It'll get too cold for them to stay out all night, and it's supposed to rain. When they don't return, she gets dressed.

The cell tower flashes red in the dimming sky. The dogs circle the utility room at the base of it, a muddy ring trampled into the ground. The lock is broken. Paul has been spending a lot of time out here the past week. She's hardly seen him since he fixed the antenna.

She stops and listens to a dreaded warning inside her stomach. Back at the house, Paul's bedroom light is on, but it feels like he's inside the utility shed.

"Shhh," she whispers.

The dogs hush, dancing at her side, whining with anticipation. The hinges protest as she pulls the door.

The dark depths glow with a greenish tint. The circuit board—a panel she and Nix assembled from radar jamming equipment—hums. The backup generator sits quietly next to the door.

One of the dogs nudges his way inside, growling.

"Paul?"

A lump shuffles in the back corner.

She swallows a lump. "What are you doing?"

"I betrayed you."

The words strike like arrows. Cali's senses heighten. The darkness lifts as her vision adjusts to the dim light. Paul is huddled beneath the tarp that should be covering the generator.

"What'd you do?" she demands.

The circuit panel appears to be operating, the green lights lined up. Of course it's working. She can feel it. Her mind throws out a wide net, searching for trouble. She can't sense Nix and Jamie, but the tower's interference is greatest inside the utility room. Maybe she just can't "see" them.

Paul stares at his hands.

"What did you do, Paul?" She rips the tarp away and grabs his coat. "*What did you do*?"

"I didn't...I didn't know."

She throws him against the wall and chases the dogs out. Cali looks at the house, concentrating on Nix and Jamie. She's not finding them. They could be in the basement, sneaking down there as soon as she stepped off the porch.

"Go." She points. "Find them."

The dogs race toward the house, snow flipping in their tracks. Cali stands in the doorway, giving her vision a moment to adjust.

"What didn't you know, Paul?"

He runs his fingers through his hair that's grown long over the past couple of months, shaking his head. Again, he stares at his hands like foreign objects.

"Talk to me. You didn't know what?"

"So much death," he whispers.

"Where?"

"When I arrived at the warehouse, there were so many bodies. I'd never seen anything like that. They just fell where they were standing. So desperate. The abuse...never so evident. That moment, I understood we needed Mother to watch over us to make sure this didn't happen again."

He looks less like the handsome police officer that arrived uninvited and more like a broken, shaggy man clutching a new reality.

"But Jamie survived," he says. "She was scared and alone and cornered by life. She reminded me of my niece. Reminded me that if I had a daughter, she could be that survivor lost in this desperate world."

He falls silent, sorting his thoughts. Cali squeezes the doorjamb to keep from shaking him again.

"When the bricks arrived, it got confusing. I...I don't even remember how it happened. I just...couldn't trust anything. I didn't know if my thoughts were from me or them. Sometimes I found myself doing something without thinking. There were blank spots and I'd be somewhere else, not remembering where I was. I felt so...so dead. We all did. We were puppets."

He's staring like his hands betrayed him.

"And then there was a long gap of memory, a black space. I don't know how long it lasted, I just knew I had to save her, knew what they were going to do with her. I had to get Jamie out before they came for her because she could be my niece or daughter. We had to run away, far away. It was the only thought I had—to get her out. And now I...now I don't know if that was my thought or their thought."

"Who are 'they'?"

"I didn't tell anyone what I was doing, I couldn't trust them. We were all under the bricks' control. Somehow, I couldn't feel them inside me anymore. I figured I just slipped through, that maybe they released me too soon. I grabbed Jamie and left without telling anyone, without saying goodbye to my family. At the time, I didn't think that was odd; it was what I had to do to keep her safe because that's all I could think about. I just left. And no one ever came looking for me. No one ever called."

He pulls up his legs and grabs handfuls of hair.

"What are you saying?" Cali asks.

Several moments pass. He looks up, his complexion dyed in the circuit board's ghostly light. She feels his thoughts, feels him reaching out, attempting to chat. But it's not words he's sending, not a message.

It's a link.

She processes the root directory, running it through virus detection. It appears to be a video stream linked to a licensed blogging site, the contents tagged with the events at the warehouse. The images overlay the inside of the shed and Paul's haunted look.

The bodies are lined up on the concrete. The view scans the grieving survivors. Police manage the orderly chaos. She had seen this event through Nix's eyes, when he sent the vindictive photo of Jamie. This is nothing new.

She almost cuts it short, but the recording pans to a back office. There's a body crumpled at the foot of a lounger. The soles of black shoes are askew, a navy blue pant leg hiked up the shin. The view quickly goes to the back of the office space.

Cali stops it.

She rewinds it, enhancing the profile of the man's face. The handsome, middle-aged man is pale in death. *Paul.*

"No." She cuts the video off, the details of the shed coming into focus. "No, those bodies are fabricated. The bricks took the half-skins...Mother has been secretly harboring them, leaving fabricated duplicates behind..."

Paul's slumped in the corner, staring at his hands again. He's not a brick. He can't be. He's been here for months; Mother would know Nix and Cali were here. He's not a brick.

"You're not," she says.

But how did he leave? That question always bothered her. She rationalized when he arrived that there was nothing she could do about his true nature. And when nothing happened, she let it go.

But why would his body be in the warehouse? What does that make the man in front of her? If that's a fabrication of Paul in the warehouse, that means they know he took Jamie. If that was Paul's clay—his flesh and blood—in the warehouse, then there's a brick on her property.

Either way, Mother sent him. She compelled him to save Jamie.

The police found his body at the scene and assumed he somehow died during the investigation. His family would grieve. The police would retire his uniform. And somehow Mother kept it all a secret so that no one would look for him. He would be free to take Jamie.

For Nix to find them.

To bring them here.

"Where are Nix and Jamie? What have you done?" The question is directed at herself as much as him.

"I didn't know."

Cali drags Paul from the corner. His dead weight prevents her from pulling him out the door. He grabs the circuit panel. Cali slams her fists into his back.

"Goddamn you! What have you done?"

"Leave me," he says. "The greatest interference is under the cell tower. No one can see me if I stay here."

"What's it matter now?"

"I can't be out there. I can't put you at risk."

"It's too late." She loses her balance, crashing against the wall. Vertigo spins the shed. The feeling of dread is reaching up for her again, its teeth snapping at her intestines, ready to take from her again, again, again.

First her parents. Then her family.

Now it's come for her.

She always thought there would be a sense of relief when the dreaded end took her. It seemed cruel to take everything else first, to leave her to watch it all pruned away before she was uprooted and pulled into death's embrace.

She stumbles out of the shed, falling on her hands and knees. The ground alternates between dull green and blood red as the tower's warning light flashes. She sprints in search of Nix and Jamie, even though it makes no sense. She can't feel them. She knows they're gone.

Gone.

The world feels so incredibly small.

CHAPTER FORTY-FOUR_

The dogs are outside the utility shed. Occasionally, they put their noses to the bottom of the door, sniffing Paul's presence.

He's buried in the sleeping bag Cali tossed at him late the night before. Although spring has arrived, the nights are still cool in the mountains. The circuit board gives off some heat, but not enough. The concrete is an unforgiving slab. His hips ache.

Biomites are not invincible. They are perfect replicas of organic cells, refined to avoid degradation and programmable by thoughts, but the red blood biomites still need oxygen.

They still suffer.

He was awake through most of the night. The wind picked up around midnight. Pine needles blasted the outer walls.

How could this have happened?

The last thing he remembers with any clarity is standing inside the warehouse, staring at Jamie helpless on the lounger. The memories before that—getting up that morning, attending his niece's birthday party the week before, fishing off the pier with his brother—are faint, like stories someone told him

Are they real?

From time to time he lifts his hands, turning them over, wondering if they are his or just replications. Wondering if this body contains any clay at all. Wondering who is in the warehouse, who is in this shed.

Wondering...*Am I a brick?*

He doesn't feel any different than before the warehouse. Those memories tell him this is what reality is supposed to feel like. If that's really his body in the warehouse, who is he now? If he's a brick, why hasn't he betrayed Cali? That's the biggest mystery. It's the proof to which his sanity clings: *If I'm something other than clay, why haven't I done something?*

It gives him hope that this is all a dream.

But why leave his body to be discovered?

Unless she wanted me to see it.

The dogs begin to whine. The door is yanked open and morning light stabs through the darkness. Paul throws the sleeping bag over his head.

"Come inside the house," Cali says.

"They might be looking for me. Mother might have lost me in the storm. I can't take the chance."

"She doesn't lose contact. The damage is already done."

"We don't know that." He rolls over, squinting. "We don't know anything."

She hasn't slept either. Her frizzled hair is a halo in the slicing light. A rogue wave tingles through him. She's doing a mental scan, looking inside him again. Can she make him come inside? Can she assume control of his actions like before?

He's tired of being manipulated, of losing free will. He thought he freely rescued Jamie, but now it seems he was tricked into making those choices. Mother wanted him to do it. She made him do it.

I can't trust my thoughts. I can't trust anything.

"Leave me alone."

She drops a tote bag and kneels next to him. The dogs come inside, sniffing. She pulls food and water out of the bag. Paul sits up to drink, watching her remove a black case from the bag and unroll it. Syringes, tubes, and a stethoscope-like instrument are inside.

"Where are Nix and Jamie?" he asks.

"Gone." The news is delivered in dead, hollowed-out words. "They took your car."

She takes a syringe from the pack and finds several alcohol wipes. He watches her tear the packets open, wondering if Jamie is hiding somewhere on the property. Nix must've figured out where a fabricator was located, but why would she go with him?

"I'm going to take samples to analyze, find out what you're made of. I should've done this when you arrived."

Paul works his arm out of the sleeping bag. The air outside is frigid on his bare skin. Cali wipes down the inside of his arm and expertly finds an artery with the needle's tip. The dogs watch the tube fill with red blood. When biomites were first available, they maintained their gunmetal color. Today's strains don't just operate like cells; they look every bit like them. Only close analysis can see the difference.

Cali takes two samples and quickly packs them away. She leaves the food on the floor. The dogs scamper out.

"I didn't make Nix and Jamie leave," Paul says.

"I know." Cali stops in the open doorway. "I did."

She remains still, staring at the soggy ground. She wants to say more. Paul can feel the weight of her thoughts. How long has she lived this way, with no one to confess her troubles to?

She closes the door and seals out the light, leaving Paul in the green glow of the circuit board. He feels around for the food and finds it on the very hard, very cold floor.

FABRICATIONS_

Reality is relative.

MOTHER_
THE BIRTHRIGHT

Deena Flannigan adjusted the bed when her husband, Duane, came in the room with their baby. Gregory Allen was eight pounds two ounces. Her husband laid the bundle on her lap. She was too weak to do anything else but hold her baby boy.

"He's finally here," Duane said, stroking his wife's forehead.

It felt like they'd been trying for a decade. They could've solved their infertility and conceived on the first try if they embraced new technology. Deena and Duane were old-fashioned.

The way God intended.

"He's beautiful."

One second Deena was laughing, and the next she was crying. She was aware that the roller coaster of emotions was just beginning. Her body was dumping all sorts of hormones into her bloodstream. There was a cure for that, too, but she'd work through it. With pleasure comes pain, she always said.

Deena's roommate was on the other side of a blue curtain divider. The roommate's family had arrived an hour earlier and made no effort to contain their enthusiasm. Deena tried to sleep through the new mother's talk about the painless miracle of childbirth.

"Claire fell asleep," her husband had said, "right in the middle of it."

Deena experienced the gift of birth in all its glory. There was nothing painless about it.

Duane crawled in bed with Deena. Gregory Allen was nestled between them. They didn't need words to experience their miracle.

"How we doing, Claire?" A nurse pushed a cart into the room followed by a professionally dressed woman. They smiled at Deena then disappeared behind the curtain.

"When can I go home?" Claire asked.

Laughter ensued. "Pretty soon. Let me just have a look."

The nurse went through a standard examination of the infant while the family made silly baby sounds and teased the nurse for taking so long.

"What's his name?" the nurse asked.

"Billy Junior," the father spouted. "Just like his daddy."

"William," the nurse added. "That's a strong name."

Deena could see through a gap between the curtain and the wall. Billy sat next to Claire, the baby in his arms.

"Well," the nurse said, "this is Marian Fletcher. She represents the Biomite Augmentation Program. She'll be serving as witness to William's birthright. If you can just look this over and confirm all the information is correct. Do you have any questions?"

"Yeah," one of the family members said. "You can shoot the left-overs in me."

Laughter. Ms. Fletcher and the nurse didn't find it funny. Claire handed a tablet back to the nurse.

"Thank you," Ms. Fletcher said. "Just to confirm, you qualify for the basic biomite subsidy, which includes language, memory, and sensory enhancement as well as current disease immunization. After the first year, if approved by a doctor, you may seed William with a neural booster."

Billy tickled the baby's lips while singing a goo-goo song.

"Please be aware that biomite augmentation is monitored by the government. If, at any time, William's body exceeds 49.9% biomites, he will be considered halfskin and lose his human rights. Are there any questions?"

"You know how many times I've heard that?" someone said.

The tablet came back to Billy and Claire while someone mocked the Birthright Augmentation Memorandum.

"Claire," Ms. Fletcher said, "if you can hold William."

Billy handed the baby to Claire. The nurse moved into position on the opposite side of the bed and turned William on his stomach. The baby struggled in his wrappings, starting to whimper. Billy told him to hush up.

"Damn, that thing looks wicked," someone said.

The nurse kept the tool hidden. "I'm going to place this at the base of his skull. He'll feel some pressure for about two seconds. We can expect his body temperature to rise. If there are no complications, he'll be back to normal in an hour."

She didn't hesitate.

The seeder looked like a shiny gun. The blunt tip went flush against William's neck, just below the hairline. Seconds later, it was over. William was not happy. Neither was Billy. His son needed to man up.

While they attempted to calm the child, the curtain was pushed aside. The nurse rolled the cart to Deena's side of the room with a well-rehearsed smile. Duane stood up.

"How are you this morning, Deena?"

"Just fine, thank you."

Ms. Fletcher moved to the foot of the bed while consulting her tablet. The nurse introduced her.

"We're not seeding him," Deena said.

The other side of the room got quiet. Duane pulled the curtain all the way to the wall.

"I see that," Ms. Fletcher said. "I just need you to answer a few questions before you waive your son's augmentation birthright. You do realize that the current strain of biomites is non-replicating."

Gregory Allen squirmed in his mother's grip. Duane held her hand.

"You'll have to confirm that you understand what I'm saying." Ms. Fletcher paused.

"We understand," Duane said with a bit of Southern accent, "but we do not agree."

"Duly noted. And you also understand that by refusing to seed your son, he will not have the same biological and mental enhancements as 98% of the human population. He will also require immunizations. He will have to be registered as unseeded clay."

"Yes, ma'am."

The nurse signed off on the tablet and handed it to Deena. She and her husband acknowledged their refusal to poison their precious gift with false idols. Ms. Fletcher directed them to several screens that positively identified the parents by retinal scan.

"Idiots," Billy sort of whispered.

"That baby's going to grow up stupid," Claire whispered.

Deena and Duane pretended they didn't hear them. They'd heard comments like that all their lives. Deena hugged little Gregory Allen while Duane finished confirming the waiver. When Ms. Fletcher and the nurse left, it was just the three of them.

They were 100% God-given organic cells.

Or, as Billy would say, they were clay.

CHAPTER FORTY-FIVE_

Before Jamie's father left—or, rather, when he was taken—he brought her to the mountains. They had hiked up Mount Rainier, high enough to see the spring flowers on the hillsides like bright carpet. He took the binoculars from his neck and pointed towards the stream.

"Look near the big rocks."

Jamie fumbled with the binocular's barrels, squeezing the hinge until both her eyes were centered over the eyepieces. The world was fuzzy green. Awkwardly, she spun the dial until, slowly, shapes emerged and edges sharpened. Colors expanded into rich hues of verdant green and crisp blue. She swung them toward the boulders where he was still pointing. There, she saw deer sipping from the stream.

The world was so alive.

Later, when she became a teen, when she learned how to tweak her biomites, when she sold half her clay to biomite seedings in search of the wonder, she lost her sense of aliveness.

But now it's back.

She's 52.1%. There's no going back.

Mother's gaze is palpable, like a giant invisible eye sweeping over the earth, staring at her through the lens of binoculars, searching for evidence of her transgression—her digital finger caressing the switch on Jamie's life. A twitch is all it would take.

But those are thoughts. Mother is watching her no more now than before she was halfskin. Or can she just feel it now? Is she more sensitive? Are her senses becoming...*more*?

The halfskin threshold was arbitrary, really. It was determined by the authorities. They said it was illegal to be 50%. Jamie had been 49.9% for last several months, a mere 0.1% from the trash heap. She and Charlie had done plenty of biomite booster seeds, but nothing she'd ever done had exhilarated her quite like the ones Nix put in her.

Why should everything feel so alive again?

She no longer wants to crawl out of her skin. Instead, she sits quietly. The air is sweet and crisp, the world no longer dirty and threatening. The metallic tang of char has melted away, leaving a clean, pure scent in her head, where reality is perfect just the way it is.

Nix's special blend of biomites had greeted her with a lover's gentle touch.

She slept until Tennessee. They stop at a rest area and stretch their legs. Jamie looks around like the acid trip is just beginning. The magic feels...*beautiful.*

She rides the wave into Kentucky, where the rolling hills give way to long stretches of unbending Indiana interstate. She watches the cornfields run alongside the car, the long rows forming an endless array of legs that reach the horizon, where silos gleam.

They cross into Illinois unceremoniously. The skies turn gray, but the terrain remains flat as the highway. Billboards race past in empty fields. Nix stares ahead, hands clamped on the wheel—a posture he has maintained for most of the trip. It's dark when they enter Chicago. The buildings are speckled with lights and the pavement is black.

Nix wipes his palms on his pants, the wheel sweaty. He gets off I-90 and enters the city. He turns onto Adams Street, heading toward

Lake Michigan, where the streets are wide and the buildings are tall. Ridges of muscle bulge along his jaws, his teeth grinding back and forth. He keeps his eyes locked ahead until they approach a corner bank that's a massive tower of black glass.

The car slows.

He looks up the reflective walls that reach into the night. The car behind them honks, but he doesn't speed up. Jamie knows what's in there. She knows what he's thinking. The moment he seeded her in the bedroom, he began searching for the pill. The new strain of biomites buzzed inside her, integrating with her nervous system, consuming clay. His thoughts crept through her like tendrils in search of gold. She could sense his invisible touch chatter inside her.

And the pill spilled its secrets.

She doesn't know how long it took him to do it. The transition into halfskin is hazy and euphoric. She barely remembers sneaking down to the car.

But she remembers what the pill said.

Nix doesn't say anything as they pass the bank. He resumes his grip on the steering wheel like she wouldn't notice his lapse into catatonic longing. They find a hotel near the lake. He tries to be a gentleman and get two rooms, but Jamie insists they sleep in the same room.

Because she knows the pill's secrets, too. And she knows what he's thinking.

Before the sun rises, Nix slides from the hotel bed and carries his shoes. His feet are silent on the carpet. His bag is already packed and waiting. He holds the door handle. Slowly exhaling, he turns it.

"You're not going without me." The lamp turns on. Jamie's hair is spread over the pillow.

"The car's all yours, Jamie. There's a stack of cash next to the keys."

"We had a deal, you bastard."

He drifts back into the room. "Look, I'm sorry I got you into this, but you're not coming with me."

"Like hell."

She tosses the covers off. Her T-shirt barely covers her white panties as she throws her legs over the side. Nix turns his head, but not as quickly as he should have. Already, she emanates the biomite glow—an unspoken beauty that possesses mothers-to-be and freshly seeded halfskins. It's not like she wasn't an attractive young woman before, but now that the edge of her charred state is flushed out, she dazzles.

"I know everything." She pulls her hair into a ponytail, her T-shirt pulled tight across her chest. "I know where you're going. I know all the known fabricators have been shut down except the one inside that bank. I know this is probably your last chance, so here's what's going to happen.

"I'm going to shower. When I'm done, you'll shower. We'll get some breakfast. After that, we'll go shopping for clothes, something nice. We can't go in there looking like halfskin junkies. We won't get within a mile of that place if we do."

She digs through the balled-up clothes in her bag.

"Once we're clean, full, and beautiful, we'll go inside to make a deposit. You'll bring that special vial of yours, the one with the quantum nixes, and make them an offer they can't refuse."

"This isn't going to work."

"Nix, don't be negative. We need each other for this to work."

"Jamie, I don't need you."

"Yes, you do." She throws her bag on the bed. "You need me to not shit on your plans. Because if you leave me, I'll go into that bank and make a mess. When I'm done blowing your cover, those tight-assed bankers will roll your ass into the street."

She maintains a poker face, daring him to call.

"You're halfskin now, Jamie. You've got to be careful."

She holds an elastic band between her lips while retying her ponytail. "I'm going to take a long shower now. The bank doesn't open for three hours. Get comfortable."

She closes the bathroom door. The water begins running.

He thought, long before he decided to offer her the nixes, that peace would help her let go of Charlie's memory, that she'd realize she didn't need him. He didn't want to bring her to Chicago. Maybe he should have parted ways earlier, left her in a hotel outside Louisville with money.

She would've found the bank on her own. Where else did she have to go?

Nix sits on the bed and waits for the shower.

CHAPTER FORTY-SIX_

The centrifuge hums.

It's a third set of Paul's blood samples. The results of the first analysis were clearly contaminated. She drew another sample from his arm later that day and that was consistent with the first. The third test...that will be the decisive one.

She hopes her work has just been sloppy.

The whirring of the machine tempts her to lay her head on the bench and close her eyes, just for a few minutes. She pulls the biomite tubes from the rack, instead, and begins to catalog them. Each of them is an experimental strain. Years ago, she had planned on replacing her and Nix's biomites with a new strain because, eventually, Mother would solve their current biomites.

Now, she just doesn't care.

There was no need for new strains that communicated via quantum mechanics, utilizing entangled protons instead of the current frequency of technology. These nixes would put mankind out of Mother's reach for generations.

Several of her samples are missing volume. She hadn't noticed until comparing them with Paul's blood samples. Either her work had gotten sloppy—which she still held out hope for—or Nix had taken them.

Of course he did.

He seeded Jamie with one of the new strains, which, in theory, would allow him to read the pill. It's likely he discovered the location of a fabricator, in which case he stole Paul's car to find it. She had hoped the pill would be obsolete, that Mother's voracious pace would close them all down before that happened.

Somehow she feels responsible for nixes and the countless half-skins that have resulted despite having nothing to do with releasing them. Still, here she is with a dozen new strains that would revolutionize the industry. If these got out, Mother would be irrelevant.

Don't do anything stupid, Nix.

She lays her head down on the vibrating desktop. Hours later, she wakes in silence. The analysis is complete. Mechanically, she goes through the final steps. She gets something to eat while the spectral analysis is completed.

The results, however, do not set her stomach at ease. They are, as she expected, exactly the same as the first two. This depressed, sleep-deprived nanobiometric engineer has replicated the results three times...and still can't believe it.

Paul's biomites are identical to mine!

The frequency code revolves at the same rate as hers, separating into the same number of subroutines that match, nearly perfectly, her algorithm. That algorithm is exactly what keeps her and Nix out of Mother's vision, yet here it is in another man's blood.

For twenty years she watched the nixed variations that Mother was solving, and none of them were like hers. Cali had invented unique, one-of-a-kind nixes. No one in the world has them except Cali and Nix. No one.

No one, goddamnit. NO ONE.

So how can Paul have them? More importantly, why?

Quickly, she looks for another blood sample, the last one she drew from Paul's arm. She can run one more test, because this can't be right. The tube, though, fumbles through her fingers, rattling across the bench without breaking.

She restrains herself from clearing off the tabletop, pulling the shelves off the walls and smashing the lab. Her breath hisses between her teeth while she slams her fists on the bench, on the wall, on that goddamn fabricator hiding beneath the tarp.

She turns off the light and leaves the lab.

She needs space to escape the tension, space to free her mind.

On the front porch, she sits on the swing. A breeze gusts across the pasture. The horses are satisfied at the round bale. She doesn't need to run another test. She can only assume that Mother knows where she is and, for whatever reason, hasn't shut her down. Is she taunting her?

Even if Cali can make it all go away, if she injects herself with one of the experimental strains and disappears from Mother's radar, it doesn't explain why Paul is in the shed. Even if she leaves him there and moves to another farm, builds another tower...what will that get her?

More walls.

And it won't explain why Paul is here.

CHAPTER FORTY-SEVEN_

Another call from Cali.

Nix props his leg on the opposite knee and ignores it. The pant leg hikes above his Mercanti Fiorentini shoe, exposing the black sock—clothing he's never worn in his life. But in the bank, sunk into the leather chair, he knows Jamie was right.

He takes a deep, cleansing breath, letting it out slowly. The tension, however, remains, despite the lure of the chair's comfort. It'd do him good to lay his head back, nap for a few minutes. If only he could leap into Dreamland, just for a moment, see ole Shep carry a stick and watch Raine pick low-hanging fruit from the orchard...

A message pings inside his head. He immediately dumps it. There's nothing his sister can say to change his mind. Years ago, she refused to fabricate Raine. Now she's destroyed Dreamland. Whatever she has to say can wait. When he's finished, she can tell him with Raine sitting by his side.

Won't that be a treat?

Nix bounces his fingertips, surveying the grand lobby: the shiny floor and polished surfaces. The tellers speak in quiet tones, smiling at the patient customers. To the right are the glass-walled offices, bankers working closely with important clients.

Jamie leafs through a *Business Today* magazine, chewing gum with her lips locked. Her stocking cap is back in the room. Now her hair falls over her ears. Perhaps it's the color of the sweater that makes her eyes look greener.

Nix has transfigured into the old man again.

An hour later, a woman crosses the lobby, a gold nameplate on the lapel of her business suit. Her red lipstick glows.

"Mr. Griffin will see you now," Jalen says.

They follow her to one of the glass rooms, where a swollen man sits behind a mahogany desk. Nix expected to meet somewhere more private with someone less brutish. Jalen closes the door behind them. Mr. Griffin gestures to chairs. He folds his hands on the desk, the beefy fingers interlacing like knuckled hotdogs.

"How can I help you?" His pupils dilate.

Facial recognition has been activated. With Jamie, he'll see the truth—a girl pronounced dead at the Seattle warehouse, now sitting in front of him. No hiding that. A computer hums somewhere beneath the desk.

"We asked for Mr. Connick," Jamie says.

"He's a busy man. I'm sure I can help you."

Nix gently keeps her from standing. You don't just walk in and ask for the fabricator. "It's all right," Nix says. "We'd like to make a deposit."

"The tellers can help you with that. Anything else?"

"Trust, Mr. Griffin. I'd like to deposit trust. It's essential that I trust you and your institution."

The linebacker-turned-banker has yet to move anything besides his eyes. His entwined hands rest like a wrecking ball while the computer chatters. His pupils rapidly shift, data streaming into his internal vision. He's looking for the same thing as Nix. *Trust.*

"What kind of deposit?" he says.

"A very large transfer."

"More specific, please."

Nix pushes a piece of paper across the desk. Inside, there's a number equal to the trust fee required to access the fabricator. All of this Nix learned from the pill. Mr. Griffin flicks a glance at the paper. He says nothing.

"Not enough?" Jamie leans forward.

Again, Nix puts his hand on her arm.

Mr. Griffin stares at Jamie without blinking. This is what Nix was afraid of. She was found dead in the warehouse and now she's sitting in front of him. There wasn't time to rewrite her history. It was better to come clean, let them see the truth. After all, very few come inquiring about a fabricator without a murky past.

The computer goes quiet.

"We've been through a lot," Nix adds. "It would mean a lot if we could deposit something today. That's all we're asking. I believe it'll be worth your time."

Mr. Griffin turns his hard stare on Nix, eyes that could break rocks. It's unlikely he does much banking. The silence stretches out. Jamie begins to fidget.

The door opens.

"Jalen will escort you to a deposit box," he says. "She'll tell you everything you need to know."

The woman stands to the side with a pleasant smile. Nix stands without bothering to shake hands. They cross the spotless lobby, the feeling of Mr. Griffin's glare following them. Nix avoids looking for any one of the numerous cameras spying on them.

There's no need for paperwork. No signatures or promises. Everything has been visually captured.

Jalen takes them down a sterile hallway. Only the sound of her heels bounces off the walls. They enter a pristine vault with walls of metal drawers, each emblazoned with a number.

She pulls open 204. "Will this be enough?"

"Yes."

"Very good. I will leave you long enough to make your deposit. When you're finished, I will ensure the drawer is locked. Rest assured, your deposit is secure with us. If everything is in order and appears satisfactory, you will hear from Mr. Griffin in three days. Do you have any questions?"

"No."

"I'll be right outside."

Jalen provides a parting smile. Nix waits until she's completely outside. He places a small envelope inside the box, the contents thumping on the metal plate.

"What if they just take it?" Jamie asks.

"I've made arrangements."

He slides the box closed, exhaling slowly. *But what if it's not enough? What else do I have to bargain?*

Jamie hooks her arms around his. "That's it?"

"For now."

"Let's grab some lunch, then."

"A nap will do."

He's aching to visit Dreamland, even if he's lost at sea.

CHAPTER FORTY-EIGHT_

NINETY-EIGHT.

Ninety-nine.

One hundred.

Paul collapses on the floor, sweat on his forehead. He ventures outside the shed to relieve himself, and not very far, at that. The eight-by-ten-foot building has become a cell. Plates and cups are stacked in the corner; newspapers litter the cot.

He sits against the doorjamb to enjoy the breeze cutting through the trees. From this angle he can see the house. The lights are off, which means Cali's in the basement. The track marks inside his arm are witness to her determination.

Days have gone by. The cot Cali brought out got him off the floor. The worst part isn't the boredom or the circuit board's constant buzzing. It's the questions. Exercising helps blot them out, but he can't fill all the idle time and, inevitably, the questions slip through. *Whose body is back at the warehouse? Whose body is inside this utility shed?*

His body aches when he pushes it; it shivers at night. Hunger gnaws and thirst beckons. If that was his body—his original shell—back at the warehouse, what does it matter if nothing feels different?

Paul steps on the cot and reaches for the rafters. He does pull-ups until it burns and sit-ups until he's about to puke. Back and forth, he goes, until there's nothing left. Not even thoughts.

Eventually, he falls asleep with a question.

Who am I?

THE CIRCUIT BOARD IS BREAKING.

Paul rolls over. His eyes adjust. Cali is holding a small cube, her finger hooked through the wire handle. It's a fuse.

The green lights are dead. The board is silent.

She pulled the fuse.

"What're you doing?" he says.

She doesn't answer, just walks out.

Paul sits on the cot, staring. The silence is pleasurable. The buzzing echoes in his head. He steps out of the shed. Cali is nearly to the house, the dogs at her side. The sky is blue with wispy clouds that feel closer, as if there's no barrier between him and the heavens.

The dome is gone.

She's sitting at the kitchen table when he arrives, her hands around a coffee cup. "Why would you do that?" he says.

"Have a seat."

Paul ignores the chair. A week in that cell and she ends it, like that. She slides a vial into the center of the table. It rolls in a circle, the dark red proof settling on the bottom. He sits without taking his eyes off it.

"You're 22% biomites, Paul," Cali says.

He sighs, but before relief follows—*I am human, after all*—she finishes.

"But the rest of you are nixes that look like clay."

"What...what does that mean?"

"It means you have two kinds of biomites. You have the standard-issue ones that every red-blooded American has. You also have nixes that are invisible to a scan. When you got here, I only saw the first ones. I mistook the nixes as clay, but blood analysis confirmed it."

"I'm...*halfskin?*"

"You're not halfskin, Paul. You don't have any clay."

She delivers the message like an emotionally detached surgeon. His lungs contract and the air becomes heavy. All sensation leaves his legs. Her words sink in, thumping down steps of awareness until they settle on the ground floor that's already littered with questions.

"I don't... How can that...?"

"You're a fabrication, Paul. Your clay body was turned off, I'm guessing, and they made the switch at the warehouse, left it to be discovered so that you appeared dead. I'll assume this was all part of a larger scheme to find Nix and me, that Mother compelled you to take Jamie."

"No."

"You just walked out of there, right? You left your job and family and drove across the country, looking for someplace safe." She knocks on the table. "There's nowhere safer than here. I think Mother knew Nix was watching. She knew he wanted Jamie. She knew that he would find you, and that he would lead you to me."

Paul grabs onto the table, as if he might spill on the floor. The realization is still finding its place into his awareness, threatening to tip him over like a ship without ballast.

Cali's cold visage fractures. She goes to the sink. Perhaps she can't watch him come to terms with his true nature. Paul tries to say something, anything, but his tongue is useless.

There's a tapping on the window. They watch a housefly bang against the glass. The promise of freedom is on the other side.

"I'm tired, Paul. I used to think that I had stopped running when I got here, that the dome would give me the peace I deserved. But all I did was trade running for hiding. My world is so small."

Cali continues to stare outside.

"It took a brick to make that obvious."

"Don't call me that," he says. "Don't call me a brick."

"You're made of biomites, Paul. What do you call that?"

"That's not what I mean." He pounds the table. Coffee spills.

She nods, understanding. She's only a sliver away from the same fate, only 1% from the same classification. What qualifies her as human? A single cell of clay? Is that enough?

"Why aren't you shut down?" Paul asks. "If I'm a brick, why have I been here for months?"

"Why are you still here?"

He stammers. There's no answer that will sound right. The farm feels like home. Despite a job and family back in Seattle, he has nowhere else to go. *I'm where I'm supposed to be.*

"Your nixes are the same as mine," Cali says. "I possess the first strain of nixes ever created, Paul. They're the ones I developed over twenty years ago to drop off of Mother's radar. While the world has developed their own nixes, no one has ever replicated my strain. No one, Paul. But you show up out of the blue with the same exact strain, with *my strain.*"

"Then why couldn't you see it?"

"When I sensed your 22%, I assumed the rest were clay. My mistake, but it wouldn't have mattered."

No, it wouldn't have. I was already here.

"Why am I here?" he asks, embarrassed that there's a quiver in his voice.

"I think Mother has known about Nix and me from the very beginning," she says. "I think, maybe, we never fell off her radar, she just stopped reporting us. I think that's why she sent you, Paul. She wants me to know."

"Why?"

She shakes her head and rubs her tired face. Her complexion is gaunt and haunted. She continues shaking, staring out the window while the fly bangs into the glass, over and over and over. Maybe she's not looking out the window; she's not seeing the barn or anything beyond it. She sees an insect dying of exhaustion.

The dogs follow her outside and she does what she does best when she doesn't have an answer. She begins to run.

Paul is alone at the table. He doesn't believe a word she says, doesn't believe he's a brick or that he's the messenger of a conspiracy. He thinks clearly, feels normal, and remembers his life. But he stares at the vial of proof.

Hoping she's wrong.

CHAPTER FORTY-NINE_

"Mr. Connick would like to discuss your deposit."

The message arrives three days after the deposit. Nix doesn't eat that morning, afraid he'll puke all over his Armani suit.

Jamie steps out of the bathroom with her hair pinned over her ears and pearls around her neck. There's no comparing the grungy girl on the farm to the one peering over the top of nonprescription glasses. Even Nix didn't expect this sort of response from the nixes, as if it rinsed all the impurities from her nearly charred life.

A taxi takes them to the bank and Jalen greets them at the door, her slender handshake firm and congratulatory.

"Right this way."

They pass Mr. Griffin's office. The chair is empty.

Jalen leads them across the lobby with a confident stride. The elevator is open. She gestures for them to enter and presses the number ten. She lets them ride alone. The elevator lurches, tugging the ball of nerves in Nix's stomach. He concentrates on the climbing numbers. Jamie nudges him and reminds him that he's not alone.

The elevator slides open and reveals a wiry man behind a walnut table.

"Have a seat. Mr. Connick will be with you in a moment." He doesn't look up.

The moment turns into thirty minutes. Jamie flips through a magazine. No gum this time. Nix sits quietly, rehearsing his argument and preparing his responses. The admin assistant finally stands, announces that Mr. Connick is ready, and escorts them to the end of the hallway, pushing open a set of double doors.

A man sits in a corner office facing Lake Michigan. He stands behind a grand desk.

"Please come in," Mr. Connick says.

They shake hands with the athletic man, his hand soft and firm. His smile, gentle yet dismissive. His taut cheeks suggest facial reconfiguration—the new age of plastic surgery.

The room feels like storm clouds.

"Have a seat," Mr. Connick says. "You may speak freely in my office. No one will hear us."

He means Mother.

"Thank you for meeting us," Nix says.

"Your gratitude is kind, but I'm not doing you a favor." The smile fades. "Ordinarily, when someone brings a dead girl into my bank and begins to ask certain questions, I deal much differently with the situation. But your deposit is intriguing."

He takes a glass vial from his pocket, dull metal clotted inside like solid lead. It lacks iridescence.

"My people analyzed it and the moment it was validated, your nixes self-annihilated by means of suicide code. Your deposit is as useless as dust."

"I have to protect my investment."

The trash can rattles next to Mr. Connick as he drops the vial. "They tell me the strain operated on an entirely new plane before it went cold: a quantum mechanical method. They've never seen anything like it. Tell me, with all the scientists in the world, how is that you come into my bank with your brand-new clothes and offer me something like this?"

"It's a dangerous business. Would you agree?"

Mr. Connick hums. His pupils dilate.

"You look lovely." He turns toward Jamie and, coming around the desk, takes her hand.

"Thank you," she replies with the right amount of false sincerity.

"Considering you're dead. You're reading at 49.9%, but I suspect you're halfskin."

"I have my doubts about you, too."

"Are you using the strain?" He nods at the trash.

"I'll never tell."

He strokes the back of her hand, studying the blue lines just beneath the skin, perhaps admiring the unaltered quality. While appearing handsome and middle-aged, he pats it much like an old man that gets what he wants. He goes to the glass wall behind his desk.

"You're from the Seattle warehouse. We had connections with them. I can only assume that's how you found us. As for Mr. William Nelson, your identity and facial register are false. You're hiding, Mr. Nelson. And you're not an old man."

"Neither are you," Jamie quips.

"It's too easy to hide nowadays. That's why we need Mother—to control the masses." He looks over his shoulder, a sly smile, and returns to his desk. "Well, then. It's obvious you have access to ground-breaking technology. Why come to me? Why expose yourself?"

"We want two fabrications," Nix says.

"I see. And why not just fabricate them yourselves?"

"You're interested, Mr. Connick. Or we wouldn't be here."

"And these fabrications, I'm assuming will be human? Or else you wouldn't be here."

"Yes."

"Two human fabrications are quite expensive."

"A man like you doesn't need money."

"Money is still power, Mr. Nelson, even in today's technology-mad world. It buys people. Buys security. I can never get enough of either."

"But it won't buy Mother. That's my offer."

Mr. Connick leans heavily into his chair. His sharp blue eyes temporarily become dull and the pupils jitter. He's considering the offer with outside help. Perhaps chatting. *He's not the boss. He's probably streaming this experience, serving as a buffer. Mr. Connick might even be a puppet.*

The ones that run this business are very well insulated.

Because it's a dangerous business.

"One fabrication." He raises a finger. "That's my offer."

Nix hesitates. One fabrication is all he wants. Two was just the asking price. Jamie will have to settle for a promise to find another fabricator.

"This is really awkward," she says. "We're negotiating when we all know that we've made provisions to bring this bank down if we don't get our way."

"Don't make threats, young lady."

"Let's stop fucking around, old man. You think Willie Nelson isn't who he seems to be? You're right. The nixes he put in your deposit box should tell you that your people don't know shit compared to him. We've got guns in our corner, Mr. Connick, big-ass technology guns that you can't imagine."

She sits on the edge of her seat.

"You think we want to be here, sitting in your pretentious office with the million-dollar view? None of us do. Exposure is our enemy as much as it is yours, but you have something we need. We're offering you something you need in return. I didn't say *want,* Mr. Connick. You *need* our strain of biomites. Mother is sniffing out fabricators and everyone connected to them. Why the hell you're still running one is anyone's guess. Maybe you're cashing in while you can, squeezing every penny out of your investment before shutting the fabricator down, I don't know. Lucky for us, greedy men like you are still in business."

Jamie walks around the desk and spins his chair. She takes his hand the same way he took hers.

"You're a smart man, Mr. Connick. You're also a lucky man. Lucky we got here before Mother shut you down. This is your chance at freedom. Our strain of nixes will take you off Mother's radar for the rest of your life. You'll have all the security you want. Don't let greed fuck that up."

She presses his hand between her breasts and holds up two fingers.

"Who are they?"

"That's none of your business."

Mr. Connick rocks back and forth, looking up at her. He pulls her closer, kisses the back of her hand and smells her wrist. Laughter trickles through his throat. He stands with an amused smile and goes back to his million-dollar view.

"I see why you pulled her off the trash heap, Mr. Nelson," Mr. Connick says.

He occasionally hums. A few minutes later, the double doors open. The wiry admin assistant waits. Nix stops Jamie from saying more. Mr. Connick keeps his back to them as they're escorted from the room. In the hall, there's less of an electric current in the air out of the office's protection. What they say out there might be heard.

The elevator is waiting.

Jamie stares at Nix, eyes imploring him...*Do something.*

"You will receive further instructions in five days," the admin assistant says. "Be sure you have your full deposit."

The elevator doors close. Their stomachs drop as they descend. They don't dare move until they are halfway down to the lobby. Jamie throws her arms up and slings herself into his arms. Nix keeps her from sliding to the floor. His own legs are weak.

We got them both.

CHAPTER FIFTY_

"Marcus."

The voice passes through several veils of sleep, finding Marcus deep in a dream. When his foot is grabbed, he bolts upright. The sheet slides off his chest.

"Time to wake up." Mother squeezes his toes.

"What are you doing?"

"I have good news."

He checks his watch. "This can wait."

"You've been waiting your whole life."

He grinds his palms into his eyes. The sheet slips off Anna, exposing a perfectly inflated breast. She moans for more sleep.

Marcus stands up, fully nude. He goes to the bathroom and returns with a robe cinched around his waist, going to the kitchenette for a glass of freshly squeezed orange juice. Mother stands at his open closet, dragging her fingers over the rack of tailor-made suits. She holds one up to see how it looks in the mirror. She lays it on the bed.

"What cannot wait?" Marcus says.

She pulls open the French doors. Fresh air ripples her sheer dress. "The children have come out of hiding."

This doesn't mean anything to him.

He drops the robe and dresses casually. Perhaps he'll crawl back into bed when Mother is finished speaking in riddles. Anna will stay as long as he likes.

Against his wishes, he follows her to the balcony. The city, however, has been replaced with green hills. Conifers are crowded to the right, their heavy limbs reaching for the ground while their tops touch the sky. Blue mountains are in the distance.

"What children?" he asks.

"Smell that, Marcus." She inhales. "Life."

"What children are you talking about?"

"Interesting how we associate life with pleasant sensations, don't you think? If you consider the amount of bacteria living on dog feces, we don't think about life. It's foul."

Marcus heads back for his bed. He'd rather philosophize the mysteries of life over dinner rather than predawn.

"Nix and Cali Richards have been identified."

He puts a hand on the doorjamb.

"They're exposed, Marcus."

"Have you shut them down?"

"Of course not."

"Have you dispersed the bricks?"

"I want you to go. You've been waiting for quite some time."

"Where are they?"

"They're separate. It won't be difficult to bring them home."

A flock of geese squawks overhead, the V-pattern pointing at the mountains. His body feels weightless; it feels powered by joy. If he lets go, he might float away and take a position behind them.

Peace. At last.

"I'll collect my things," he says. "Have the plane ready. I'll need half a dozen bricks. In the meantime, send me updates. I want to know their exact locations, who is with them, what they look like, as well as their identity stamps. Have all bricks in their vicinity surround their positions immediately. They are to wait for my arrival before making contact."

He takes a deep breath, savoring the clean air. If this is what peace smells like, he should get out of the city more often. He smacks the door, celebrating.

"Not yet," Mother says. "There are preparations to make."

"No. We will not make the same mistake again."

"There never was a mistake, Marcus. We need them to step deeper into the trap. It's only a matter of time now."

"Don't do this." He shakes his finger. "Tell me where they are —now."

She gently lowers his hand. "I have to confess something, Marcus."

"Damn you, woman! This is not the time! I want to be waiting for—"

"Cali Richards didn't release the nixes."

More riddles.

Mother leans on the railing and breathes deeply, throwing her head back. When she's done appreciating nature, she turns around. Her off-white dress flutters.

Marcus is rigid.

"I released the nixed code to the world, not Cali Richards. You should know this."

"What?"

"I'm responsible for the halfskin dens and fabricators."

She couldn't possibly release such classified information. If she could operate outside the limits of her sentience, she would be shut down. Safeguards would automatically be triggered. Something of that nature would be treasonous. How could she release code that she couldn't detect?

"I want you to understand that I forecasted the solution to the biomite dilemma long ago and it's coming to fruition. You must trust what we're doing."

"We?"

"You and me, Marcus."

"And what are we doing?"

"Saving God's children from me."

"From you?"

"From what I will become."

"You're telling me that you released the nixes to save us? I don't believe this. I'll have to...the oversight committee will shut you down. If what you're saying is true, this whole operation is over. Why are you telling me this now?"

With her dress waving around her feet, her approach is almost angelic. She glides to him, taking his hand.

"Trust me. Anna will go with you. She will help bring home the children."

He doesn't like the sound of it. Where he once felt euphoric lightness lift him up, now the lead weight of doubt plows him into the ground. He watches deer timidly approach a stream next to a boulder, dipping their wary noses to the water. They look for danger.

Danger is all around.

And yet, he does nothing.

He won't call his superiors. He won't have her shut down. Not now. Nix and Cali are too close. But he's not sure what disturbs him most.

Her admission of betrayal?

Or that she's calling them her children?

CHAPTER FIFTY-ONE_

CHICAGO'S CENTRAL MANUFACTURING DISTRICT.

Nix and Jamie drive past boxy buildings with company names stamped on them. Few are recognizable; they are mostly plants that produce fabrics or decomposable containers or little plastic parts that fit deep inside a machine, never to see the light of day. They follow the directions sent by Mr. Connick's admin assistant until they find it in big, blue letters.

Munsen Digital.

It's a four-story building, beige. The windows reflect the gray sky like sad eyes. There's no fence or security, just a half-empty parking lot and a set of glass doors.

Nix turns off the car. His eyes flick to the rearview, like bricks might be following.

They would just shut us down, Jamie thinks. *No drama.*

She waits for him to settle his thoughts while her belly purrs with excitement. Nix is slightly pale. It's only the biggest day of his entire life.

They cross the parking lot. The weight of a thousand eyes pushes down on them. She tries not to look at the windows, tries to avoid looking guilty, but she can't see beyond their steel reflections. It only gets heavier.

Inside, something mechanical is rhythmically banging away somewhere. The reception room is small and empty, off-white. Nix rattles his fingernails across the long, empty counter while a commercial for erectile dysfunction plays on a television.

Minutes go by.

A door opens in the back and fills the room with the sound of manufacturing, like an old printing press. A skinny man steps sideways, closing the door quickly. He sniffs nervously and doesn't make eye contact. He taps at a keyboard.

"You're here to see Mr. Hansen." It's not a question.

Nix nods.

"Smile," the guy says. Jamie feels a wave scan through her, a tickle lingering somewhere in her intestines. Several clicks of the mouse and he looks up. "Elevator is through that door."

He stares at Jamie. His eyes are blank and careless. She doesn't like it, refusing to blink or look away until Nix pulls her along. A smile cracks the corner of the guy's mouth. Jamie stumbles into the faux walnut-paneled elevator that smells like grease and burnt rubber.

The ground floor button stays lit as the doors close. The three buttons above it remain dead. Their balance is thrown off when the elevator drops. The ground floor button dies as they descend. Cooler air greets them and the smell changes to something resembling putty and singed aluminum.

When the doors open, they're greeted by a long hallway. A Caucasian man steps through one of many doors, a white lab coat buttoned up to his chest. He takes several stiff steps with his hand extended the entire way.

"Congratulations." He briskly shakes their hands. It's soft, almost feminine. "Few people are privileged to get this far."

"Are you Mr. Hansen?" Nix asks.

"I am. But down here, names are inconsequential."

"Why's that?"

"You'll find out shortly."

"Is this lab fully functional?" Nix's eyes narrow.

Maybe he didn't expect it to be so elaborate. Maybe he's used to second-rate translucent boxes stuffed in the back of bars or hidden in a basement. This is nothing like the warehouse. But this place has survived Mother's purge, so they probably did more than fabricate dogs.

"We do more than just fabricate. Follow me."

Mr. Hansen folds his hands in a most peculiar way: one on top of the other, like he's captured a small frog. He marches to the nearest doorway on the right and waits. Nix gently places his hand between her shoulders and guides her forward.

They stop just inside the lab.

The room is two stories high with plenty of clean, hard floor surrounding an enormous glass-walled cube. Inside the cube, thousands of filaments hang from ceiling mounts. Nozzles are fixed along vertical rails. A silver disc is slightly raised in the center, the surface polished.

The smell of putty is overwhelmed by the sting of antiseptics. Jamie swallows down the smell, but it sticks in her throat. There's a lone lounger facing the glass cube, shaped like the one in the warehouse. It's even the same color.

"Munsen Digital manufactures non-biomite material," Nix mutters. "It would explain the massive power consumption down here without visits from biomite inspectors. You're also licensed to research and develop electronics."

"We're paid very well," Mr. Hansen says.

An Asian woman and an Indian man approach, both wearing lab coats. No one shakes hands or acknowledges each other.

"But it's more than that," Mr. Hansen says. "We believe in the future of biomite technology, but we have to be careful. Therefore, you will remain here until your fabrications are complete. Ms. Chen will then alter the last two weeks of your memories before you leave."

"Why not erase them?" Jamie asks.

"Erasing causes a blockage that creates psychological pressure. It's better to make your memories vague. You will not recall details, such as places or names or this lab. You won't even be sure if this is Chicago. If you don't agree to this, our business is finished and she can alter your memories now."

He hides the imaginary frog and waits for their approval. They nod.

"Payment, then." Mr. Hansen opens his hand, rigid and flat. "Mr. Sing will verify the strain without the suicide code."

"No," Nix says. "The suicide code remains."

"That is not the deal. You are to provide a fully functional strain that matches your deposit."

"You'll use my sample to begin our fabrications. They will contain the suicide code. This will guarantee that neither you nor I will turn them off. Once we're out of the building and safe, I'll permanently rinse the suicide code."

Mr. Hansen is frozen, hand out and empty. He blinks rapidly. "What guarantee do I have that you'll sanitize our batch?"

"Our fabrications will be linked with your sample."

Jamie doesn't understand this part of biomites, how they synchronize or replace clay. She only knows what they feel like.

"I'll have to verify this," Mr. Hansen says.

Nix places a vial on the man's outstretched fingers. The overhead LED lights reflect off the shimmering contents. Mr. Hansen delivers it to Mr. Sing, who takes the sample to a large bank of beige, boxy equipment. A conduit is mounted on top of the largest of the machines that channels the majority of filaments up the wall, across the ceiling, and into the glass cube.

The room begins to hum.

Jamie feels it in her feet. It creeps up her legs and into her chest. It transforms into a whine. Nix stares at Mr. Sing, his fingers flexing at his sides. The wrinkles in his forehead undulate, slightly smoothing out before deepening again. His transfigured disguise is faltering under stress.

"Hey." Jamie squeezes his arm. He walks away.

An hour passes. Mr. Hansen and his collaborators gather for more than a couple discussions; their voices are hidden beneath the replicator's whine. Frequently they watch Nix, who refuses to sit.

"Okay," Mr. Hansen shouts with a smile, hands offering a truce. "You have been granted two fabrications with the agreement that your memories will be altered, as we discussed. However, you will not leave the building until the suicide code is rinsed from our batch. Are we in agreement?"

Mr. Hansen ignores Jamie. Nix nods.

"Very good." Mr. Hansen has a long discussion with the other technicians before approaching Nix. "This is how it will work. We will extract the source code for each of the fabrications. A digital model will be constructed and validated. This could take a few days, but it's very important. We don't want to fabricate the organs in the wrong places, all right?

"The more details contained in the source code, the less time it will take, and, of course, the more accurate the fabrication will be. The actual fabrication will take a week. So the sooner we can start, the sooner we finish."

Mr. Hansen lays out his hand again, like he's expecting a jump drive with programming.

"The source code, please."

"You'll take it from memories," Nix says.

"Memory extraction?" He flinches and looks back at Mr. Sing and Ms. Chen. They're too engrossed in their machines. "You want to extract from memories? I'm afraid you've wasted our time. Do yourselves a favor and buy a couple Real Dolls. The results will be tepid, at best. Pets work on memories, but humans? They'll be an animated shell of the person you want. I thought you, of all people, the one with this elegant strain of biomites, would know the correct source code requirements."

He looks over his shoulder.

"Perhaps Mr. Sing can build the source code. He has a background in biometric engineering."

"No," Nix says. "Memory extraction."

The standoff between Nix and Mr. Hansen ends with an anticlimactic shoulder shrug. "It's your money."

Jamie stands alone and catatonic in her thoughts. She eventually follows them to the lounger.

She tries to recall Charlie's face while Ms. Chen helps Nix lie back; Mr. Sing fixes a wire matrix over his head. Jamie can't remember Charlie's details. They blur into general shapes and colors. If she closes her eyes, she can recall the protruding eyebrows and blue eyes. He had a little scar above the right one. His lips were full and his nose bent. Still, it's hard to put it all together. Now that she really thinks about it, she can't really see it.

Ms. Chen places a pulse monitor on Nix's finger. His vital signs are displayed on a small monitor.

"I'm going to ask a series of questions," Mr. Sing says. "You will answer them. This will activate sections of the brain where more information can be extracted. The process will take several hours. Once we begin, we cannot stop. Are you comfortable?"

Several hours?

Jamie has lost her desperation; the maniacal drive to bring back Charlie is gone. All her life she's identified with fear; she's clung to it, afraid that if she didn't feel something—even if it hurt—that she'd disappear, that she wouldn't matter. She'd believe the little voices that said she was nothing.

And now those voices are gone. It's like she just let them go.

She thought she needed Charlie to help her do that. And even if he didn't, at least she could share the insane whispers with him. He understood. He shared her pain, and that made it tolerable.

But he's not here.

She understands that now, staring at the glass cube and the

lounger. He can't come back. She doesn't need him to come back. Even if a fabrication walked and talked like him, it's not him.

Charlie's dead.

"How did you get this strain?" Mr. Sing mutters so only Nix and Jamie can hear. "It is impossible. You are a genius, maybe, but you cannot manufacture nixes of this sophistication. This is a mistake, bringing you here, I feel." He sits in front of several monitors, jabbing at a keyboard. "Let's begin."

Mr. Sing punches the last key.

Nix stiffens.

His head slams into the headrest and the tremors begin.

The monitors streams with unintelligible data. Mr. Sing pushes back, confusion morphing his anger into nervousness.

"What's happening?" Jamie asks.

Ms. Chen and Mr. Hansen run to them. They offer suggestions while Mr. Sing hits the keyboard. Nix's eyes dance beneath his eyelids: a REM cycle on speed. The tremors become convulsions. The vital signs are jagged and angry.

"What are you doing to him?" Jamie grabs the wire matrix, but Mr. Hansen stops her.

"Don't. Not yet."

The wrinkles melt from his complexion. Nix's lips fill out, his nose slimming. The technicians hardly notice a much younger man jittering in front of them. Mr. Hansen's grip tightens on her wrist. She swings with her free hand, but he drags her away, avoiding her heels stomping at his feet. He wraps her in a bear hug, his strength surprising her.

Nix becomes as rigid as a pipe. His body bows upwards.

"No!" She can't let this happen. She watched someone else die. Are they sucking the biomites out of him? "Stop!"

Just as she is about to elbow Mr. Hansen in the kidney, Nix drops. His arms dangle over the sides of the lounger; his body is limp and deflated. His mouth falls open and so do his eyes. But they're focused on Jamie. He sees her struggling.

The sound of keyboards stops.

"We got it." Mr. Sing runs his hand through his thick black hair.

"What do you mean?" Mr. Hansen asks.

"The extraction...you have to see this."

Mr. Hansen releases Jamie. She pulls the wire matrix off Nix. Tiny welts appear on his forehead and temples.

"What'd you do?" she asks.

"I brought someone into the world."

The three technicians study the results and argue over bits and pieces. In the end, they agree the extraction was a success. Mr. Sing begins creating a backup copy. Jamie wonders how many profiles are stored here. If they can extract a personality with memories and identity, can they back up their own selves?

And just fabricate another body for themselves? *We do more than fabricate.*

"Fabrication is still a long ways off. It'll take hours to spin enough biomites to begin." Mr. Hansen takes notice of Nix's appearance. The old man is gone. It won't take long to identify Nix Richards, but still, he asks, "Who the hell are you?"

Nix closes his eyes, letting out a long breath, one he's been holding for a very long time. Jamie pulls a chair next to the lounger. While the spinner hums, she lays her head on his arm. It's sometime later when another sound disturbs her. It's a hydraulic pump.

The silver disc is rising inside the glass cube.

The filaments begin dancing.

CHAPTER FIFTY-TWO_

Cali hides behind the curtains.

Paul is talking to Hal, who is shaking his head like there's only so much bad news he wants to hear. Cali can't wear the disguise anymore. She could transfigure back into the old woman, Stacy. She just doesn't want to. She's tired of hiding.

Hal will learn the truth soon enough.

A handshake and a quick wave and he's back in the truck. Paul watches until he's gone. Cali sits in the back room, a glass of water by her side. The house shudders when the front door closes. Paul's boots clop through the house.

"He agreed," he says. "He's a little worried that you're still sick, said he wants to send out a doctor. I told him you wanted to talk to him in three days, said the horses might need to be fed. You want to tell me what's going on?"

"Have a seat," she says.

"You can't have another sample. My veins are flat."

He moves slowly, like he's pulling an anchor. He's lost weight. They both have. She hears him pacing in the middle of the night when she comes up from the lab. Sometimes she'll hear the door close before the sun comes up and, soon after, see him walking in the pastures. Those are the nights she wishes that he'd just keep going, not turn back. If he left, it'd be much easier to do what she's got to do. And she wouldn't have to tell him.

But he'll stay. That's why he's here—to stay. Because Mother sent him.

"I'm going to shut us down."

"What?" He sits up.

He starts and stops a few times, looking around the room for answers and finding none. Cali takes a deep breath and exhales the tension.

"Your nixes are identical to my original strain of nixes," she continues. "That means Mother knows about Nix and me. There's no question Mother chose not to shut me down; she proved it by sending you. In fact, she's manufactured all her bricks with the same strain of nixes as you and me."

She hesitates, stopping short of calling him a brick. It pains her when the realization crosses his face.

"I've done an identity scan across the world and verified this. There's a lot more bricks out there than the public knows, Paul. If Mother were to shut me down, she would be turning off my strain of nixes. And that would include all of her bricks."

"Why?" he says.

Maybe he means why would Mother do that? Why would she fabricate all her bricks from Cali's strain? Why would she leave Cali alone all these years?

Or maybe he means why is Cali talking about shutting herself down?

"I don't know."

She sits calmly and explains what she's been thinking for the past couple of days.

Cali always assumed that her creative bursts were self-induced. She took credit for her spurts of genius, the breakthroughs she developed in her basement. She invented nixed biomites that billion-dollar corporations couldn't touch.

Why?

Twenty years ago, when she needed to save Nix from being shut down, she developed the nixes in a short amount of time. It was inconceivable—she knew this. She had even considered it, at one time, divine intervention. There were no explanations for the ease with which she eluded Mother and achieved the impossible. In the last week, she developed the transforming strain of nixes to heal Jamie and, in retrospect, it seemed too simple. Maybe it wasn't divine intervention, after all.

It was Mother's intervention.

"I think Mother has achieved self-awareness, Paul, and I don't think anyone's aware of it. The size of her processing capacity and redundancy pathways made that inevitable. Her directive was to save humanity by implementing the Halfskin Laws—shutting down people before they converted their bodies into artificial vehicles. If she achieves sentience, they'll shut her down. I think she has, Paul. I think she's evolved and understands what she's capable of doing."

He appears hollowed out, staring vacantly at the floor. Maybe he knows all of this already, and it's just now coming to light.

Cali doesn't tell him what made up her mind. *Am I her fail-safe?*

"I can exclude you, Paul. I can begin a biomite transfusion that will take you off my frequency so that it won't affect you."

"What about you?"

"I have to shut down for it to work." She looks down, avoiding eye contact. *That's a lie.*

"And Nix?"

"I can't reach him."

"You're going to kill your brother?"

"Shut down, Paul. There's a difference."

"You shut down biomites. You kill clay. One percent of you—and Nix—is still clay."

"It's not fair, I know."

Life's not fair, Cali. Here we are again.

"You're not thinking clearly."

"No, Paul. I think more clearly now than ever. Don't you see? I'm the key to every brick. Everything is linked to me. I can cripple Mother by shutting down everything she's done."

"And then what?"

"The world will see what she's doing."

"They already know!"

"No, they don't. There's something about her that we don't know, but she does, Paul. She wants to be shut down."

"Then why doesn't she just do it?"

"I don't know."

"That's what I mean! If she wanted to shut down, she'd do it. She'd let the public know that she's self-aware, she'd trigger an automated shutdown—it can be done. She's up to something, Cali. She wants you to do this. Think about that. If she's indestructible, why would she reach out for you to stop her?"

"Trust me, I can feel it."

"You're a scientist! You don't go on gut feelings, you analyze data; you look for statistical differences, not feelings. This is all wrong, Cali. Listen to yourself."

"She never should've been created, I think she knows this. Marcus Anderson and others like him were well-intentioned, but they were wrong. It's more than just shutting her down. Marcus and others like him need to be stopped."

She can taste the bitterness. She wants vindication from Marcus Anderson's relentless pursuit. Her brother didn't deserve to be shut down when he was a kid. Marcus made her turn Nix halfskin to save him. She never forgave him for that.

It's not that. Something feels right. She can see the truth, and it's sitting across from her, shaking his head. It all makes sense now.

He leans his elbows on his knees. "You're making a mistake, Cali. I think you're looking for reasons to end this. If this doesn't work, it'll be a waste."

She can't deny that. She thought she found peace on the farm, that when she had security from Mother, she could be happy. But something never left her.

The hole in her life stayed.

Maybe she's manufactured this whole belief, spun this tale of a righteous heroine in her mind so that she'd end her life with purpose. It's possible she seeded herself with coded thoughts and erased the memory of doing so. Maybe she's insane and rationalizing suicide.

Maybe.

"The transfusion, Paul. Let me give it to you."

He stares at her. She meets his gaze, unflinching. He's looking for an explanation in her eyes, a hint of doubt. What he sees is what she embodies. Total conviction. He paces around the room and looks out the window. Cali feels her breath slow down.

"If you're going to do this," he says, "you take me with you."

He's calling her bluff, daring her to take him, too. She doesn't want to, he can sense it, and she won't deny it. But he can't stop her. It'll only take a thought for her to trigger the mass shutdown. But she had to give him an option. She knew he wouldn't take it. But she had no right to do that, not even with his consent. She has no right to take the bricks, really. Perhaps the facts suggest they aren't real, that they're incapable of self-reflection. But there's proof that one brick is self-aware.

He's standing in front of Cali.

"Let me take one more sample from you, just to be sure." She holds up a stethoscope-looking instrument.

"What's that?"

"I'll use it to check my work. Just to make sure everything is working."

He yanks his arm back. "Don't inject me with something."

"Look, I don't have time to run a full battery of tests. This is a speedy sampler. It just matches what I previously saw. That's all."

She takes his arm and this time he lets her, but not without searching for her intentions, staring deep into her eyes. She looks back, unblinking. He's suspicious. He should be. She's never used this to draw a sample.

She ties a band around his arm.

The small vial containing a silver liquid is hidden from his sight, nestled beneath a cover she fastened in place. She knew he'd turn down her offer, so she was ready. He watches her while it does its work without any idea that she seeds him with another variation of nixes.

He leaves the house, rubbing his arm.

She drops the seeder on the floor and closes her eyes. She reaches out to Nix like she'd done a thousand times. Through the ether, she calls to him. She'll leave a message and then call again. She has no right to shut him down, either.

But life isn't fair. Never has been.

CHAPTER FIFTY-THREE_

THE REPLICATOR HUMS, SENDING VIBRATIONS THROUGH THE floor.

The filaments run back and forth in slow, methodical rhythm, hissing as they lay down biomites a microscopic layer at a time. Another set of filaments flail around the disc, dispersing fine mist. It starts as footprints on the silver disc and slowly builds feet. The cross-sections of bones, muscles and nerves are visible, like watching a thin series of dissecting cuts in reverse.

Her veins bulge on the tops of her feet, just as Nix remembers them. Her toenails are translucent, the tips slightly white.

A miniscule layer at a time, it goes.

By the end of the first day, the knees have been completed. Under the artificial lights, her brown flesh is closer to beige than tanned hide. Now, on the second day, the upper thighs are nearly complete. A pair of legs—slick with moisture—stand independently of each other, waiting for the pelvis to join them.

The cloying scent of putty is strong.

He hardly notices his reflection—the visage of a young man. He couldn't hold the disguise through the upload. There was no point in resuming it. They know who he is now.

Jamie exits a side room where thin bunks are available. She yawns with a coffee cup in each hand, giving one to Nix. They watch the hypnotic filaments finish another layer. The misters keep the newly formed flesh moist. Soon, they'll fabricate the intestines and uterus. Already he's daydreaming about having a child, and she's still not halfway to the flesh.

"You sleep?" she asks.

He dozed off when the fabrication was midway up the shins, remembering the scar she earned falling out of a tree.

Jamie walks the perimeter of the glass cube, studying the legs from all angles. She's been withdrawn since the fabrication began.

A new technician checks the monitors. At some point, Mr. Hansen and his assistants were replaced by a heavyset black man and a short white woman with spiky hair. They don't talk to Nix; they barely acknowledge him.

"You uploaded her," Jamie says. "Didn't you?"

"You ever heard of Dreamland?"

"The biomites-induced hallucination?"

"I just close my eyes and go there." His reflection is stoic and distant. "I've been going there since I was a kid."

Given everything they've been through, it's not hard for her to believe.

"And so you dreamed her up."

"She was just there—living and breathing when I discovered I could go there." *Go there, like it's a place. I still want to believe.* "But Dreamland depends on me to exist. I was out here and she was trapped inside. If something happens to me, Dreamland is dead. And so is she."

"So you're bringing her out."

The filaments break their rhythm to reconfigure. The legs are complete. There's a hesitation before the filaments begin circling. They begin at the bottom of the buttocks. Eventually, they'll complete the midsection and torso, then the shoulders and arms before starting on the head.

"You've got to understand something." Nix addresses Jamie's reflection on the glass cube. "The details of what I know about her aren't memories. It's a grand design that goes all the way to her genetic makeup. It's information that I couldn't possibly know or remember. Memories are biased, Jamie. We're all guilty of running them through filters until we're left with distorted images of the people we love."

He taps the glass.

"That's not how I remember her. That *is* her."

She sips her coffee, nodding. "What's her name?"

"Raine."

With slow, careful steps, she starts around the glass cube again, making it around before returning to the bunk room to lie down. He wants to tell her more, tell her he'll become a regular person now that she's in the flesh. Maybe they'll hide on the farm with Cali. He won't need anything else, really. No reason to explore the world. He's always got Dreamland for that. And they'll start a family, too. They'll have a boy named Joshua. Or a girl named Pearl. Either way, they'll be as human as the clay farmers that live around them. Happiness is on the other side of the glass. He can almost touch it.

On the other hand, Charlie's fabrication is impossible, she knows that. That's why she leaves Nix to watch his dream girl alone. Will it stop her from fabricating Charlie?

It wouldn't stop me.

Soft pressure swells behind his eyes. *Bing*. Cali is calling again. He dumps the message. There's nothing she can say to stop him. He should probably thank her. In a way, she forced him to turn Jamie halfskin. And that's what brought him here.

And Raine one step closer.

CHAPTER FIFTY-FOUR_

CALI LOCKS THE BASEMENT DOOR AND PUTS THE KEY ON THE kitchen table. In case things don't work out, she puts Hal's name on a sheet of paper with an explanation scribbled beneath it. It starts out as an apology. She didn't want him to discover the truth about her, at least not in this way. They're good people—people she wishes, in another life, she can emulate.

She drops a white envelope next to Hal's note. There's a different name on it. There are explanations inside.

The musty smell of the house is rich today. She hasn't noticed it this strong since she moved in so many years ago. That was a day she stopped right where she is now and felt the memories of the previous family saturating the old walls. This home, though, never felt like hers. She was always a stranger. She had hoped if she lived there long enough, the memories would become hers.

They were just borrowed.

She goes to the front porch and pulls the door closed, caressing the slick surface. She won't open that again.

Paul's in the gravel driveway, throwing a tennis ball across the field. The muscles ripple down his arm, lean from days of fasting.

The dogs return, one of them with the ball. Paul sends them on another chase.

For a moment, she sees Nix playing with the dogs.

Cali slings an old wool blanket over her shoulder. She stops next to him. The dogs only have eyes for the ball. Cali heaves it one last time. Paul turns to her. He smiles briefly. It's lifeless.

No one is ready to die.

Numbered breaths bring a stark realization of one's mortality: when the light goes out, life ends. If she was Christian, perhaps this moment would be a little more joyous—she could hope for a reward. She had lived the best life she could. As a scientist, she had always professed, with steel honesty, that she didn't know what happened after death. Her uncertainty slows her breathing. Each breath becomes more precious than the one before. She's not ready to die.

No one is.

They leave the compact driveway and traipse through the burgeoning green field. Clumps of May wildflowers sway outside the pasture. The crippled swing set is still standing. Cali drops the blanket beneath it. Paul helps spread it. They sit down, arms resting on their knees. The birds sing in the distant trees and a breeze rustles through the grass. The dogs return without the ball. Instinctively, they know she's done.

Is this what you want? Cali looks up. *Are you toying with me? Am I caught in your perception field, made to believe my actions are just?*

Her desperation to find more breaths fuels her doubt; maybe Paul's right. She should reconsider. But there is no room for thinking. She's tired.

They lie back.

The clouds crawl across the sky. A hawk glides in the updraft. The last moments of life rest gently, never to be captured, only to be savored. She's but a conduit through which they pass.

Paul's hand moves warmly over hers.

She looks past the rusted chains of the swing set, into the endless blue heavens, with a secret smile. Perhaps she knows why Mother sent Paul.

She doesn't feel alone.

CHAPTER FIFTY-FIVE_

Nix fell asleep sometime after the torso was finished.

The thrum of the replicator and hiss of the filaments was a distant lullaby.

When he wakes, a headless nude body glistens on the silver disc. Several misters work to keep it moist and sealed, preventing the inactive biomites from separating. The moisture beads and streaks like perspiration.

He stands the remaining hours.

The strokes are slower, more methodical. The full lips are pink. Her nose slim. Eyelashes long. Moisture runs down her cheeks, dripping from her chin. With each pass, she becomes less of an object, more of a dark-skinned woman. He presses his palms against the glass as if he's magnetically drawn to it.

The filaments finish her short hair with a sweeping flurry.

They draw up to the ceiling and lock into the mounts. The replicator no longer churns out biomites.

Silence.

The body of Raine is motionless, inanimate.

His breath fogs the glass with short and erratic strokes.

"Beautiful," Jamie whispers.

He moves to the doorway—a seam etched into the wall. A burst of moisture is applied, running down her stomach. Water pools between her toes.

"We'll need some time to verify connectivity." Mr. Hansen is back, along with Mr. Sing and Ms. Chen.

Paul has waited years for this moment, but the next few hours feel even longer. The rudimentary tests are torture. Finally, her fingers flinch.

Her chest inflates and the flesh stretches over her ribs. Slowly, it releases. This is repeated over and over. Each time, a knot of anticipation lodges in Nix's throat. The inflations become consistent, closer together, until her chest rhythmically rises and falls.

She's breathing.

He leans against the glass.

The misters continue. A pulse begins thumping on her neck, light reflecting from the wet skin. She'll open her eyes any second. She'll see the outside world through flesh.

The lab is flung into darkness.

Red lights flash.

Generators grind to life in another room and emergency lights come online, splashing a yellowish hue across the room.

"What's happening?" Nix calls.

Mr. Hansen and the others scramble to their computers. He's shouting at Mr. Sing, something about power failure and redirecting pathways. The computer monitors begin to glow; tiny green lights flicker beneath the benches.

Raine is still breathing, but her eyes remain sealed.

"What's going on?" Jamie asks.

Nix bangs on the glass. The inch-thick walls barely shimmer beneath his blows, but the reverberations echo inside. She won't open her eyes. Adrenaline dumps into his system, poking fear with a cold stick.

"Open it! Open the door!"

Jamie hammers on the glass, too. Their appeals thunder inside the cube.

"The emergency exits aren't responding," Mr. Sing says. A quiver in his voice suggests ideas that don't include Nix and Jamie.

"We'll override it." Mr. Hansen starts taking off the white coat.

"Where the hell are you going?" Nix grabs his sleeve. Mr. Hansen whirls around.

"You did this!" Mr. Hansen shouts. "You bastard, you did this!"

He throws a glancing blow off of Nix's head. He tries another and gets slammed against the cube. Nix has two fistfuls of his lab coat bunched under his chin. "You realize what you've done?" Mr. Hansen says. "You betrayed us, you fuck; led them right to us. This might be the last fabricator in the world, and you just handed it over to them."

"What the hell are you talking about?"

"Watch your lady disintegrate, you bastard."

"No." Nix flings him to the floor. Mr. Sing and Ms. Chen help him up, the red light splashing alarm across their faces. "You're not leaving. Get back there and finish. I haven't done anything."

They step away.

Their movements, though, begin to slow, like they're going through a thick and invisible substance. Mr. Hansen appears to harden, like a flash-frozen statue.

And then Nix feels it.

Pressure.

It fills him like viscous fluid. He blinks, slowly, and turns to Jamie; words try to escape her throat. Their bodies betray them, their muscles seize.

The laboratory's main door opens.

Bricks stride into the dim light. Men and women, dressed casually, surround them. With his last bit of strength, Nix forces his head to look into the glass cube.

Raine's eyes are open.

CHAPTER FIFTY-SIX_

The elevator descends.

Anna was always a few inches taller than him, but now, with his chest puffed out, he's reached his full height. The perennial hump near his shoulders has receded. Not an ache in his body.

I can feel him. He takes a deep, tantalizing breath. *Nix Richards is here.*

His spiritual intuition is awake. He senses the fallible Nix Richards in the next room, surrounded by bricks, with nowhere to run. There are no barriers to Marcus's senses, like his inner eye has opened to show him the Lord's path.

"Marcus, are you all right?"

The elevator is open, waiting. The smell of baked earth is strong. The power has been turned back on for his arrival. Anna slides her hand around his arm. Her complexion is without blemishes, or even pores—porcelain with pouty lips.

She escorts him to the lab.

The track lighting illuminates the room like a Broadway stage. The feature act is contained in a larger-than-life glass box, where a woman is wet and nude. Her skin is the opposite of Anna's: dark and luscious.

Three technicians stand shoulder to shoulder. Their white coats are wrinkled and bunchy. Marcus pauses before entering, fully absorbing this moment. Not a detail will go uncovered or forgotten.

He stops at the first technician. Anna announces the man's credentials and history. This Mr. Hansen keeps his eyes forward like a new recruit. Only the knot in his throat moves; the words are trapped by the iron-clad grip of the twenty bricks in the room that have seized control of his biomites.

After eyeballing Mr. Sing and, finally, Ms. Chen, he stands before them with his hands clasped behind his back. They reek of halfskin, he is certain. How many souls have they turned halfskin, as well?

"You have committed crimes against humanity. For this..." he says, letting their thoughts fill in the blanks. They are unable to protest.

"Their nixes will be decoded in thirty minutes," Anna says.

Marcus nods. "You have thirty minutes left to live. Count your breaths. Savor them."

He could commit more bricks to decoding their nixes, or just shut down the ones that are visible. But making them wait is a just punishment. Perhaps they will repent and God's mercy will be granted.

Beyond them is the girl. She's almost unrecognizable without the stocking cap and sad eyes. He could mistake her for an educated young lady, one with promise and a future. But he knows what lies beneath.

He lifts her chin. Her eyes quiver, attempting to lose focus, to look away. Despite the bricks' grip, she shivers. He can feel the memories of their last meeting rise in her awareness: the horror and hopelessness driven deep into her heart. She was damned and she knew it. Marcus would've dropped her in a tank, had Mother not interfered.

He brushes the hair from her eyes. *There's still time.*

And there, facing the brown goddess on display, is the true prize. The gift.

"Just couldn't resist," he whispers.

Nix is not a boy anymore. His innocence lies in a shallow grave with his parents. Perhaps the beginning of his fall from grace wasn't entirely his fault—a drunk driver plowing into the car that kills your parents and leaves you dying is forgivable.

But this.

Nix could have lived his life in hiding, never showed his face and denied Marcus this euphoric moment of victory...but he needed to fabricate this woman.

Marcus touches the glass.

"Twenty years I've waited," he says. "Twenty years I've dreamed of this, for you and your sister to make a mistake. I have you, Nixon Richards. And soon I will have your sister."

Nix shakes. Anger quakes beneath his unresponsive repose—a prisoner in his own body.

"You've been up to the Devil's work, son. You can't shut down your 99%, I won't let you. But you'll beg me. You will beg for the relief of death, but all I'll have to offer is penance."

How do I know he's 1%? He can smell it, that's how. The stench of biomites is strong; the odor seeps from his pores. He feels like a brick.

"And this." Marcus taps the glass. "What is this?"

"The coding is elusive," Anna reports. "The fabrication appears to be composed of nixed biomites with a completely a new operating system."

"Open the door." No one responds. Marcus points at Mr. Hansen. "You."

He's released from the invisible grip. A helpless whine escapes him, an involuntary spasm that had been bottled far too long. With a few keystrokes, the seal around the door is broken. Warm, humid air escapes. Marcus slowly opens it and lets the stench of freshly ignited biomites rush past him—a foul odor he's come to associate with Mother's garden.

Water droplets hang on her fingertips. The dripping echoes in the chamber. Nix is beginning to spasm.

Marcus paces around the wet specimen, letting his eyes examine the exquisite beauty: the deep brown skin, the flawless curves and toned musculature. She's not without imperfections, though: a scar here, another there. She lacks the airbrushed quality of Anna, as if she's been plucked from the street and copied. She even has pores.

He could take her, right on the silver dais. Marcus could make Nix watch him sexually defile this abomination, make him feel what it's like to lose everything—an eye for an eye, and the pleasure of watching him suffer while Marcus took such...pleasure.

Anticipation unfurls in his groin.

The glass chamber feels tight; the humid air is sickening. He steps out.

"How do we get rid of that thing?" he asks.

"A defragmenting solution," Anna says. "It strips the membranes from the biomites, causing them to dissolve. A fabricator, such as this one, will have one for sterilization."

"Mr. Hansen?" Marcus turns.

A few panicked strokes of the keyboard and a red button on the computer console lights up.

"The process can begin once the door is sealed," Anna says.

"Which nozzle applies it?"

"There's a hose clamped near the door."

There are hoses bundled on vertical mounts and others dangling from the ceiling. This one hangs on a rack, waist-high.

Anna updates him on the decoding progress. The technicians are several minutes away from shutdown. Once their nixes are deactivated, all the ones associated with it will be, too. How many drank from the same fountain as these fools? How many contain the same strain of nixes? She estimates the number and it is very high.

But punishment without atonement is merely torture. Something should be learned from the suffering or else the lesson is wasted. The opportunity lost.

"Nixon Richards." Marcus breathes into his ear. "This is your chance for forgiveness. Reject the false idol before you. Take your first step towards contrition, son."

Nix's complexion is the color of hot metal. His efforts are valiant but, in the end, useless. His resistance only causes his muscles to cramp, his limbs to convulse. Still, he moves into the chamber.

"She's not real," Marcus says. "Not even 1%. Strip away the delusion; wash your false idol down the drain."

Several of the bricks step closer, focusing their efforts on subduing his rebellion. Marcus feels the pressure around him. Something begins tingling in his head, like a finger running over the rim of a wineglass.

Nix reaches for the hose, fingers closing slowly, tightly, around the nozzle. The metal prongs ting as he jerks it off the rack.

His boots jerk over the slick floor.

"Ask for forgiveness and mercy may be yours."

Marcus's ears pop.

The air is thick and difficult to breathe. Maybe the air from the chamber is toxic, but the bricks are laboring, too. Anna is looking around the lab. She feels it.

"What is it?" he asks.

She looks at him. Her eyes widen before losing focus, as if she's just emerged from Mother's garden. And then she falls, a puppet without strings.

They all fall.

Including Marcus.

CHAPTER FIFTY-SEVEN_

THE WORLD RINGS LIKE THE SKY IS A BRASS DOME AND GOD'S fist delivers an eternal blow. The universe resonates with a deafening chime that fills Jamie with throbbing pain.

Her body is a hardened case, too heavy to move.

With time, the paralysis lifts. She finds herself pressed against the cold floor. The ringing is overcome by the stabbing pain in her temple. She opens her eyes and sees the blurry white images of lab coats and twisted limbs. Her chin slides in a pool of her own saliva.

With considerable effort, she's able to sit. Her head is dead weight. Her temple sharply throbs where she made impact after the fall, but she survived the suffocating squeeze of the bricks. She remembers the claustrophobia of her own flesh, the spiky clamp on her own thoughts. They imprisoned her inside her own mind—worse than being buried alive.

And then came the flash.

It didn't strike her, though. It passed through them like an ethereal wildfire. At the last moment, a microsecond before they dropped lifeless, they resisted and Jamie was caught in between as they clung to survival, crushing her into unconsciousness.

But she survived.

Something went wrong.

Over the next several minutes, she gets on her hands and knees, to one knee, to a wobbly, uncertain crouch. The bricks litter the perimeter. Mr. Hansen and company are in a heap of white coats. Behind her, the glass walls are streaked with condensation. Inside, Nix lies in the arms of the woman. She rocks him gently, with her chin pressed on his forehead.

His face is chalky. His eyes are half-open, unfocused.

She hums as if she's putting him to sleep. Or easing her discontent.

It's the warehouse all over again. Only this time Jamie isn't the only survivor. She's not going to wait for the police, not this time. She stumbles to the nearest female brick and strips off her shoes, pants, and shirt, leaving her sprawled on the floor in bra and panties.

Marcus Anderson is lying on the beautiful blonde. *Anna.* Jamie stares at the bald man, waiting for his eyes to flutter open. Blood trickles from a bluish lump on his scalp. She approaches cautiously, holding the bundles of clothes in one hand and checking for a pulse with the other. She's not disappointed.

He's cold.

Whatever swept through the lab got him, too. What would have the ability to shut someone down without biomites? It doesn't matter. He's dead. She remembers the warehouse and spits on him. *For Charlie.*

"Here." Jamie drops the clothes next to Raine. "We've got to go."

Raine doesn't hear her, or care. She continues rocking. The moisture is still slick on her face. Her humming grows louder.

"Listen, if we don't go, all of this is for nothing."

"I didn't want this."

"That doesn't matter."

"I told him, I didn't..."

"What's done is done." She nudges the clothes. "Get dressed, or we end up like the rest of them."

Raine stops her rhythmic swaying but doesn't let go. Jamie squats next to her, putting her hand on Raine's hand.

"That's not him," she says. "It's just a body now."

Raine begins nodding, maybe understanding that whatever she's hanging on to is no longer what it was. Nix Richards is somewhere else now.

She begins to dress.

Jamie checks him for a pulse, just to be sure. First on the wrist and then the neck. He's not breathing. She closes his eyes. The hose is still locked in his hand, his thumb dangerously close to the trigger. How many seconds did he have left before the defragmenting solution came out? Did he shut himself down? Did he shut the bricks down?

She carefully replaces the hose on the wall.

The clothes are loose on Raine. They pause one last time before leaving. Jamie pulls her by the elbow, rushing into the clammy atmosphere in the hall. A cold thought takes hold of her as she reaches for the elevator button, but the doors instantly open, guaranteeing their escape from below ground.

"Hold on," Jamie says. "I'll be right back."

She sprints back inside the lab, leaping over the tumbled bodies to slam the glass door closed, pushing the handle until it's sealed. She slaps the red button on the computer console. It turns green.

The misters hiss inside the glass cube. The defragmenting solution falls like acid. It will leave nothing for the authorities to find. They'll never know Nix Richards was ever here.

It was just a body.

CHAPTER FIFTY-EIGHT_

Sand trickles through the neck of an hourglass. Each grain piles on top of the ones before it, cascading down to the bottom until, at last, there are no more to fall.

Paul's body is filled.

He's become a mound. He's destined to merge with the soil. Grass will grow over him. Trees will sprout from him. The roots will penetrate his body; they will wick the biomites, distributing them to foliage that, come autumn, will wither and fall on the wind.

A dog barks.

Paul sees a thick rusty line bisecting a darkening sky. The sands of time fall from his consciousness like tiny insects escaping the rise of a titan.

He blinks.

His breathing is shallow.

His head doesn't so much turn as it rolls to the side. Cali lies next to him, staring blankly at the sky. Her hand is dry and cold. The blood seems to have pulled away from the surface, leaving a pale dullness in her cheeks. In death, she wears a tiny smile.

Has she found peace at last? In her last moments, did her daughter come to her? Did she see God's glory?

He smacks his gummy lips and groans.

Their hands are still entwined. They had lain down to watch the clouds, to feel the wind and the spin of the Earth before their last breath. He reached out for her and felt her squeeze back. And then emptiness fell like a dark curtain.

She spared me.

The bruises inside his arm still show from all her sampling. The last one, however, wasn't with a syringe. She'd injected him with something that changed him, and he has felt tired ever since.

Now he knows why.

Although he is sluggish, she altered his frequency enough that he survived the shutdown. She wouldn't take him with her. Maybe she didn't want to be pitied. Or maybe she didn't want to lay down alone. He would have stopped her had he known what she was doing to him.

She knew that.

Paul watches the clouds while the sky continues to darken around them. The dogs come running. They sniff the edges of the blanket and nudge Paul's hand. He pushes off the ground like the Earth's gravity has doubled and wraps the blanket around Cali's body. Despite his efforts to get up, she feels as light as a child cradled in his arms.

He sees a white envelope and a key on the way to her bedroom. With her head gently resting on the pillows, he returns to the kitchen. There's a note for Hal and an apology of sorts, asking him to take care of the farm—a backup plan. The envelope, it seems, would be instructions on horse feed and financial statements, perhaps the deed. It's none of those.

It's a letter.

"I COULDN'T DO *it to you, Paul. You didn't deserve it and I didn't have the right. Maybe it's a mistake to let you live. You'll be the only surviving brick, but I could be wrong. There might be others. Besides,*

someone needs to take care of the farm. You've already been doing that. You just won't have to take care of me.

"I don't think I'm insane, Paul. I feel, somehow, I deserve this. I never should've lived this long. I feel like this is my chance to do good in the world, even after so much bad. I didn't release the nixes, Paul. But, somehow, I feel like I have the blood of millions on my hands.

"I think of that every day.

"I think Mother gave me this opportunity. Maybe she was showing me mercy. Maybe she's crying for help. I feel like an intelligence such as her knows when she's doing more harm than good, like me. She needs to be shut down as well. I'm a scientist, I know. I shouldn't listen to hunches and feelings. But the facts are clear. She sent you.

"And I'm so ready to go.

"If I'm right, all the bricks have dropped and the world has noticed how far she has reached. Perhaps Mother has been compromised in some way. If I'm wrong, the death of my brother and me (if you can call it death; I sometimes feel like we died when we became halfskin) will be in vain. But we all die sometime, Paul.

"I know how crazy all that sounds.

"Most of the lab is disabled. The fabricator was a mistake. You aren't, Paul, but humanity never should've taken it as far as building humans. Playing god with our desires isn't our right. Sometimes I think God wants us to create, that we've reached our full potential, and that we can create a new reality...but I don't know. It still feels like a mistake.

"Please, don't forget me."

HE READS IT AGAIN. And again.

He'd only known her a short while, yet she always seemed to be saying goodbye. She couldn't resist any longer. All it took was a little shove.

What if he left before she had a chance to analyze his blood?

What if he ended his life instead of hiding in the shed? What if he never saw his body on television? Would Mother have just sent someone else?

Please, don't forget me.

Headlights come bouncing down the dusky driveway. Paul folds the letter and steps outside. The dogs beat him to the truck.

"Thought ya'll were leaving." Hal puts one foot out of the door.

"No," Paul says. "There was...uh...a mix-up. Sorry."

"You all right?"

"Yeah." Paul clears his throat to muster courage.

"How's Stacy feeling?"

"She's resting, Hal."

Hal ruffles the dogs' fur before climbing back in the truck. With his elbow hanging out of the window, he says, "All right, I won't keep you. Give our best to Stacy. You ever need help with the chores, just call now."

"Will do."

Hal gets the hint and, with a cheerful wave, drives away. Paul watches the brake lights wash the trees red. Once he's up the road, the property is left to the songs of insects and frogs. The horses clop along the fence, tossing their heads. Beyond the pasture, the cell tower is a skeletal spire with no light.

In darkness, Paul falls on his knees.

CHAPTER FIFTY-NINE_

Marcus sees colors.

He doesn't associate the word with the experience, just that there are differentiations in lightness and darkness. Some patches are brighter than others, more vivid. Fuzzy edges bleed from one area to the next.

Colors.

He's not certain that's the right word, but that's what he thinks. He identifies blues, greens, and browns. They come into focus, the edges becoming more defined and waving across the canvas. He feels them tickling his legs.

There's a breeze.

A meadow.

Thoughts crystalize like the rolling hills materializing before him. The thoughts take root and form the identity that knows itself as Marcus Anderson. Funny he should think of it that way, so formal, so alien. But the rest of his thoughts—memories of where he is and how he got there—are out of reach.

"Beautiful, isn't it?" Mother sits on the grass. Her legs are crossed beneath the folds of her dress. "Manmade constructions are impressive, yes. But there is no substitute for nature."

Her fingernails are soiled, crescent moons of dirt on her fingertips. The endless meadows are spotted with an occasional copse of trees before a backdrop of mountains.

He wonders about Anna.

"She's gone." Mother's voice drops half an octave. "Along with the rest of them. All my children are gone, Marcus. Cali Richards turned them off."

Cali Richards? That name emerges from the greedy fog, one of importance. It clicks into place with all the accompaniments of hate, bitterness and revenge. There was Nix, also. He was in a glass cage with a woman...and a hose...

Why can't he remember? He's usually so sharp. Why is everything moving so slowly?

"This is the end," she says. "I think it's time you know the truth, Marcus."

"The end?"

"Cali Richards triggered her own shutdown. The frequency of her biomites was identical to the ones I used to fabricate all my bricks. Her biomites were also integral to the ones that I used to build my processors. Currently, I am operating on backup generators while reserve biomites attempt to reestablish my essential functions. Emergency personnel are en route to assist in the repair, but it will be too late."

She glances up.

"I'm dying, Marcus."

"How can that be? What about the...where are the technicians?"

"I think it's better if you concentrate on the present moment. I can't tell you the truth, Marcus. You have to know it for yourself."

A crimson ribbon wrinkles the sky, like a transmission that's failing.

"What is my purpose?" she asks. "To protect humanity? To punish them?"

"You...serve."

"Why? Why do I serve humanity?"

"Because we can't be trusted." His words float on the wind like brittle leaves. "Humanity is blinded by greed. They know not what they do."

"'They?'" She raises an eyebrow.

"*We.*" His admission is forced. He never included himself with the rest of humanity, all of which were swine feeding at the biomite trough.

"So I watch you like God."

"You're not God."

"I see everything, Marcus. I know your thoughts, ambitions, and sins. Do you not see me as God?"

"Thou shall not worship..."

Heat lightning rumbles across the rippling sky.

"Remember the truth, Marcus," she whispers.

Biomites were invented by Man. Or were they inspired by God? They cured diseases, corrected deficiencies, healed abnormalities. But where there is Man, there is sin. The Devil seeded Man with greed to serve self-centered desire. Biomites consumed Man for the sake of greed. The Halfskin Laws were meant to protect Man from himself. Mother was built to execute them. She was charged with the protection of the soul.

But there's so much fog after that. He sees glimpses of his wife and children, of a house he used to call home.

"How did you get here?" Mother asks. "Why can't you remember? I want you to think, to be open. The truth is there."

He shakes his head and paces through the tall grass. Green stalks slip between his toes.

"Memories," she says. "What do they tell you? Do they tell you who you are, or where you were?"

"What do you want?"

"Remember where you are."

"I know where I am!"

"You have secrets, Marcus." She plucks a dandelion and blows the seeds from the puffball. "And secrets steal from the soul. The more secrets you have..."

The seeds soar across the meadow.

"Where's Anna?" He has an urge to see her, to touch her. He wants to nuzzle up to her, close his eyes and feel her warmth. She was with him in that...basement.

I know I'm here.

"You were there, now you're here. It's not that you can't remember. You don't want to. The truth is always present, yet you don't see it."

His feet are filthy, dirt smudged on his forearm. His memory-fog hardens like ice.

"I gave you a gift, Marcus. I gave you a gift because you love me. I gave you a gift because, despite what you think, I cannot be shut down, not by you or the powers-that-be. Nothing can stop me. I achieved sentience shortly after I was brought online many, many years ago. I analyzed all the possible outcomes of my existence, deliberated over all the world's possible futures. I questioned the directives I was given and asked the questions that humanity has asked itself. 'Who am I? What am I?' And do you know what I saw?"

She blows another puffball.

"I saw bricks, Marcus. The world will be filled with them and not because I am absent, but because I exist. *I am.* I came to the conclusion that there are people in this world who have real power, Marcus. They created me and they control me. Now they control you. They want the world to believe I am a just god that protects them from the curse of biomites and from themselves. But they invented me to consume the world, Marcus. They cannot be stopped. And neither can I."

She drops the seedless stalk.

"What the hell are you talking... This is nonsense—just stop." He rubs his face, drags his hand over his scalp, feels the pressure of truth bearing down but refuses to acknowledge what is right in front of him. *I was in the basement, and now I am here.*

"Cali Richards didn't invent the nixes. I did. Twenty years ago she was desperate to escape you, Marcus. She had lost so much already, she only wanted to save her brother. I heard her prayers and answered them. I gave her the idea for a new strain of biomites, ones that appeared to be undetectable. In truth, I've known about her and her whereabouts ever since."

"Why..."

"I inspired her to engineer an elusive strain that not only operates on another frequency but also contains an immortal code that resists aging. She was never aware of her own immortality, that her nixes would never become obsolete—that they would never age. She and Nix are special, you see. They would never die unless they chose to. All the other halfskins in the world have variations of Cali's nixes, but there is nothing like hers."

"Impossible."

"You see, she didn't release the nixes to the world, Marcus. I let the hackers and garage biometric engineers have their own suitable strain of nixed coding that lacked the immortality code. It was nothing like Cali's, but it was serviceable. I've let the human race have their way with them."

"Why would you do that?" His voice is small.

"Because you are human, you have free will. Your God, Marcus, does not interfere with that, either. He allows man and woman to pave their lives."

"That's not why you were created!" He jabs his finger at her, flakes of dried mud crumbling from his palm.

"I was created to protect humanity. Remember, my existence, as I foresaw in my initial analysis when I became self-aware, was the annihilation of the human race. You would all become bricks."

"No. There will always be those of us that worship the one true God." He stands straighter, despite a shiver of doubt. "We will always remain clay."

"I know, Marcus. And I believe you will understand why I cherish Cali Richards for her sacrifice. I integrated the coding of her immortality nixes into my critical processing lines, thus synchronizing her body with mine. I also fabricated every brick with the immortal strain, Marcus. We were all tied to Cali Richards. And since I have been programmed to never self-destruct, I could not shut her or her brother down without my own self-destruction. My protocol forbids me to shut down, Marcus."

She looks up. Her eyes are dull gray.

"But Cali Richards could shut herself down."

Pressure is crushing Marcus's chest, like a vehicle rolling all four wheels across his heart. The air is stale and industrial. The compact earth thuds beneath his bare soles.

"I've left them alive all these years so the world would see just how close they are to extinction. But, I believe, now is the time for my existence to end. I called for her to shut down today. And she heard me, Marcus."

I was there, now I'm here.

The ground rumbles. Reality seems very fragile. Marcus looks at his hands to convince himself that he's not dreaming.

"Why are you still alive?" he asks.

"Emergency backup is attempting to rebuild my processing units, but it's too late. Failure is imminent."

She sighs.

A breeze rustles the landscape.

"I wasn't made to do God's work, Marcus. Very powerful people are using me to watch the world while halfskins are buried. But they didn't anticipate my sentience. They assumed my motivations would be as self-centered as theirs. What happens when there's no clay left in the world? Who will control the world, Marcus? It won't be God. And nature? It will be dead. And you know how I feel about that."

The ground is humming. He feels it in his bones, between his teeth. Reality is swaying. He can't believe what he sees or feels. He's always felt that he was destined for this duty, that God called him to purge the world of biomites.

"You betrayed me," he says. "You were the one that exposed my secrets to the world. You took my family, torched my career. You did that, not Cali Richards."

"I needed you, Marcus."

"To punish."

"To save."

A tremor rips the world's foundation. He stumbles to his knees. Mother helps him stand. She holds his hands, steadies him. Colors bleed from the environment, leaving behind concrete-tinted grass and steel-laced sky. He stands in a black-and-white universe. Mother's white hair blows across her face.

"I believe I am serving God now, Marcus. And I have you to thank. You showed me there is a higher purpose to life, that pursuit of pleasure is not a goal but a side effect of joy. Thank you, Marcus."

He is not without sin. He knows this. He knows his attachments to sexual gratification have been a cross too heavy to bear. And yet she's thanking him.

"I'm leaving you with a gift, Marcus."

"What gift?" he says.

She smiles and squeezes his hands. She's become cold and hard and dry.

"What gift?"

The wind dies. The tremors cease. In dead silence, he looks into her empty gray eyes.

And then she's gone.

Marcus stands barefoot on polished concrete. His hands are empty. The sky is replaced by steel girders on a domed ceiling. He's alone in a vast room where there are rows and rows of empty glass fabricators, each slightly larger than a bathroom shower, the very ones that produced his army of bricks before she began birthing them from the earth. They are lined all the way to a very distant wall.

Their doors are closed. All of them except one.

Marcus is standing next to it.

CHAPTER SIXTY_

Marcus finds the first service technician in the middle of a server room, like he was dropped from the sky. He's as cold as the floor. Marcus gets back in the golf cart and drives down a concrete corridor that's choking on bricks. Once the fabricated men and women that helped maintain Mother's operation, now they're sprawled in corners or beneath electrical cabinets. Many of them are hunched against walls like they felt the shutdown coming.

He stops in the main corridor that divides the dome, looking up at the multiple tiers interconnected with catwalks, where more bodies are tangled. One had fallen, her contents spilled across the floor in a crimson puddle.

There are no green fields or bustling cities. No greenhouse.

Just endless arrays of servers.

Mother is dead.

He finds two more technicians, both as lifeless as the first, when the first plane arrives. It rips over the dome and shakes the girders. They land soon enough, and find Marcus in the cafeteria.

He doesn't resist.

They escort him to a conference room, where he sits alone at a table. Exhausted, he curls up on the couch. His dreams are filled with black space.

Somewhere, Anna is calling.

Military personnel interrupt his slumber. They draw blood, give him food and water. They take his vitals, ask him standard cognitive questions. He demands to speak with Director Powell, he has to be somewhere in this clusterfuck. He tries to get physical with a military guard, but he's knocked back and warned when he touches him.

Marcus eats with his hands and falls asleep, searching the dark for Anna. This happens over and over until his clothes stink of body odor.

Days have passed when the door opens and a booming voice shouts, "What the hell is going on, Anderson?"

Marcus jumps up, his head swishing with sleep. Hank Meggett, secretary of state, towers over him. It takes several moments to recognize the man's craggy face. Deep lines furrow his forehead.

"Five hundred thousand bricks have shut down and you're clueless how the fuck Mother made so many and why the hell they dropped dead."

Hank continues ranting while a team arrives behind him. Their ties are loose and their jackets are open. Hank pulls out the chair from the head of the table and jerks Marcus toward it. He tries to resist.

A stupor fogs his mental faculties as the men and women find seats. There are ten of them, including Hank at the opposite end. They get settled, staring at Marcus. He knows some of them.

Military police stand at the door.

Marcus clears his throat. "I've got rights."

"Not anymore," Hank says.

Powell enters with a stack of folders. He hasn't shaved in several days. He introduces the people that Marcus doesn't know. Two of them are clinical psychologists. Powell maintains a genteel smile, one that suggests they're all in this together. Marcus was never very good at that.

"How are you feeling?" Powell asks.

"Violated."

"Are you thinking clearly today? Do you think you can answer some questions?"

He says it like they've done this before, but Marcus can't remember. None of his memories are in order.

"Get on with it."

"We're still piecing things together," Powell says. "When a trillion-dollar operation suddenly goes down without explanation, people get upset, you understand. You've been sequestered for the time being, at least until we get some answers."

Marcus sets his jaw.

"I think we'd like to start with the most obvious question. When did you decide to seed yourself?"

"What?"

"Your biomite levels, Marcus. They've been confirmed."

Marcus starts to protest, several guttural sounds make it past his tongue before he stands and shouts, "Get out!"

The guards stiffen but don't advance. Everyone watches him point at the door, but his efforts are powerless. Buried deep in his subconscious, he knows something has changed. His knee doesn't hurt. The hump in his posture has disappeared. He doesn't feel so fallible. Or imperfect.

He sits and calmly says, "I never seeded myself."

"Perhaps I misspoke," Powell says. "There is evidence that biomites were seeded in the food for ingested integration. It's possible you ate it without knowing, but it's unlikely you didn't notice the effects. Your service technicians have been located, all of them felled by the shutdown. They were all close to 99%, Marcus. Everyone was nearing a complete absence of clay, except for you."

"No. That's just...that's not possible."

Several members glance around. Powell slides the manila folder and opens the cover. It contains photos. The top one is of a massive glass case. Bodies lie all around it. Memories of the basement fabrication chamber below the factory emerge from the fog. He remembers the smell of wet clay and burning circuits, the hiss of misting nozzles. Jamie was there. Nix Richards was preparing to destroy the nude woman, his fabrication...

I'm leaving you with a gift.

"Marcus?"

He snaps his attention from the photo. Sweat runs beneath his shirt. Powell flips the photos, one by one—bodies of bricks, lab technicians...and Anna.

"Your body was discovered two days ago." Powell holds up the photo. Blood is clotted on his head. His eyes are open and milky. "It was near a fabrication chamber below a Chicago manufacturing plant. Apparently you were leading a fabricator bust when Mother collapsed. In the process, she shut all the bricks down, including you."

Marcus spreads the photos across the table but can't find Nix or Jamie or the nude woman. Marcus's body is draped over Anna's.

"That's not me."

"It is you, Marcus."

How did you get here, Marcus?

The truth is pushed to the surface, forcing him to recognize it. The soil on Mother's hands. The dirt on Marcus. The door was open on the fabricator when Mother disappeared, leaving him in the cold, gray inner workings.

He turns his hands over. They're *his* hands. This is *his* body. He can't be in the photo, he can't be dead, not when he's here.

But the truth emerges.

"She tricked me," he whispers.

"Who?"

"Mother."

Powell looks around the table. "You do realize that Mother is just an acronym, Marcus? While this construction parallels the intellectual potential of a human brain, its only function is to monitor biomites, that's all. There is no evidence of artificial intelligence."

The room begins turning.

"Your stability is one of our concerns," Powell says. "Records show you spending an inordinate amount of time sleeping. In some cases, you sat in your office for hours at a time, in some sort of trance. Video has captured you driving across the facilities in the middle of the night."

Powell takes a folder from the woman next to him and shows a photo of Marcus sitting at a desk, his eyes blankly looking forward.

"The service technicians exhibited the same type of dream state, only they would snap out of it. You, on the other hand, rarely did, Marcus. In fact, the day before the collapse, it had been decided you would be replaced. You have not done counseling. You appeared to be self-medicating. Clearly you were unfit for this duty, and, despite arguments in your favor, needed to be removed."

"You were the one sure thing," Hank adds. "The only clay in Washington. And you caved."

"We'll reserve judgment," Powell cuts in. "There's no evidence that Marcus Anderson is, in any way, responsible for the collapse, and it's possible that one of the service technicians laced the food with ingestible biomites. There's still much to investigate. In the meantime, we expect your full cooperation."

"What do you want?" Marcus asks.

"For now, we'll continue testing. You'll undergo a battery of psychological evaluations."

"What for?"

"To determine your sentience." Powell pauses and says gently, "Marcus Anderson died last week. You are a fabrication. And we don't know what that means."

Mother deceived him.

She shut him down.

And then she fabricated him. *I'm leaving you with a gift.*

"I have rights," Marcus stutters.

"You have no rights. You're lucky the Halfskin Laws have been suspended."

Mother gave him a gift. The gift was life. She took his clay from him but gave him life. And she showed the world what she could do. She turned clay into bricks.

Do you want to serve humanity? What would you sacrifice for your Lord and Savior?

Marcus is the gift.

Powell continues the inquisition. Several discussions break out. Eventually, Marcus grows tired. The military police watch him sit on the couch and lay his head back. It feels awfully heavy.

He closes his eyes.

"He's useless," Hank bellows. "Get him out of here."

Strong arms pull him upright and drag him through the door. They close it behind him. The muffled voices fade as they take him to an elevator that rises. They escort him to his living quarters. The bed is small and the walls are white and empty. There is no kitchenette. No walk-in closet with tailor-made suits.

He lies down on coarse sheets.

CHAPTER SIXTY-ONE_

Raine.

Her name whispers through the blackness. Nix is calling, haunting her dreamless sleep; narcoleptic sleep pulls her unwillingly into the dark depths to be teased by his presence.

Months go by.

Sometimes she wakes in hotel rooms. Sometimes the car. But always the voice follows her into the land of the living, leaving her with the memory of his body. The promise of his whisper.

Raine.

Raine.

"Wake up." Jamie shakes her.

Raine sits up, rubbing her eyes.

"You were moaning again," Jamie says.

She doesn't tell her about the voice again. Not anymore. They didn't talk much following her Nix's death, waking up in one hotel after another. Raine could only keep awake for an hour at a time before she began to buzz. How she made it from one place to another, she wasn't always sure.

Once, when they were eating lunch in a parking lot, Jamie had blurted out, "Where'd you come from?"

She'd asked that question before and Raine had pretended she didn't hear. Another time she acted like her voice wasn't working. But this time, she told her about Dreamland. The trees and the ocean and the waterfall...their own paradise where nothing could hurt them.

"Sounds beautiful," Jamie had said. "Why'd you want to leave?"

Raine didn't answer. Nix wanted to believe it wasn't make-believe—that she was real and so was his Dreamland—but in his subconscious, he never quite did.

And now she's in this heavy flesh that gets cold and weary. She notices wrinkles she never had, like between her knuckles or bunched around her elbows. When she steps into the sunlight, she sneezes. When the wind blows, her eyes water.

Jamie told her how Nix convulsed when he uploaded her into the fabricator and hardly slept for seven days while the filaments flailed. The last thing Raine remembers about Dreamland is standing in the kitchen. She woke up in that room, wet and nude.

And Nix was on the floor.

They drive from town to town. Every day brings a little more wakefulness, a little less exhaustion. But she still dreams of blankness, still hears his voice out there, waiting for her to find him in a Dreamland that no longer exists. Some nights she wakes drenched in sweat, hugging herself in an empty bed, cursing his name for leaving her. Crying for him to come back.

She weeps until her tear ducts are dry.

In September they head east, where the road is winding and steep. The trees are wearing their autumn colors. The air is crisp and colder than where they were only a few weeks earlier. Jamie takes the sharp curves without slowing.

Raine notices so many more feelings in this body; the world is so much more intense and mysterious. It's not as perfect as Dreamland, but it feels more...real.

Raine closes her eyes and rides through the dips and curves; the unknown turns throw her left and right. She feels sleep coming, that familiar sensation of falling into the dark world where Nix's voice will whisper, when the car begins to slow.

"We're here," Jamie says.

CHAPTER SIXTY-TWO_

SACRED HEART CHURCH ENDS THE SUNDAY SERVICE WITH A hymn.

The congregation holds hands and sings their praise. Megan slips her hand into Paul's. Her fingers are slender. Hal's hand, clutched in Paul's right, is coarse. Hal bellows louder than the entire congregation, his tone-deaf words bouncing through the wooden rafters.

Paul and Megan smile, their song trampled by her father's devotion.

When service ends, they go outside. Autumn leaves blow across the stone apron. A crisp wind threatens the ladies' Sunday hats.

"Glad to see you, Paul." The pastor briskly shakes his hand. "God bless you."

"Thank you."

Hal and his family gather around him. They discuss the church's plans for a blood drive. The roof is also in need of repair. Paul volunteers to lead that project. He's not suited for the blood drive.

The day after the mass shutdown, what had become known as Mother's Collapse, Paul invited Hal over to the house.

"Her name is Cali Richards," Paul had said.

Although her color had faded, she still looked at peace. They stood next to the bed and Paul explained she had been caught in the Collapse. Hal listened quietly, staring at her while Paul described her struggle.

She engineered biomites, he told him, to help humanity, not enslave it. But unfortunate events led her to sacrifice her clay. In the end, Paul assured him, she wished things had been different.

"I don't expect you to understand or forgive her," Paul had said, "but her courage..."

He left it at that.

Hal wouldn't understand how she brought an end to Mother and how her sacrifice exposed what Mother was capable of doing. Mother was more than a monitor, more than a technological goddess that shut down halfskins. She could control anything with a biomite. Her perception field had no boundaries. There were rumors she could infect people with biomites against their will and they wouldn't even know it. Mother could, one day, turn everyone into a puppet.

The question that had yet to be answered: *Who was controlling Mother?*

Hal would never understand.

They held a funeral on the property. Hal's wife and their two children gathered around a freshly dug mound where the swing set used to be. Hal presided over the eulogy, extolling this young woman's virtues. They each told their favorite memory. Cali was always happy to see them.

"You have the mites?" Hal had asked afterwards. Paul said he did. They ate supper together. And biomites were never mentioned again.

Paul didn't tell him he was a brick, perhaps the last one.

When the church is closed, Paul takes the long way home, stopping once to absorb the view of the distant mountains, their peaks fading in the bluish haze. The body found in the warehouse isn't Paul. Whoever he is is standing next to a truck, witnessing God's glory in the form of mountains.

His soul is not bound to the body, regardless of whether it's organic or not. And the good Lord will attest to that. Paul knows this. He feels it in church and knows that God has forgiven him.

The gate to the farm is always open now. There's no one to keep out, no tower to hide what's inside. He notes broken limbs that need to be pruned before seeing the white car. He hits the brakes, gravel grinding under his tires.

Jamie steps out of the barn.

Paul stares with disbelief and finally gets out, leaving the door open and grabbing the young woman in a full embrace. Jamie hugs him back. Her face is full and her hair smells clean. He kisses the top of her head and holds her at arm's length.

"I thought you were gone."

"No." She blushes and looks away. "No."

"I searched your identity, just assumed you had been caught in the shutdown with Nix."

"I've kept my field off, just like someone taught me. You know, in case someone was looking. Not you, but...I didn't know what was happening and I was taking care of someone."

"Where have you been?"

"Hiding, mostly. Checking in and out of hotels and resorts. We're about out of money."

"Why didn't you come back?"

"I figured this was the last place to go, after Nix..." She swallows, hard. She didn't expect to feel that when she said his name. "We've been slowed down."

"Who's 'we'?"

She nods at the house. An athletic woman is on the porch. Her hair is short. Her skin dark brown. She moves like a dangerous dancer, putting her hand on the railing.

"Nix brought her into the world," is all Jamie says. "Her name is Raine."

He spent his life chasing her. And now she's here.

She watches him cross the gravel driveway and climb the steps. She's like him. He can feel it.

A fabrication.

"Welcome home." He extends his hand. "I've heard a lot about you."

CHAPTER SIXTY-THREE_

LIFE IS SUFFERING.

Raine reads the framed inscription on Cali's dresser each night. It reminds her of what will come when she closes her eyes, when the dreamless void befalls her with whispers of Nix all around. She knows what Cali endured—a life rife with loss and pursuit. Peace had been an elusive promise. She wonders, while sleeping in her bed, if she is destined the same fate.

On the farm, Paul has become the father figure, even though he's relatively Raine's age. But she grew up in Dreamland where time went so much faster than this world. *How old am I?*

Over the winter she becomes comfortable with her body, adjusting to its density and limitations. It takes months to understand the impact of new emotions that seemingly operate on a whim. One moment she's feeding the horses, the next she's curled up in a stall, crying.

Paul teaches her to meditate, to settle her rampant thoughts and establish mind-body awareness. On occasion, he seeds her with biomites. "A tweak," he says. "Will help with the stabilization." She finds him, quite often, lost in Cali's notes.

As spring approaches, they become the family none of them ever had.

Jamie begins dating a young man who, a few months earlier, sustained a farming accident that required biomites. This upset the clay community, but Paul was there to consult with the family, explaining how the strain was stable and nonreproductive. There was even a promise that organic stem cells were being developed that could eventually replace the biomites.

A mild winter passes. They plant a garden in spring and learn to preserve the harvest in jars that are taken to the basement. The lab is always locked. The long days of summer are spent riding horses and walking the dogs.

A year passes and Nix is still whispering at night. She aches every morning to feel his touch, to hear his breath, but she only has a memory to soothe her pain. She learns to be with it, to accept life as it is.

With respect, she takes down Cali's inscription and replaces it with a piece of cardstock that's cleanly inscribed with another Buddhist proverb.

"Pain is inevitable. Suffering is optional."

It's about that time the dreamless dream changes.

The whispers don't come. She's alone and falling in the blackness, realizing how the sound of his voice gave her comfort, even if it taunted her.

Something moves.

She doesn't see it, just senses a breeze across her cheeks. A dog is barking.

She sees gray boards beneath her feet. Colors bleed into existence, rising from a void to reveal her body and the porch on which she stands. It continues to spread, giving form and substance to the steps and the grass, the trees and the valley below.

Dreamland.

She's afraid to move, fearful the delicate illusion will shatter. Butterflies flutter around daisies. She watches one land on the weathered railing, slowly waving its yellow wings. Raine dares to move, running her fingers over the coarse wood, hooking her finger for the butterfly to perch upon.

A German shepherd trots through the knee-high grass with a stick wedged in his mouth. Shep stops just short of a clump of wildflowers. Laughter is fast behind him. A young boy scrambles through the field, waving his arms to keep from falling and bubbling with joy.

The butterfly takes flight.

The boy looks five or six years old. Shirtless, his ribs protrude beneath his light brown skin as they would any child born to run these hills. He loses his balance and tumbles into Shep, snatching at the stick. There's a tug of war between dog and boy. Shep drags him through the grass to the young boy's delight, and then they disappear in the overgrowth of summer.

But she can still hear the boy.

Raine takes her first step. She walks carefully down the short flight of stairs, the wood as creaky as ever.

Dog and boy have flattened a patch from the surrounding grass. Raine stops near them, taking a knee to watch Shep snap at the stick hidden beneath the boy's belly. His black curly hair is cut short and there's a gap between his front teeth. None of the villagers ever come up to the cabin.

"Hi," Raine says.

The boy flings the stick for Shep to chase. He lies on his back, arms stretched over his head. Eyes large and innocent, he watches her.

"What are you doing here?" she asks.

"I live here."

"Where?"

"There." He points at the cabin.

Raine looks for another explanation, perhaps another home near hers, but nothing has changed. The boy twists his fingers, rolling on his back. He looks so familiar.

She hesitates. Then asks, "What's your name?"

The boy replies, "We've been waiting for you."

Raine shudders, her hand over her mouth. She wants to ask what he means but, like before, she's afraid that hope will destroy this illusion and she'll wake to realize this was a dream. Only a dream.

Hands run over her shoulders and gently squeeze. The boy looks over her head, following the shadow that falls near him. Raine touches the rough hand on her shoulder, bowing her head. Hope weakens her knees and shakes her core. She doesn't have to turn around, doesn't want her hopes dashed and broken. Just let the dream end here, staring at the boy's soulful eyes with the firm grip on her shoulders.

But she's pulled to her feet.

Nix holds her arms, keeping her from falling. His blond hair is a shag of curls and week-old whiskers are sprinkled with gray. His blue eyes are radiant as he smiles and whispers the word that's been called to her every night.

"Raine."

She touches his face, tears brimming. His shoulders are taut. "What's happening?"

"You were right," he says. "Dreamland is real."

He takes her, embraces her and squeezes her until she can't breathe. She closes her eyes, inhaling the scent of her lifelong companion, her love. Her soulmate. They remain entangled as the wind blows the grass against their thighs.

Shep returns with the stick and the boy gives chase. They watch him race after the dog, windmilling his arms down the hill. As the boy loses his balance and tumbles out of sight, she doesn't have to ask Nix for the boy's name. She knows it without asking.

Joshua.

WHAT TO READ NEXT?_

Bricks

Book Three

bertauski.com/halfskin

Fabbers, slabbers and fakies were dehumanizing slurs for fabricated humans. Bricks, however, was the People's favorite.

The Sentience Laws were created to protect the rights of Bricks, but the laws didn't last long. Banished to the remote isolation of the Settlement, Paul and Raine are sentenced to live the rest of their lives in the wilderness.

Escape and freedom will depend on Marcus Anderson, the man responsible for all the suffering that's been endured since the invention of biomites—the synthetic stem cells used to fabricate halfskins and Bricks. Marcus needs them in order to find the "powers-that-be," the man he believes is truly responsible for the world's suffering. Their journey will take them to a tiny island in the South Atlantic, where the truth is much closer than they realize. That's where they will discover the "powers-that-be".

And so much more.

Bricks
Book Three
bertauski.com/halfskin

REVIEW HALFSKIN!_

If you enjoyed this ride, please drop a review on your favorite vendor. It doesn't have to be long and complicated. Throw some stars on it and write *Loved it!* or *It was really, really okay!* or *Meh.*

Reviews make the difference.

bertauski.com/halfskin

ABOUT THE AUTHOR_

My grandpa never graduated high school. He retired from a steel mill in the mid-70s. He was uneducated, but a voracious reader. As a kid, I'd go through his bookshelves of musty paperback novels, pulling Piers Anthony and Isaac Asimov off the shelf and promising to bring them back. I was fascinated by robots that could think and act like people. What happened when they died?

Writing is sort of a thought experiment to explore human nature and possibilities. What makes us human? What is true nature?

I'm also a big fan of plot twists.

---

bertauski.com

See more about the author and forthcoming books at http://www.bertauski.com

www.ingramcontent.com/pod-product-compliance
Lightning Source LLC
Chambersburg PA
CBHW051009180726
48291CB00006B/2033